Limping Along

a novel

Ryan Stallings

OAKLINE BOOKS

DEDICATED

To You

but mostly…

To Me

ON INTERNET SECURITY (AND WHY YOU NEED ME)

A Whitepaper by Vijay Kumar

Approximately 3 billion people in the world have access to the Internet. Roughly, this represents only 40 percent of the world's population, meaning there are more than 4 billion additional people who will eventually go online.

Among this massive population exists a criminal class of thieves, thugs, dilettantes, charlatans, and no shortage of Internet hackers, who will either steal or otherwise be responsible for the theft or loss of nearly $1 trillion annually across global industries.

A trillion dollars, and that is a conservative estimate, because most companies and individuals are too embarrassed to report a breach in their Internet security.

In the last year alone, two major retailers in the United States have had their websites and point-of-sale systems attacked, resulting in the theft of credit card and social security numbers. Estimated damages reached into the hundreds of millions of dollars for these two companies alone, and that is before factoring in loss of trust in their brands.

This is only the tip of the iceberg. The point of the spear. The opening salvo in a world war for which very few are prepared.

Retailers are just the appetizer. The main course will be the banks and global financial institutions.

Governments of the world's independent nations will provide the dessert.

As the globe becomes more and more connected, and everything seems to be controlled through Internet technologies, we have already seen the rise of the miscreants, malefactors, greedheads, anarchists, and perverts who seek to profit in their own sick ways from the porous battlements protecting our Internet interests today.

Imagine a world where an entire bank account can be liquidated with the push of a button.

Imagine a world where health records can be breached and medications surreptitiously changed at the click of a mouse.

Imagine a world in which a missile can be commandeered and fired from someone's laptop.

Now wake up, because there is nothing to imagine.

This world already exists.

But fear not, for one man stands above the filth and rabble who would do you harm.

One man can design and build the fortifications necessary to withstand the onslaught of bad actors with bad intentions.

Only one man can truly secure your network.

Me.

CHAPTER 1

Coleman entered the conference room in a rush, barely glancing at the eight individuals seated around the table. His eyes wandered past the dark wood oval, beyond the uneasy looks from his colleagues, through the windows and out to the pond, where a fountain sprayed in fits and starts, until the system cleared itself and streams of water steadily traced the shape of a flower, rising and then gently falling in an arc.

He cleared his throat and spoke toward the star-shaped speakerphone.

"It's Rob. Who's here?"

Three seconds passed, then five.

"Hello?" His tone was short.

"Hey, Rob," a nervous voice piped through the phone. "We're all here."

"Where are we?"

The colleagues seated around the table looked down at their laps. The phone remained silent. Coleman moved briskly toward the head of the table.

"Where are we, people?"

After another tense pause, a voice with a slight British lilt spoke through the phone.

"Rob, this is Vijay. Simply put, we need more time. I'm afraid we need a lot more time."

Coleman stared at the phone from his perch at the head of the table. Leaning in, he clenched his fists and rested the knuckles of both hands on the waxed wood.

"We don't have more time. I don't need to remind you what this deal means to the company, to everyone in this room, to everyone on the phone, and to you personally, Vijay."

Coleman now balanced his weight on his fingertips as he leaned farther in toward the phone. "Whatever it takes, Vijay. Work nights, work weekends, work holidays. I don't care – just do the job, do it on time, and do it right the first time."

Another pause, this time longer, before Vijay answered.

"This is not fair, Rob. It simply is not fair. We are all, everyone on this team, working ourselves into the ground. I have personally been writing and testing code on nights and weekends already. It would be impossible to work any additional nights and weekends, because they don't exist! You have given us limited specs, no project plan, no outside resources. The only thing you have given us is a hyper-aggressive timeline and more pressure than any one of us can take!"

Coleman looked at his reflection in the wood and shook his head.

"It's a $100 million deal over three years, Vijay."

"Yes, I know that, Rob. You have mentioned a few times."

"The deal is worth $100 million over three years, Vijay."

"Sorry, was I on mute? I said I am aware of that, Rob."

"$100 million, Vijay."

Silence.

"$100 million, Vijay. You said you're aware, but are you actually aware of how much money that is?"

"Rob, do not patronize me. I understand the implications, loud and clear."

"$100 million, Vijay. Have I mentioned that?"

"You act like it is already done, Rob! We have not even been given a seat at the table yet, let alone won the job. You want us to kill ourselves over something that may not ever happen."

Coleman stood straight up and glared at the phone. The team members seated around the table all buried their gazes in their phones and laptops, desperate not to make eye contact. Coleman breathed deeply through his nose and waited a good half-minute before speaking in a tone that was clear, concise and ice cold.

"Vijay, you are weak."

"Rob, this is ridiculous..."

"You are lazy."

"Come on, this simply is not true..."

"You are annoying."

"This is completely unprofessional..."

"You are a deterrent to success."

"Rob!"

"And, Vijay, you are hanging by a thread. Take the next few hours and decide if you wish to continue with us. Let Steve know your decision by lunch. Our conversation is over."

Coleman pointed at Steve and then pointed at the phone. Steve reached over the table and disconnected the call.

The fountain outside sprayed water in a full plume, creating gentle ripples in the center of the pond. Coleman stole another glance at the fountain, slapped his palm on the table and left the room.

CHAPTER 2

Coleman pulled his BMW to the left of a white box truck and, within a second, accelerated past the oblivious delivery driver and moved back into the center lane. The car was quiet. Coleman had cut off the radio, and his passenger had no designs on drawing the driver's ire.

The dark leather was cool against his skin, and Steve Wellman allowed himself to relax as he watched the pine trees flashing past him through the car window. Spring started early in the Carolinas, and Steve noticed the flowers beginning to bloom, and the popping pinks, blues and purples reminded him that his wife was due a nice bouquet. The last few months had been some of the most difficult of his career, and he had no illusions that those difficulties had remained at the office. It was a miracle, Steve thought, that she still spoke to him.

"Nice day," Steve muttered, mentally wishing himself outside of the car.

"There are no nice days until we cross the finish line."

Coleman coolly handled the BMW, leaning into turns and winding the car through traffic until they eased into a stop at the red light. He had gone with the four-door 6 Series, but his patience was wearing thin with the terms of his lease, and he was ready to move up to the M5 once the deal closed. He was torn between the Champagne Quartz and the Silverstone Metallic color packages, but it wasn't something he worried too much about. If they won the deal, he thought, he could get one of each.

Though he contractually pulled 10 percent of his sales plus salary, the company had a $1 million yearly cap on commissions. This year, Coleman intended to make every penny of that $1 million.

"$100 million," he whispered, accelerating as the light flashed green.

"It's a big deal." Steve agreed.

"Huge."

"Massive."

"Enormous."

"Well, maybe for you," Steve said.

"Hey, you're looking at a six-figure bonus out of this thing, Steve."

Steve turned back toward the window and pondered the numbers, before speaking softly.

"You know, Rob, that's the only reason I'm doing this. These last few months haven't exactly been paradise."

"What is it with you guys? A few freaking weeks of hard work and you all start crying like a bunch of little girls. Is Vijay rubbing off on you? I can fire him. I would love to fire him."

"Vijay isn't the problem. He's been killing himself. We all have."

"We are bidding to run network security for one of the three biggest banks in America. It's not Romper Room. We're not drinking Mai Tais and hula dancing. That will all come after we win. You sacrifice up front so you can reap the rewards later. Why am I explaining this to you, Steve? You've been with me every step of the way here."

"I know. I know."

"You know?"

"I know. But, Rob, come on. At the very least, try to motivate the team."

"I am motivating the team."

"Through fear and intimidation?"

"If it does the job."

"Well, the way it's going now, everyone will quit the day the deal closes and we get bonused."

Coleman considered this last point for about three seconds while he weaved around a minivan that was driving the speed limit. When he spoke, he looked at Steve with a big, mocking grin on his face.

"Do you need a bottle, Steve? Do you need a diaper? Should I read you a bedtime story?"

"Rob..."

"Does Vijay need a massage? Should I get him a pedicure? Should I tell you all how pretty you are? How nice your hair looks?"

"This is low, even for you..."

"Should I send you flowers? Do you want chocolates and candy hearts? Come on, Steve, give me a little kiss..."

Coleman reached over and placed his hand on the back of Steve's neck. Steve swatted at Coleman's arm and pulled away, fixing his brown curly hair and adjusting his glasses once the unwanted advance was over.

"Seriously, Rob. You know I'm with you, but this attitude isn't helping. At least try and be positive. Try to thank the team once in awhile. This is Management 101. You know all this. Just try and create a nicer environment for everyone involved."

"Yeah, and you know why those people write Management 101 books? Because they can't close $100 million deals!"

"Is it completely about the money for you?"

"Yep."

"No other reason? Like you're still trying to prove yourself to Armstrong?"

"Nope."

"Are you sure? No other reason at all?"

"What are you fishing for here? You want me to say it's all for my family? Okay, fine, Steve, it's all for my family. Does that make you happy? Does that please you?"

"You're a piece of work."

"Do tell, Steve. Why are you doing it?"

"For my family."

"For your family?"

"For my family."

"Ugh," Coleman shook his head. "Remind me to recruit men next time, okay?"

"Where are we going?"

Coleman had turned off the highway and was cruising an access road near the airport.

"We're gonna go put some hair on your chest. I need a drink."

"A little early, no?"

"Sure is."

Coleman pulled the BMW into a nearly empty lot and parked across the painted line, right in the middle of two spots, so that his 6 Series would have plenty of space on either side. Punching Steve in the shoulder, he climbed out of the car and walked toward the rundown club.

"See you in there," he called back.

Steve frowned and looked through the windshield at peeling paint on the establishment's pale purple siding and a small mountain of crushed cigarette butts swept into a pile near the front door.

A blinking neon sign, which hung slightly off-center near the entrance, announced the club's name and offerings:

"Girls, GOODIES, Great Times."

Steve reluctantly followed Coleman inside.

CHAPTER 3

The Carolina sky glowed rust red, with streaks of yellow and white highlights, as dusk settled over the Silver Creek neighborhood, nestled just outside of Raleigh in a lush, wooded corner of the Research Triangle Park. After entering the security code and negotiating the gates at Silver Creek's entrance, Steve Wellman pulled the BMW into a flat, expansive drive, where decorative lighting led to a three-car garage. Sprinklers wet a group of unruly shrubs fronting an attached breezeway that stretched from the garage to the main house. Coleman stumbled out of the passenger seat and stepped directly into a soggy patch of Bermuda grass.

"I'll pick you up tomorrow morning," Steve said, throwing the car in reverse and hitting the accelerator as soon as Coleman was safely outside.

Coleman watched until the taillights faded into the early evening, ignoring the cool wetness that seeped through his leather loafer and moistened his sock. He took a deep breath, in through his nose and out through his mouth, and adjusted his shirt beneath his waistband. The house looked pretty good, he thought, as the sky's remaining light gave way to the coming darkness.

Coleman had purchased the 6,500-square-foot estate home immediately after closing his last big deal, with a nearby university that needed a comprehensive wireless solution to holistically integrate Internet access and services across campus portals and platforms for 30,000 students and faculty. That was the way they sold these things: "Comprehensive wireless solutions that holistically integrate Internet access and services across campus portals and platforms..." Basically it meant that he sold the equipment and subsequent day-to-day management of the university's wireless Internet access. But, for Coleman, it meant a $1.2 million estate home in Silver Creek. With his bonus from the wireless deal, he had written a $600,000 check for the downpayment. Though 20 percent was the norm,

Coleman wanted to stay in this house in case things ever went sideways for him, and he figured he could manage a $600k mortgage in his sleep.

He admired his purchase and thought about how much he loved the house, as he continued to ignore the water sprinkling around him. The bank deal would get him his beach house.

Coleman heard a little voice coming from the backyard. He drew another deep breath and did his best to walk a straight path around the garage. The house came with an actual white picket fence, and when Coleman came to the swinging gate, he clumsily fumbled with the latch until he was able to open it on the third try.

"Dad!"

Coleman took a few wobbly steps forward and, with an awkward hug, greeted a little boy with a shock of blonde hair so light that it nearly matched the white socks pulled up over his bulging shinguards.

"Hey champ, how ya doing?"

"Good! Dad, check this out!"

The boy ran toward the middle of the yard, where floodlights shined a stadium-quality halo on the soccer ball resting near an intricate stone patio, complete with firepit and outdoor grill and kitchen. The boy picked up the ball, held it at waist-level, then dropped it. When the ball had nearly reached the ground, he kicked it with his black cleat, sending the ball high in the air before it descended again. With the same foot, he kicked it again, sending it higher this time, and when it fell back toward the ground, the boy missed it and the ball rolled toward Coleman, who stood watching with a glazed look and a goofy grin.

"Son, that is a gooood start," he said, unintentionally drawing out his words. "But let me show you how it's done."

A little off-balance, slurry, and with one wet shoe, Coleman rolled the ball backward, flipped it up on his foot, and began to juggle with the skill and precision of an elite athlete. Over and over, he kept the ball bouncing in crisp, tightly controlled kicks. The rhythmic staccato timing of the kicks continued until Coleman grew bored and sent the ball looping high over his head. Performing a makeshift pirouette, he spun to meet the ball and, just as it was about to hit the ground, began the same juggling routine on his other foot. Coleman's son loved it.

"Awesome Dad! Now over the top," he requested with a few claps of his small hands.

Coleman complied, booting the ball high into the air again. This time, he did a half-turn, and met the descending ball with the back of his heel. Giving it a soft thump, he popped the ball up, did another half-turn beneath it, and met it with his forehead, then his chest, to his knee and, finally, back to his foot. As the ball touched down, Coleman began juggling again, just as before, in a short, tight pattern, while his son looked on, amazed.

"Awesome!" the boy said. "Mom, did you see him do that?"

"I sure did," she said, stepping out to the edge of the patio and crossing her arms. "I also saw him let another man drive away in his car."

"Hey," Coleman greeted his wife, still juggling the soccer ball.

"Was that Steve?"

"Yep."

"How bad are you?"

"Not too bad," Coleman said. "Watch this."

Closing his eyes, he extended his arms at his sides and began alternating feet with each kick. Like someone suspected of driving under the influence, he touched his nose with the index finger of his right hand, then made the same motion with his left arm. When he was finished, he opened his eyes and smiled at his wife. Throughout the demonstration, the soccer ball never touched the ground.

"Cool!" his son said.

"Very cute. Now can you put the ball down so we can talk?"

Coleman juggled a few more times, then softly tapped the ball over to his son, who picked it up and tried to mimic what his father had just accomplished. Three consecutive bounces was the best he could manage.

"I don't really want to talk," he said, his eyes fixed on the boy.

"Great," she replied, her arms still crossed and now grimacing. "Well, what is it that you do want?"

He didn't reply right away, and in the cool Carolina evening, while the sprinklers registered at the edges of his lawn, and his son tried and tried to imitate his father, and his wife impatiently waited for an answer, Coleman thought about the question, rattled it around in his head and, despite his thick tongue, spoke with purpose and certainty.

"I want $100 million," he said, finally looking at his wife.

Despite his display of soccer prowess, fresh in his son's imagination, Coleman wobbled a little as he made his way from the lawn to the patio. She pivoted to watch him, her arms still folded and her tone unamused.

"Sleep it off, okay," she said.

Coleman dismissed her with a flippant wave and slowly ambled across the patio, crossed through the open French doors and disappeared into the home he had built with bonus money.

CHAPTER 4

Morning came faster than Coleman would have liked. Reaching over to turn off the smartphone alarm blaring beside him on the bedstand, he groaned and drew a deep breath through coarse lips and a dry mouth. Like most other days, Angie had beaten him out of bed and was, no doubt, already squeezing in a 30-minute session on the elliptical in their home gym. Fortunately, she had left the lights off and shut the door behind her, so he wouldn't have to hear Nickelodeon, or Disney Junior, or whatever awful cartoon Connor was watching in his room down the hall.

Coleman forced himself to pull the covers away and swing his legs off the bed until they touched the ground. He realized that he was still wearing the same clothes from the evening before – all but the shoes. He unbuttoned his blue dress shirt, tugged it off, and let it drop to the ground beside the bed. Angie would get it later.

After a pit stop in the bathroom, where he splashed cool water on his face and gargled with mint mouthwash, Coleman made his way down the left side of the dual staircase that seemed like two arms embracing a grand foyer. Shuffling his socked feet onto the polished hardwood floor, he scooted into the French kitchen and drained a strong mug of morning brew from the coffeemaker. From there, he traipsed through the family room – she had already opened the tall curtains, and morning light poured through the windows – and made his way down a connecting hall to the bonus room at the back corner of the house.

The door was open, and Coleman propped himself against the door jamb while he took a long draw from the hot mug of coffee. A low *whirr whirr whirr* emanated from the elliptical machine as Angie pumped her arms and churned her legs to keep the rhythm. Her pace was good, and a light film of sweat clung to her forehead, yet her soft, controlled breathing barely registered. Her eyes were fixed on the television mounted to the wall, where an overly perky morning news anchor informed the audience that property tax rates were likely to rise again as part of the state's drive to fund new schools throughout the area.

"Awesome," Coleman mumbled sarcastically into his mug.

Angie turned her head and squinted her eyes, but continued with her workout. She looked terrific, decked out in skin-tight yoga pants and a form-fitting white tanktop that accentuated her olive skin tone. Her wavy hair, light brown with just a hint of auburn when the light hit it at the right angle, was pulled back into a ponytail, and the end bounced softly between her shoulderblades with each *whirr* of the elliptical. Even in the morning, without a hint of makeup, her skin was nearly flawless. Coleman hardly noticed, fixing his attention instead on the TV.

"Is that what you're wearing today?" she said with a smirk. Her green eyes disapprovingly looked him up and down.

Coleman grunted and took another gulp from his mug. Angie turned her attention back to the news, but spoke to him through the *whirr* of her workout.

"Listen, we need a few things."

"What things?"

"Well, we need to hire a landscaper. I want to get the mulch down before too much longer."

"Mulch?"

"We also need the windows cleaned, and I'd like to get the exterior of the house powerwashed after the pollen has settled down."

"Isn't that what rain is for?" Coleman said.

Angie ignored him. "You also promised me that we could go to a weekly cleaning service instead of the housekeepers coming monthly."

"I did?"

"You did. Last week."

Coleman slurped from his mug. "How much?"

"Probably less than whatever you spent with Steve last night."

Coleman frowned.

Angie continued churning the machine for a few more repetitions. Neither of them made a sound until she finally spoke.

"Rob, you have to slow down. It's not good for Connor to see you like that."

"Like what?"

"Stumbling home drunk every other night."

"I was hardly stumbling."

"You were a mess."

"Stop overexaggerating. I was fine."

"Look, I don't care if you unwind once in awhile, but it's starting to become a routine, and it's not good."

"You don't care if I unwind?" Coleman snorted. "Oh, well thank you for your generosity."

"I'm trying to help you."

"Help me? What, by spending all my money? This is fantastic – in one breath, you ask me to pay for every service in the Yellow Pages, and in the next breath you're telling me how to live my life."

"Your money?" Angie glared at him.

"Oh, I'm sorry, let me think for a moment..." Coleman made a display of looking toward the ceiling while he counted single numbers on his fingers. "That's right...you made ZERO DOLLARS last year. Forgive me for thinking it was my money."

"Just stop it. We're supposed to be a partnership."

"Sure, and apparently I'm the silent partner." Coleman finished his mug. "Actually, I'm worse than a silent partner. I make all the money, AND I'm told what we'll be spending it on, AND I'm criticized for my behavior in the pursuit of the money that you get to spend. This is really cute, Angie."

"Hey..."

"No, let me make this really simple and really clear for you, dear. There are two ways to do this – one, you leave me alone, and you can spend the money on whatever you want! Doesn't that sound good?"

"Seriously, stop..."

"Or two, you can continue picking at me and telling me what a horrible person I am and, in return, I will give you an allowance based directly on how well you treat me. All things being equal, your allowance is currently about 85 cents."

Angie looked away in disgust and began cranking the elliptical faster. Her legs churned in double time, and her breathing became noticeably heavier.

Coleman immediately regretted his words, but didn't say as much. He looked toward the ground and exhaled through his nose.

"I need another cup of coffee, then I'm going to take a shower, and then Steve is picking me up for work."

"I'll be sure to post your plans to the Internet, for all the world to see."

Coleman clenched his jaw, but didn't engage. Instead he loudly slapped his palm against the door jamb, cleared his throat and turned to go.

"Oh, and sweetheart?" Angie said mockingly.

Coleman turned back toward her.

"While you're out there simultaneously making it rain and determining what my allowance should be, it's probably a good time to remind you that during our lovely marriage, I did, in fact, bear you a son, and he has his Spring Concert this evening at the school. Perhaps in the course of your affairs, you can find it in your busy schedule and in your glowing heart to attend in support of your only child."

After a long pause, Coleman said, "What time?"

"Six o'clock."

"I'll be there."

He was gone by the time Angie had composed herself enough to look toward the door.

CHAPTER 5

Coleman had no interest in driving and gladly slumped into the same passenger seat that Steve had dumped him from the night before. This was nothing new for Steve, and he merely nodded as Coleman fastened his seatbelt. The soft, self-important voices from the morning news channel filled the BMW's cabin and allowed the two men to ignore each other throughout the drive to work.

The Carolina pines zipped past as Coleman stared, glassy-eyed, out the window and tried to shut off his brain for a few minutes before the normal workday machinations claimed his attention. The argument with Angie, however, prevented him from entering a zone of mental inactivity. As much as he would refuse to admit it, her mockery had stung. Even worse was the creeping guilt he felt for essentially classifying her as a free-loader. It hadn't always been that way.

Many years ago, before Connor, before the estate home, and before the reputation had been cultivated, he had been a doting husband with a gorgeous young wife, fairly big dreams of soccer stardom, and absolutely no income whatsoever. They had lived in a modest one-bedroom apartment near the university training facility, and Angie's entry-level marketing job for a local mall had kept them afloat while Coleman chased the fading wisps of a professional soccer career.

He was hardly unique in that regard – just about every player with a pulse gave it one shot at a paying gig – but Coleman straddled the line between dreams and delusion longer than most. He had been a terrific striker, helping guide the team to the College Cup during his senior year and garnering Honorable Mention All-America honors along the way, but pro soccer is a much different animal and the competition is fierce and crushing. College standouts from America rarely beat out their international peers, many of whom have been training since age 10 or 12 in futbol factories, where all expenses are paid, soccer is the curriculum, and the best of the best are identified and targeted for the top European clubs. Coleman had been good enough to earn a few tryouts with this caliber of player, but not good enough to advance.

For three years he had tried to make it, all the while supported by his wife, and it took several long discussions with her, with his parents and, finally, with his college coach before Coleman realized that it wasn't going to happen for him. She had stayed with him during the ensuing six months, when he completely dropped out of polite society, grew his hair long and became a barfly, and she was there to buck him up when he finally snapped out of it, cut the hair, polished his somewhat sparse resume, bought a suit, and then failed to land four or five junior sales positions in several different fields. "Working on your soccer" for a three-year post-graduate stretch hardly excites the hiring managers, who routinely must choose between MBAs and PhDs for the technology and biotech jobs available in the Research Triangle Park.

And then, one day, everything fell into place. Coleman's coach put him in touch with a former player, 10 years Coleman's senior, who had an open position. He got the job, found his groove over the next few years, and became a top earner. It wasn't long before the headhunters sought after him, and Coleman eventually landed where he stood today – as a rising client executive for one of the top tech companies in the world. And if he followed the breadcrumbs to the beginning, Coleman's path led back to Angie. Without her, there was none of "this."

While he wrestled with the pangs of conscience, Steve pulled into a parking spot near the front of the building.

"You have to take me home, you know?" he said, engaging the emergency brake.

"No problem," Coleman smiled. "Maybe after a stop at Goodies later."

☺

Neal Armstrong's office looked like it was stolen from the Smithsonian's Air & Space Museum. Framed portraits of the moon, the Apollo spacecraft and a signed photo with a smiling Neil Armstrong graced the walls. The gratuitous inscription read, "To Neal Armstrong: One giant leap for OUR kind. Yours, Neil Armstrong." His exuberance for all things aeronautical had, of course, been inspired by sharing a name with the great NASA spaceman, and instead of shunning the connection, Armstrong had embraced it with zeal. Tall, thin and bald, with a nose as prominent as an eagle's beak, Armstrong greeted his visitors like he greeted everyone who visited his office – with a spin of the moon.

Placing his thin, pale fingers atop a waist-high rendition of his hero's former stomping grounds, Armstrong gave the moon globe a strong spin. Coleman and Steve, like everyone who entered Armstrong's office, stood just inside the door and stared, mesmerized, as the contours and craters rotated in a blur, then slowed, then finally came to a stop. Never tiring of the reaction to his piece de resistance, Armstrong beamed and beckoned them inside.

"Good morning, gentlemen. To what do I owe the honor? Oh yes, I called this meeting, didn't I?"

"Morning, Neal," Coleman said, pointing to a set of chairs before a large cherry desk topped by models of the Space Shuttle and Apollo spacecraft.

"The couch is fine," Armstrong said, moving them toward the office's sitting area. "How are you today, Steven?"

"I'm well, Mister Armstrong. Hope you are?"

"Just fine. Have a seat," he said, directing his employees to the couch, which sat just below a giant framed photo of the Milky Way Galaxy, taken by the Hubble Telescope. "Robert, you look terrible. Goodies again?"

Steve nodded enthusiastically.

"Would you stay out of that joint? What a waste of money. The girls don't even touch you."

Now Coleman nodded knowingly, before cutting off the small talk. "What's up, Neal?"

Armstrong placed his hands on the back of a chair and looked them over. Coleman had reclined and rested his head just below the Milky Way, while Steve sat on the edge of his dark green cushion and fidgeted with a signed copy of Buzz Aldrin's autobiography ("Dear Neal: Our walk on the moon was the highlight of my life! Buzz Aldrin") resting atop the coffee table that separated them from the boss.

Armstrong took a deep breath and gave them a long stare. "$100 million, gentlemen."

Coleman and Steve nodded in unison.

"That's a lot of money, guys."

Coleman and Steve nodded in unison.

"A whole lot of money."

Still nodding.

"This is a highly competitive situation. Three years of IT and data security services for one of the top five banks in the United States. Two other competitors..."

"IntelliSec?" Steve said.

"Yes."

"SecureIntell?" Coleman added.

"Correct."

Coleman and Steve nodded, this time a bit more grim.

"The good news, gentlemen, is that I've been on these bankers like white on rice. Like a bee on honey. Like..."

"Like Coleman on happy hour?" Steve said.

"Exactly," Armstrong smiled. "And, gentlemen, I believe that we are uniquely placed for victory."

"How's that?" Coleman asked after a pause.

Armstrong moved toward his moon globe and tapped his fingers around the Sea of Tranquility. Staring deep into the globe's rendering of the dark basalt basin, he grinned and said, "They're athletes, gentlemen."

A confused silence lingered before Steve spoke up. "I don't follow, boss."

"Athletes, Steven. The men at The Bank – the executives, the decision-makers – are all athletes."

"What does that have to do with us?" Coleman said.

"Everything, Robert. EVERYTHING." Armstrong gazed out the floor-to-ceiling window and watched the fountain spraying the pond in a full floral bloom. Turning back, he moved toward the couch, unable to contain his glee.

"I'm sorry, Neal, but what in the world are you talking about?"

"Robert," Armstrong said, clapping his hands, "these men at The Bank are what are known as 'Extreme Athletes.' All of them! The CEO, the CFO, the CIO and, hell, pretty much all the top-level VPs."

"Extreme athletes?" Steve said. "What does that even mean?"

"It means marathons, triathlons, 50-milers, mud runs..."

"Mud runs?" Steve said.

Coleman interjected. "Yeah, you've seen them. Those races where they climb up hills and run through ponds. Mud the whole way. Stupidest thing I've ever seen."

"But what does that have to do with us?"

"Victory!" Armstrong punched the air. "That's what it has to do with us, young Steven."

"I think I know where you're going with this, Neal."

Steve turned to Coleman. "Where is he going? I don't get it. Who cares if they're part of some athletic cult?"

"That's how they're going to make their decision, isn't it?" Coleman looked toward Armstrong.

"Robert, there is a reason I made you the lead on this account."

"And this is the reason?"

"This is the reason."

"Not because of my numbers? My experience? Because I'm the best guy you've got?"

"Well, I took all of those things into consideration..."

"But this is the reason?"

"Yes."

Coleman shook his head and looked at the floor. Sitting beside him, Steve raised his hands and looked at Armstrong. "I still don't get it?"

"You see, Steven, these men — these cultists, as you put it — will be making their decision in large part based on how well they get along with our team." Armstrong pointed at Coleman, who still stared at his feet. "And on our team, we have precisely one gentleman who can keep up the pace."

"You gave me The Bank because I was a soccer player," Coleman muttered to himself.

"An All-American soccer player!" Armstrong clapped his hands together.

"And soccer players have to run for miles and miles," Steve said, finally joining the conversation.

"They're some of the most finely-tuned athletes in all of sports," Armstrong agreed. "And our friend here — he's still got it. I've seen him running around the pond at lunch."

"So you want him to beat these guys?" Steve said.

"Nooooo, Steven, not beat them! I want him to keep up with these guys, just so they understand how tenacious we are, but then he will give them the glory at the finish line. Give them the glory, and they will give us the money!"

Armstrong's grin was wider than the moon's Crater Tycho.

Coleman raised his eyes, a blank stare painted on his face. "You picked me because I can run?"

"Well, it certainly wasn't for your temperament and pleasant demeanor. If that were the case, I would have promoted Steven. You're here, Robert, to win this account by showing these guys that we share the same culture, the same interests, and the same lifestyle."

"Thanks so much," Coleman snarked.

"Calm down, Robert. You know you're a jerk."

Steve nodded knowingly.

"But look at the bright side — all you have to do is run. All that money...for running!"

Coleman considered it and nodded. "When?"

"That's the best part!" Armstrong stood and spread his arms. "You're meeting them this afternoon."

"This afternoon? Where?"

"You'll see."

CHAPTER 6

"Welcooooooome to The Asylum!"

A shaggy-haired DJ, dressed loosely in a mud-splattered tank top, and wearing tinted ski goggles over his eyes, greeted each new arrival with his loud, guttural salutation. Some sort of Japanese techno-pop piped through the speakers erected behind his table, and the DJ himself seemed to be the only congregant enjoying the music.

They parked alongside Armstrong's silver Benz, stepped out of Coleman's BMW, and took in the surroundings.

"What is this place?" Coleman said, warily surveying the course.

"The Asylum!" Armstrong said, clapping his hands together.

Steve exhaled and smiled. "It's awesome."

"Welcooooooome to The Asylum!" Another group of participants had pulled up and parked next to Coleman.

"Welcome to the Asylum!" A large man with a shaved head and a red Van Dyke beard stepped from his truck. "You guys look new."

Coleman grunted affirmatively, but kept his gaze firmly affixed to the course before him.

"Hey guys, fresh meat!" Redbeard gestured to the newcomers as his buddies piled out of the truck and they all took off in a jog toward what Coleman could only describe as giant mounds of mud.

The Asylum looked like a cross between a rodeo corral, a military training facility and a BMX racetrack. Hills made of mud, a few standing 50-feet high, descended into slick muddy ramps that bottomed out into sloppy mud trenches connected by mud-caked ladders, which led to tall muddy walls with single mud-flecked ropes dangling from their heights. All throughout the course, additional mud-splattered obstacles presented slippery challenges to the smattering of competitors practicing their rounds.

"It looks muddy," Steve said.

Armstrong cackled and slapped Coleman on the back. "You're gonna be great! Just don't be too great, understood?"

Coleman said nothing as he lifted the trunk door and reached inside. He pulled out a pair of black soccer cleats, walked back to the driver's seat, sat and slowly removed his running shoes.

"What are you doing?" Armstrong said.

"I need spikes to run through that muck."

Armstrong and Steve nodded their understanding as Coleman laced up his soccer boots. Coleman didn't look at them and took his time as he extended his legs and went into a few routine stretching exercises.

"Welcoooooome to The Asylum!" The DJ was shaking his hips and doing a robot dance as the speakers thumped and Japanese techno voices warbled from the black boxes. He had shouted his greeting into the microphone just as a black Cadillac Escalade parked near the BMW. Steve and Armstrong watched as a driver in a black suit stepped from the vehicle, opened the back door, and three nearly identical-looking men bounded from the back seat.

"It's them!" Armstrong hissed at Coleman. "Get up! Look alive!"

They were all tall, each wore a black full-body spandex running outfit, and they all sported bizarre shoes that looked like nylon casts of gorilla feet, with each toe perfectly defined, as if they had painted their feet black and glued plastic moldings to the bottoms. They would have blended in at any fitness center, and the only way to tell them apart was by their hair.

"Gentlemen!" Armstrong greeted them with a warm smile and a strong handshake, as he motioned toward Coleman, who was loosening his back. "You guys look like you mean business. You'll have to take it easy on my young buck over here."

The leader, who sported a head of thick salt-and-pepper hair, returned the handshake and smiled back.

"Mister Armstrong, it's a shame you won't be running with us."

"Oh, no, no, not me," Armstrong said, reaching for his side. "This hip has seen better days. It's reinforced with the same steel that NASA uses on the space shuttle, which is great for orbiting earth, but doesn't help too much in the Asylum."

"Welcoooooome to The Asylum!" Another car had arrived and the DJ greeted them with a slide step and some air drumming.

"Well, we've heard much about Mister Coleman, and we can only hope that he'll be gentle with us on the course today. We understand that you are a fierce competitor, Mister Coleman."

"Hey, I'm just hoping to keep up out there. And, please, call me Rob." Coleman shook hands with the leader, and then exchanged salutations with his men, a Nordic-looking giant with longish, nearly white hair that covered his ears, and a slightly shorter, but more muscular, Italian with jet-black hair that was slicked straight back from the prominent widow's peak at the top of his forehead.

"You can't fool us, Mister Coleman," the leader said. "When Mister Armstrong informed us that you would be managing the proposed account for our security business we, of course, performed an extensive background check on you, and we know all about your prowess on the soccer field."

"All-American," said the Swede.

"Honorable Mention," the Italian corrected him.

"Well, I, uh, don't know what to say." Coleman looked at Armstrong for help, but he had turned toward the Asylum and left Coleman on his own. "It sounds like you guys did your homework. I guess I'm flattered."

"You should be flattered!" the leader said. "It's a tremendous accomplishment. I don't think it will help you much on the course, but it's certainly something that should fill you with great pride."

"Well, thank you, that's very kind," Coleman said, adopting the most humble posture he could muster. "You know, I've done a little bit of homework, too, and I really think we can help you guys. You're already familiar with the strength of our product platforms, but I would really like to dig in and demonstrate to you how our code quality and robust software strategy can positively impact your business..."

"That will be quite enough, Mister Coleman," the leader interrupted.

Armstrong had wheeled around and his eyes beckoned Coleman to restrain himself.

"We are not here to discuss business. There will be time for that later in a more formal capacity. Today, we conquer The Asylum."

"Welcoooooome to The Asylum!" the DJ shouted into the microphone, as he did the worm with his arms.

The leader patted Coleman on the shoulder and started in a brisk jog toward the entrance of the corral. "See you at the finish line."

The Swede nodded and mimicked his boss's gesture, patting Coleman condescendingly on the shoulder.

The Italian leaned toward Coleman as he walked past and whispered, "Honorable Mention."

Coleman watched them go, his jaw clenching and his fists curling into tight balls. He took a deep breath and then started jogging in place, bouncing on the balls of his feet.

"Whoa," Steve said, when the three men were beyond earshot. "Those guys are weirdos. Did you see those shoes?"

Coleman nodded and handed Steve his car keys. "Nobody with shoes like that is beating me. Steve, there are a couple of towels in the trunk. Have them ready for me at the finish line. This is going to be muddy."

Armstrong stepped in front of him. "Easy there, Robert. You know the deal. Take it easy, and let them win. Especially the President! Let. Him. Win. Are we clear?"

Coleman didn't respond as he continued warming up.

"$100 million, Robert! It's a stupid race. Don't let your pride get in the way of this!"

Coleman only looked at Armstrong as he bounced past and headed for the starting area. About 20 runners had begun congregating near the starting line of The Asylum, and Coleman found a good spot near the front and filled in, on the opposite side of where the gentlemen from The Bank stood. Back near the car, Armstrong looked like a ghost.

"He's going to blow this for us, isn't he?"

Steve nodded and began collecting the towels from Coleman's trunk. "It's part of his charm, Mister Armstrong."

Coleman's lack of experience with The Asylum showed immediately. When the gun sounded, he took off at a pretty good clip, expecting to be somewhere in the middle of the pack. What he couldn't have known was that running The Asylum was as much about strategy and positioning as it was sheer speed. And so Coleman found himself all alone, about 30 yards out in front of his competitors. Surprised, he stole a peek over his right shoulder, and became a little rattled when he spotted the three men from The Bank jogging shoulder to shoulder with an easy stride. The President flashed him a knowing grin and nodded, while the Italian gave him two enthusiastic thumbs up.

When Coleman turned back to face forward, he had begun the ascent of a steep hill. The packed dirt, pounded by the daily stampede of runners, and lightly moistened by a recent rain, had turned into a thick, gooey mud. Coleman likened it to charging up a hill made of pumpkin pie. His soccer cleats dug for footing, but he couldn't maintain a firm grip and his feet nearly slid out from under him as he crested the hilltop. Meanwhile, The Bank team expertly planted their gorilla shoes in a cross-country skiing snowplow fashion, with their feet flared out and the arches dug deep into the mud. They didn't so much run up the hill; they climbed ladders of their own making.

As he reached the top, Coleman turned his attention to the next obstacle, but it was already too late. The hill was steeper going down than coming up, and it had been specially watered for the occasion. Coleman took a cautious step that yielded no foundation, and he immediately slipped and tumbled, landing on his back with a muddy squish, then rolling in a loose, frenetic ball down the entire slick face. Behind him, the other competitors, led by The Bank team, each seemed to execute a perfect head-first baseball slide, which took them softly from the hilltop, all the way down to the bottom, where they caught up with Coleman, who struggled to regain his legs and find his upright balance.

Rushing past him in a hurry, the President gave Coleman a pat on the shoulder, the Swede ignored him entirely, and the Italian leaned down so Coleman could hear him whisper, "Honorable Mention."

Coleman jumped up. He had fallen back to about the middle of the pack and he jogged with the group as he recovered his footing and reviewed his position. Shortly ahead, the next obstacle was a 4-foot-deep trench, half filled with water the color of chocolate milk. It was about a 6-foot jump to clear the other side, and a wooden gallows spanned the length of the trench. Four single rope swings hung from the gallows, and some of the runners had already reached for them. They grasped the ropes tightly, held on, and allowed their momentum to carry them to the other side, where they released and landed, slipping, in the slick mud. Coleman keyed in on the guys from The Bank, who ignored the ropes altogether. With their height, they had no trouble clearing the trench without a lifeline, and they landed on their feet, safely beyond the trench's edge, and continued onward. Coleman followed their lead.

Building up speed, he got as close to the edge as he dared, planted his foot, and felt the mud give way. Slipping slightly, just as he went airborne, Coleman flailed his arms, desperately tried to maintain his balance, and splashed down into the chocolate milk, about six inches short of the landing area on the other side.

Wiping water from his face, he quickly scrambled over the edge and pulled himself out of the trench. He was now about as far behind the group as he had been ahead at the start of the race. He spit twice to rid his mouth of the muddy drink and, seething, he took off in a sprint. Coleman was a strong runner, and the ground before the next obstacle was largely flat and packed down tight. It didn't take him long to catch the pack, but The Bank team had surged ahead and ran about five seconds ahead of him. Coleman kept sprinting, making up ground with each stride.

The next obstacle was a larger trench, too wide to leap across. Beyond that lay another high hill, steeper than the first, followed by a good stretch of flat ground and, finally, one final trench that marked the finish line. Coleman could see that there was only one way across the trench directly before him – a wet log that would create a time-consuming, single-file backup if he couldn't get there ahead of the pack.

Because they are constantly chasing the path of the ball, which can change direction and speed at any time, soccer players are skillful and adept at reaching top speeds in just moments, sometimes from a standstill or a light jog. Coleman summoned every bit of this training and expertise, and gave a huge kick to separate himself from the greater pack in advance of the log bridge. He watched as the President gently bounced across the log, followed by the Swede and, finally, the Italian. Just as they had crossed, Coleman broke through the group and reached the log in fourth place. He slowed just enough to maintain his balance, and safely made it across.

He was still about three seconds behind but, this time, on this hill, Coleman was able to mimic their ascent. Just as they did, he adopted the cross-country skiing technique and, when he reached the top, he witnessed how they traveled down the slippery slope head-first. Coleman did the same, and pulled himself up at the bottom of the hill. He hadn't gained any ground, but he hadn't lost any either. There was still time to catch them.

Covered in mud, from head to toe, with soaked shoes, wet socks, and the soggy clothes sticking to his body, Coleman gave chase across the flat section of ground. The last quarter-mile was wet and slightly muddy, but his footing held and he seemed to draw closer with each powerful lunge. His soccer spikes churned the ground, kicking up a rooster tail of mud behind him. Three seconds became two. Two seconds became one. And then he was upon them.

The far side of the final trench marked the finish line, and it came into sight as Coleman reached the Italian's shoulder. He said nothing and kept his eyes on the finish line as he surged past, brushing against the Italian. Coleman sunk his cleats deeper into the ground so that, on his way past, his muddy backwash would splash the taller man.

Now clear of one opponent, Coleman charged for the Swede. The final trench was about 100 yards ahead of them – the length of a football field. Coleman dug deep inside. His chest heaved, his lungs were on fire and his hamstrings felt like they could snap at any moment. But he kept on, driving his legs through the mud, pumping his arms, racing to the line.

He caught the Swede with about 50 yards to go. The Swede gave an extra kick and stayed with Coleman for a few more strides, but he had nothing left to give. Reaching out, Coleman patted him on the shoulder and kept on. Only the President stood between him and the finish line.

He was tall and fit, lean and muscular, with graceful strides and a competitive drive. But Coleman was younger by at least a decade, and possessed more stamina. This made the difference. Coleman was on his heels with 25 yards to go. He came around to his right side, and they stood shoulder to shoulder with 10 yards to go. Just like the Swede, the leader sprinted harder upon being caught, but Coleman stayed right with him.

Five yards to go.

They lunged together, drove their legs harder, ferociously pumped their arms, and they reached the launch point at the same time. Whoever jumped across the trench faster would win.

The President, having done this before, fluidly took off on his right foot and extended his long left leg through the air. It was only about four feet to the other side, and it would take only a second to cross.

Coleman knew the man was taller and he sensed the advantage of experience. He knew it would take a desperate maneuver to beat him.

With a little hop, Coleman planted both feet hard in the mud and pushed off as hard as he could. With his head up and his hands together, he sailed across the trench, hands first, like an Olympic swimmer diving off the blocks.

They crossed together, airborne, flying at the same speed toward the row of multi-colored triangular flags that marked the finish line.

However, the President was vertical.

Coleman was horizontal and closer to the ground. His arms and chest reached the other side first, and he curled up and rolled through the mud beneath the colored flags.

The President's left foot arrived just a fraction of a second later.

"The new dude wins!" yelled the DJ, pumping up some fresh house music. "Welcooooooome to The Asylum!"

"You stupid, stupid, stupid fool!" The vein in Armstrong's neck throbbed and threatened to rip through his collar. "Do you know what you've done?"

Coleman was unable to respond. He rolled on the ground, still at the finish line, and began heaving. The first two were dry, but the third time was the charm, and he vomited everything in his stomach onto the ground. It mixed in with the mud and formed a soupy, toxic gruel.

"You had one job. One! And you just blew the biggest deal of our careers because you had to be the star. You stupid, stupid fool."

Steve had joined them, and leaned down to cover Coleman with one of the towels. They were the only people still at the finish line, and when Armstrong turned to see if he could spot The Bankers, Steve leaned down and said under his breath, "That was awesome."

He helped Coleman into a sitting position and handed him the second towel. Coleman wiped his face with it, then draped it over his head, like a bloodied boxer after a fight.

"I'm not kidding," Armstrong continued. "Clear your desk out by tonight. If you sabotaged this thing, you're done. You'll never work in the industry again. I'll see to that!"

Armstrong had just completed his rant, when The Bankers walked up, looking none worse for the wear after such a grueling event. Their spandex bodysuits had deflected much of the mud, and they had cleaned themselves up so that they carried the appearance of men who had just finished a routine workout.

"Guys, I sincerely, from the bottom of my heart..." Armstrong stuttered through an apology. "I don't know what happened out there, but please believe me, this was not..."

The President raised a hand and interrupted. Stepping past Armstrong, he addressed his opponent directly.

"Mister Coleman, that was outstanding. Just outstanding."

Armstrong's eyes grew wide and he watched as the Swede reached down, grabbed Coleman's hand and helped him to his feet. "Nice job," the Swede said, patting Coleman on the shoulder.

Coleman, with his chest still heaving, nodded and pulled the towel from his head, then half-heartedly smoothed his hair back.

"That was a determined and inspired effort," the President continued. "We've never had someone come in here with the fortitude or the skill to beat us. Normally they let us win, or at least they think they let us win. But that shows weakness and a lack of integrity."

Armstrong teetered somewhere between laughter and tears. Steve audibly giggled.

"Your effort, Mister Coleman, was a first for us. It showed dedication, honesty and guts, and we admire that. We like winners at The Bank."

Coleman wiped his mouth with the back of his hand. "Well, if it means anything, I feel like I almost died trying to beat you guys."

The President smiled. "It does. If you and your team possess that kind of determination, then it's probably a safe bet that you have what it takes to protect our network security interests."

"Really?" Armstrong exhaled.

"Now, please don't be misled. The discovery process will continue, and we will still invite a few of your competitors here to gauge their spirit. But you've guaranteed yourselves another meeting. Plus, I think we all want another shot at Mister Coleman, don't we?"

The Swede nodded and even appeared to crack a smile. The Italian looked Coleman in the eye and said, "All-American."

"Gentlemen," the President said, "we need more honesty in this world. Honesty in all things. Mister Coleman demonstrated honesty today, and it will be difficult for the others to match that. We will speak again soon."

They watched them go. Armstrong, breathless and overjoyed, clapped Steve on the back.

Coleman bent over at the waist and vomited on his shoes.

CHAPTER 7

"Clear my desk? Seriously, clear my desk?" Coleman reached for another shrimp from the cocktail glass and washed it back with a big tug from his pint glass. "Why don't you clear your desk? Huh? If it weren't for me..."

"Okay, okay, okay. I may have been hasty in my assessment." Armstrong raised both hands in surrender.

"Hasty? You think you were hasty? I think there's another word you're looking for..."

"Okay, you've made your point. I may have erred, but let's not belabor it, shall we?"

Armstrong was pleased to be interrupted by the waiter, who cleared their plates and asked if he could bring them anything else.

"Yes!" Coleman responded, pointing to his drink. "I'll have another beer. Steve will have another beer, and please bring a cup of bleach for my Dad here."

"Robert, that's enough," Armstrong muttered, turning to face the waiter. "Ice water will be fine, please."

"And we'll also have another round of shrimp cocktails, another plate of the mussels, and we'll split a plate of the crab cakes. Broiled, not fried, please." Coleman drained the rest of his beer, wiped his mouth with the cloth napkin and leaned back in his chair.

The Carolina Oyster Bar had a healthy mid-week crowd in for dinner, a mix of well-dressed young professionals, college students pounding drinks and beginning to congregate on the dance floor, and the older set, who were finishing up their meals and eager to head out before the band arrived and the music started. Coleman had cleaned up after The Asylum and changed into a pair of jeans, loafers, and an untucked pink button-down dress shirt. He undid another button near his chest and took a deep breath as he surveyed the bar and dance floor. It didn't seem too long ago that he had been among the crowd mustering near the stage. He missed it.

"Look, Robert, you really demonstrated your value today. There's no question of that."

"I know what I'm doing, Neal."

"That remains an open question."

"I know what I'm doing." Coleman leaned forward, emphatic. The waiter had returned with their beers and Armstrong's water. Coleman drank deeply, draining half the pint glass in one gulp. He indicated to the waiter that he wanted another, but Steve stopped him.

"Here, have mine," he said, sliding his glass over.

"We need more honesty in this world," Coleman said, staring at Armstrong. "Honesty in all things. Mister Coleman demonstrated honesty today. Did you miss that part, Neal?"

Armstrong was silent for a long moment, returning Coleman's stare before he continued. "You've made your point, and you did well today. Now it's time to move to the next phase. We need to make sure we have the software ready to go."

"I'll set up a meeting and have Vijay fly in," Steve offered. "He's in London at a conference right now, so it shouldn't be an issue."

Armstrong nodded. "Thank you, Steven."

"We don't need to see Vijay," Coleman said. "It's in the bag."

"We haven't won anything yet, Robert. You got us off to a great start..."

"Yes I did."

"Yes you did. But we still have to do the work. We'll bring Vijay in and iron out the kinks."

"Super, can't wait," Coleman said, finishing his beer and reaching for Steve's glass. "Nothing like some good quality time with Vijay."

The band had arrived, a rough-looking crew from one of the local universities. Coleman watched as they hauled their instruments and sound equipment from the front door to the stage, the black cases decorated with stickers of other, more successful bands. He drank from Steve's glass and his eye began to wander to some of the college girls, who all seemed to be having conversations on their smartphones rather than with the people standing directly beside them.

Armstrong watched Coleman watching the crowd and frowned. He wiped his hands on a napkin, neatly folded it and placed it in the center of his empty plate. As he stared at the table, the waiter returned with the seafood. He placed a shrimp cocktail glass in front of each man, and set the steamed mussels and broiled crab cakes in the middle of the table. Smells of garlic and hot butter wafted up from the steaming dishes, and Coleman inhaled deeply before attacking a crab cake with his fork.

"Can I get you gentlemen anything else?" the waiter asked.

"One more of these," Coleman said with his mouth full, clanging the fork against his pint glass.

Armstrong waited until the waiter had gone. "Go easy, Robert."

"How many is that?" Steve said, thinking about the drive ahead.

"Who cares?" Coleman bit into two shrimp at once, and pointed at the plate. "Have some mussels before they get cold."

Steve winced and looked at Armstrong. "I'm good," he said.

"Me too," Armstrong said. "I need to get going. Steven, do you need a lift?"

Steve looked back to Coleman. "Yeah, uh, that would be great, Mister Armstrong. But how are you going to get back?"

"I'll be fine."

"Take a cab," Armstrong said.

"Yes, definitely take a cab," Steve added.

Coleman finished the last shrimp from his glass, and reached for the mussels. "I'll take a cab."

Armstrong stood and brushed off his pants. He walked around the table and placed a hand on Coleman's shoulder. "Expense this okay?"

"No doubt," Coleman said, slurping another mussel.

"See you tomorrow," Steve said, inching away from the table.

"And Robert," Armstrong said. "You did well today."

"No doubt." Slurp.

"You landed on the moon. But now we have to make it back to Earth. Understood?"

Slurp.

"Be safe," Armstrong said, patting his shoulder once more.

Slurp.

The black shells from the mussels lay scattered and wet on the tablecloth. The crab cakes were completely gone, with just a tin of tartar sauce left on the plate. Only the tails from the shrimp cocktails remained among the crushed ice in their glasses. Four empty pint glasses surrounded the flatware. Coleman raised a napkin to his mouth and stifled the sound from his belch.

He looked toward the dance floor and watched as the co-eds swayed with the music. It was a long-haired jam band, and they were playing covers. Coleman couldn't tell what song it was, but he thought it sounded like the Allman Brothers.

Rising from the table, he wound his way through the dining room and walked around the edge of the dance floor to the bar on the other side. He ordered a beer, grabbed a stool and sat there for a while, watching the band, watching the dancers, watching the band, watching the dancers...

"Hey you."

He snapped out of his trance and turned around. A young woman in a red dress smiled down at him. Her hair was long and light blonde, highlighted by either the sun or a good colorist, and it curled into soft twists that fell against her bare shoulders. She had a good tan, either from the sun or a salon, and her white teeth gleamed in contrast. Her eyes were a blueish-gray, and Coleman lost himself staring into them for a moment before recovering and pointing to himself.

"Yes, you," she said, playfully brushing her fingers against his arm. "Is anyone sitting next to you?"

Coleman shook his head, and she didn't so much sit as she glided onto the stool beside him. Her dress rested just above the knee, and it slid up to mid-thigh as she sat. He watched as she crossed her legs and let the top one bounce up and down. She had toned legs, not quite athletic but definitely exercised in some way, and his eyes followed them down to the ankles. She wore black heels, strappy and open, and her toes were painted red.

She was still smiling when he lifted his head and looked back into her eyes. Coleman smiled back.

"I saw you having dinner," she said. "You poor thing. Did your friends leave you?"

"Oh, those were my colleagues."

"Work friends."

"Something like that."

"Well, I'm glad they left," she said, still smiling.

"Me too." He held up his beer. "Can I get you something to drink?"

"Aren't you sweet? I'd love a martini. Extra dirty."

"Extra dirty?"

"With two olives."

"Yes ma'am," he said, waving for the bartender.

"So are you going to tell me your name, or do I have to call you Mister Pink?"

Coleman ordered the martini and turned back to her. "Mister Pink?"

"For your shirt," she said, reaching for his open collar. Her fingers brushed against his neck.

"Oh," he smiled. "I'm Rob."

"Robby," she looked in his eyes and let her hand run down his arm.

"And what shall I call you?"

Coleman's face was hot and flushed, and he took a drink to calm himself. The bartender had returned with the martini and placed it on the bar. The woman lifted the toothpick from the drink and wrapped her mouth around an olive, tasting the vodka and licking her red lips.

"Call me Ashley."

"I will call you Ashley."

She smiled and sipped her martini. Her lipstick left a light impression on the glass. Behind them, the dance floor had filled and everyone moved to the music. Coleman thought it sounded like The Grateful Dead.

"Do you go to school around here?" he said.

"Maybe."

"Maybe?"

"Maybe not."

"Okay, I'll play along." Coleman leaned closer. "What brings you out tonight?"

"You."

"Me?"

"Maybe." She smiled and winked at him, then took another sip. "Maybe not."

Coleman downed his beer and waved to the bartender for another. Even though he was intoxicated and feeling powerful and alive, his nerves had just surfaced and his hand trembled a little when he received his beer.

"So what made you sit down next to me?" He took a long drink.

"You ask too many questions," she said, resting a hand on his knee. "You should just go with it."

"Go with it?"

She leaned closer to him, and Coleman could smell her perfume – perhaps a bit too much, but nothing too distracting. His eyes had wandered lower, and snuck a peek down past her neck to where the red fabric had separated from her tan skin. She noticed him looking.

"Go with it," she whispered.

Coleman inhaled and drank deeply. Even in his advanced tipsiness and, despite not being the recipient of such attention in many years, Coleman still knew the deal. His mind raced, vaguely considering the possibilities, the benefits and the consequences in a gauzy haze. She had moved her hand up his leg, and was gently rubbing his thigh through his jeans. The girl was a knockout, he was there alone, and nobody would ever find out, would they?

His nerves had returned, and he reached for his phone, pulling it out of his pocket and setting it on the bar beside him. Unable to find the words to match the moment, he instead fiddled with the touch screen, when he noticed the notification that he had a new text message. Instinctively he checked it.

"WHERE ARE YOU???? It's about to start!!"

"Oh no," he cursed himself. "I have to go."

"What?" She pulled back, as Coleman stood and shoved the phone back into his pocket.

"I'm so sorry," he said, slapping a $20 bill onto the bar. "But I really have to go."

She pouted as she watched him push his way through the dance floor and race for the door, but she wasn't pouting for long. An older gentleman, with thinning gray hair and wearing a blue suit, had just seated himself at the bar, and he appeared to be alone.

She finished her drink, touched up her lipstick, and made her way over to the stool beside him.

CHAPTER 8

The Stoneridge Elementary School parking lot was jam packed. Cars filled every spot, they lined the semi-circular drop-off area, and some had been pulled onto the grass field just adjacent to the auditorium. It was a cool Carolina evening, and the last remnants of red-streaked dusk had given way to a darkening night.

Coleman drove too fast through the sea of parked cars and, unable to locate an easily available spot, he pulled his BMW to the fire zone that fronted the school's entrance. Quickly, he grabbed another piece of gum and chewed furiously. He activated the hazard lights, straightened his shirt, and wobbled out the driver's side door. The orange-ish blinking lights pulsed through the darkness and he used them to navigate his way into the school.

The halls were slick and sanitary and smelled of school lunch food — slightly boiled, possibly fried, and most certainly overcooked. His shoes squeaked as he ran down the hall. He went too far, at first, and missed the turnoff for the auditorium, but doubled back and slowed his jog as he approached the wide double doors, which remained closed. Exhaling, he slowed again to a brisk walk. He had made it in time.

Coleman gently pulled one door open just a crack and attempted to slip inside unnoticed. When he had entered the room, however, a group of beaming parents greeted him, dragging their kids along, who struggled to haul their instrument cases behind them. The flow of traffic headed toward Coleman, and he stepped to the side to let them pass. Most of the adults ignored him, too wrapped up in their own conversations to notice, but there were a few mothers who stared a bit longer, all too happy to silently judge the late arrival.

He watched a few more families exit, and then he spotted them.

"Dad!" Connor yelled, dragging his trombone case behind him as he ran to greet Coleman with a hug.

"Hey champ, you were terrific. I really enjoyed that."

"Did you see it?"

"You bet."

"I think I missed a few notes, but they said it was okay and that everyone misses a few."

"That's very true," Coleman said, tousling the boy's hair.

"Here," he shoved the long black case into Coleman's hands and turned around. "Mom, can I go play with Joey in the hall?"

Angie, who had been glaring at her husband, quickly softened and smiled down at him.

"Sure, honey. I'll come out and get you when it's time to go."

"Cool! Thanks! See ya, Dad." Connor took off out the door and down the hall.

Coleman braced himself and moved back against the concrete wall. "Hi. They sounded really good."

Angie's face had returned to a glare and she slowly approached him, seeming to grow angrier with each step.

"Don't even," she hissed, reaching for the trombone case.

"I got caught up at work! It was an incredibly biddy – busy – day. But really good things are happening."

Angie crossed her arms and looked him up and down.

"What?" he said, throwing his arms up a little too demonstratively. A couple of the mothers heard him and took a keen interest in observing the conversation.

Angie pursed her lips and waited until they had left. "You smell like a brewery."

"What? I had a couple beers."

"How did you get here?"

"What do you mean?"

"Did you drive?"

"C'mon Angie, I'm fire. I'm fine. I'm parked out front."

"You've got to be kidding me."

"What?"

"So let me get this straight," she said, raising her voice. "You miss your only child's spring concert – the one I had specifically asked you not to forget – and when you do arrive after it's already over, you arrive reeking of alcohol and unable to string complete sentences together."

"Angie..."

"Oh, and YOU DROVE YOUR CAR. TO A SCHOOL!"

"I'm fine!"

"It's a miracle you didn't kill anyone. I cannot believe you. I don't even know what to say."

"Look, I had two beers. Seriously, I'm fine!"

"Oh wait, I know what I wanted to say." She raised a hand and jabbed her finger at him. "Don't come home tonight."

She had stunned him, and Coleman stood there for a long moment, unsure of how to respond. He watched her move toward the doors and he called out softly.

"Angie, please. This is cray. This is crazy."

Just before she stepped through the doors, she turned again and pointed.

"Don't come home. I'm serious. I don't care where you go, but you're not sleeping under the same roof as your son tonight. You're an embarrassment to him."

"Angie!"

"Don't come home."

Her face was red, and her words knocked him back against the wall. Coleman watched her walk away in a hurry, and he stared at the empty doorframe for a while, thinking about what had just happened.

Raising his fist to his mouth, he loudly belched, and the sound reverberated throughout the acoustically tuned auditorium.

CHAPTER 9

Coleman opened his eyes and stared into the galactic expanse. Great and faraway stars transmitted their images to him from light years away. Asteroids rumbled randomly through space, remorseless and without regard for their celestial kin. Comets blazed across the galaxy, gone as quickly as they had come. And the planets expressed their individuality as they revolved around a fiery, unforgiving sun.

Swift Mercury taunted its larger planetary brothers, circling the orange inferno more than twice as fast as lovely Venus, its nearest competition. Majestic Jupiter stood sentinel, lording over the others, the king of the skies, while Saturn – cool, beautiful Saturn – beckoned with its rings, always just out of reach.

Coleman reached anyway.

The Milky Way Galaxy dangled from the ceiling above Armstrong's couch. Coleman extended his arm, but couldn't touch the spinning mobile, so he left his arm elevated and mentally tried to will the planets into his open palm. Unsuccessful, he reached with his other arm and pantomimed grabbing onto a rope to pull himself upright.

Armstrong kept his blinds open and the windows exposed at all times. Sitting up, Coleman could see the real sun creeping higher over the pine trees. Nearer to the building, the pond was smooth and flat like glass, with only the occasional ripple in the water from a goldfish seeking a morning snack.

Coleman swung his bare feet onto the floor and brought his hands to his aching head. He still wore the pink shirt, which was untucked over his jeans. His shoes were under the coffee table, and his keys and wallet were shoved inside either shoe. He massaged his temples as his feet pulled the shoes back toward the couch. Leaning over, he grabbed the items and pocketed them as he slid his feet into the shoes. Just as he stood, dizzy and with the blood painfully rushing from his head to his lower extremities, the office door opened and the overhead lights switched on.

"Oh good, you're early!"

Armstrong entered, holding a brown leather briefcase in one hand and, in the other, a silver packet emblazoned by the picture of an astronaut on a spacewalk. Coleman eyed the packet as Armstrong pushed a sliver of freeze-dried Neapolitan ice cream from it.

"Sorry there, Robert. I'd offer you one, but this is Astronaut Ice Cream. You know what this costs?"

Coleman shook his head and winced at the crushing pain.

"I paid $32 for 10 of these suckers. You believe that? Tell you what, though, it's worth it." Armstrong took a bite and shut his eyes as he savored the powdery chocolate, vanilla and strawberry sweetness. When his eyes opened, he took a long look at Coleman. "You look like hell. What happened, did you stay out all night?"

"Something like that," Coleman muttered and sat back down on the couch.

"You're getting too old for that sort of thing. You know better."

Coleman merely nodded. Armstrong set his briefcase on the desk and placed his snack on top of it. Reaching into the bottom desk drawer, he produced a bottle of Irish whiskey and a low-ball glass. He poured two fingers and walked the glass over to the couch.

"Drink this," he said, handing it to Coleman. "You'll feel better, and I need you on your game today."

Coleman nearly vomited when he smelled the whiskey, but he grabbed the glass and, in one swift motion, choked down the dark liquid. It burned going down and made his eyes water, but as soon as it got past his throat, he felt a building warmth in his chest and stomach.

Coleman handed the glass back. "How about another?"

"I need you alert, not drunk," Armstrong said, returning the glass and bottle to his desk drawer.

"Don't I get the day off after yesterday's shining success?"

"Nope, but I do have news for you."

"What news?"

Armstrong grinned and paused for effect. "They want another crack at you."

"Oh yeah?"

"Oh yes indeed. Ever run a half-marathon?"

"Not formally."

"Think you can manage 13.1 miles?"

Coleman looked up from the couch, his face a strange mixture of indignation and pity for Armstrong.

"Neal, a decent soccer player covers about seven miles during a single game. Do you know how much training that takes?"

Armstrong answered him with a question. "So that's a yes?"

"It's a hell yes."

"Good," Armstrong said. "Sometime next week then. The big guy called me after we left you last night and wanted to set it up. He's very eager to beat you this time."

"He can try," Coleman said, "but will we ever get to talk business with him?"

"That's the thing, Robert. I don't think he really cares. I don't think anyone on his team cares. They see so many vendors like us, and they go through all the same Requests for Proposal, all the same discovery periods, all the same margin analyses and, let's not kid ourselves, all the equipment is basically the same. We're not blowing this guy's doors off with our hardware or software. There is very, very little to differentiate us from our competitors."

"So what does that mean?"

"It means that this will come down to relationships. They trust that the technology is sound. As long as the price fits within their IT budget, then it depends on who they want to spend the next three years with."

"So I have to keep beating these guys for the next three years?"

"Robert, if we win the business, you can pay someone else to run with them. In the meantime, I need you to do exactly what you did yesterday.

"Okay."

"And, while it doesn't have to be ground-breaking, we still have to get the technology right."

"Noted."

"And that's why you're meeting with Vijay today." Armstrong yelled out into the hall. "Steven, what time does he land?"

Steve rushed over to the doorway. He saw Coleman on the couch, looked him up and down, and frowned. Coleman brought a finger to his lips, motioning to stay silent, but it was clear that Steve had noticed last evening's attire still on him. Steve turned to Armstrong.

"He's in the air right now, and I'm picking him up at three this afternoon."

"Good!" Armstrong said. "The three of you lock yourselves in a room and don't come out until you've got the plan together."

"Okay," Coleman said, resigned to the day's fate. He slowly stood and shuffled toward the door, where Steve still registered his disapproval.

"Oh, and Robert?"

"Yeah?" Coleman turned back toward Armstrong's desk.

"Don't ever sleep on my couch again. Understood?"

Coleman nodded and shuffled down the hall after Steve.

Steve and Vijay were on the way back from the airport, and Coleman took the opportunity to clean himself up a bit. He kept toiletries and a few changes of clothes in his office, so he had washed his face, brushed his teeth and changed into creased khaki pants and a white dress shirt. His hair was wet and slicked back and the redness in his eyes had almost dissipated, thanks to a nap in his car at lunch.

Steve had read him the riot act earlier that morning for driving the night before, and Coleman had let it go. He only had energy for one argument that day, and he figured his meeting with Vijay would be one long and excruciating battle. Plus, he hadn't even considered what reception might welcome him at home, but he would get to that after he had fought through his meeting with the genius.

Vijay Kumar was a brilliant guy, there was no disputing that. He held two advanced degrees and four technical certifications that were, individually, each considered the doctorate of networking – four of them together made him something of a savant and put him in very exclusive company within the industry. He also wore an air about him that announced his qualifications to one and all.

Coleman had dealt with that sort of attitude before. It reminded him of college and the arrogant soccer players from other teams who thought a little too highly of themselves. Coleman always keyed on those guys during games and made it a point to not only beat them, but to embarrass them if possible. He only put up with that attitude one time from Vijay and, ever since, Vijay had almost always left their meetings at the receiving end of a Coleman rant.

The engineers were important to every deal, Coleman felt, but they were ultimately replaceable and took their direction from the client executives. Vijay, naturally, held the exact opposite view.

Coleman knew when they had arrived by the sound of Steve's perky voice carrying through the halls.

"Look who's here, everyone!"

A smattering of polite and obligatory greetings filtered their way to Coleman's desk as Steve escorted Vijay through the cubicle farm that seemed to swallow most of the office real estate, and guided him back toward the conference rooms.

Vijay had a thick head of dark hair that he gelled and parted smartly on the left side. He wore fashionable dark-framed European glasses that added width to his narrow face. Unlike most engineers, who preferred jeans and a t-shirt, Vijay sported a tailored jacket with matching suit pants, and his crisp cornflower blue shirt was open at the collar. He rolled a black briefcase behind him and, with his other hand, checked his smartphone as he mechanically returned the greetings with an affected smile and a tight nod of the head.

"Where is Neal?" Coleman heard him ask Steve. The British accent was unmistakable.

"Out of office for another meeting," Steve said, "but he sent his regards and said he would try to meet you at your hotel for a drink this evening."

"I do not drink."

"Of course," Steve said after a slight hesitation. "Then, just for a chat."

"Fine."

Vijay followed Steve without lifting his eyes from the phone, until they had wound their way through the cubes and into a vacant conference room. They sat on opposite sides of the long table. Vijay crossed his legs, impatiently tapped his fingers on the wood tabletop and stared through the window. Outside, the fountain spit its plumes of white water into wide arcs that landed softly on the pond's dark surface.

"He should be along any minute," Steve said uncomfortably.

"Right."

Just down the hall, Coleman noted the time they had entered the conference room, and then waited five minutes at his desk. Finally, he stood, stretched his back, and then made his way toward them.

"Vijay," he said, entering the room.

"Rob," Vijay replied, without turning his head from the window.

Coleman offered no handshake. He took a seat at the head of the table and leaned forward on his elbows.

"So where are we, Vijay?"

"About the same place we were the last time we spoke." Vijay leaned forward to match Coleman's posture.

There was a pregnant pause as Coleman stared at him, before turning to Steve.

"Did you explain the situation?"

"We spoke about the need to expedite our code fixes, if that's what you mean."

"Steve was very forthcoming with the information," Vijay interjected. "But it does not change anything, Rob. As I have explained to you on many occasions, we need more time. Quite a bit of time."

Another round of silence.

"Okay, for argument's sake, how much time?"

"As it stands today, we need a minimum of six months."

"Unacceptable."

"Unacceptable? I think not."

Coleman quietly simmered before blasting off. "What is your problem, Vijay? It is beyond my understanding how you can be so short-sighted about this deal."

"It seems that many things are beyond your understanding."

At this, Steve jumped in. "Guys, please, let's try to keep this professional, okay?"

Both men ignored him.

"You work for me on this deal, Vijay. If I tell you to speed up, then you speed up!"

"I am not interested in contributing to your personal glory, Rob. The specifications call for a robust suite of security solutions, which must be stronger and more fortified than not only The Bank's current products, but also better than our competitors. Something like that does not happen overnight, no matter how hard you push or how unprofessional you act."

Coleman pointed at him. "You're going to get very rich on this deal, too, Vijay."

"In my home country, I already am, Rob. That is what you always fail to understand. I am not motivated by your riches."

"Then what does motivate you, huh?"

"Doing it the right way. Being known for developing the industry's finest solutions. Respect. That is what motivates me."

"Everyone will respect you if you finish this on time!"

Now Vijay stewed for a moment before speaking slowly and clearly.

"I have many times declined to join start-ups, and I have set my own entrepreneurial ambitions aside, because I believed that this organization would allow me the opportunities to achieve my goals. What I have learned is that all of these things are secondary to your pursuits, and I will not be a part of that."

Coleman placed his palms flat on the table and pushed himself up. "Do you know what they're asking me to do to secure this deal, Vijay?"

No reply.

"Yesterday, I had to run through mud and muck to get these guys interested, and soon I have to run a half-marathon. I'm physically killing myself for this deal, while you sit there all smug and difficult and don't even try to help."

"I always did view you as something of a circus act," Vijay said.

Steve was up and around the table before Coleman could get there. Running in front of Vijay, who was still seated, Steve braced himself for the rush and grabbed Coleman around the torso, pinning his arms to his side.

"Let me go, Steve! He's a dead man."

Vijay watched the spittle fly from Coleman's mouth and he slunk back in the chair, rolling it back out of Coleman's increasingly violent reach.

"Let me go, Steve!"

Steve held him until he had calmed a bit, and then he pushed Coleman toward the door. Vijay remained silent, knowing that he had said too much, and dabbed his forehead with a blue handkerchief.

"When'd you get so strong?" Coleman said, still trying to fight his way out of the bearhug.

"I've been working out," Steve said. "Now get out of here, and I'll talk to Vijay. You need to go home."

Home.

The thought made Coleman's shoulders slump and he stopped fighting. Steve walked him back to his office, and waited until Coleman had grabbed his car keys and returned to the hall. On his way toward the exit, Coleman turned back and looked at Steve long and hard.

"I'll take care of Vijay," Steve said.

Coleman nodded, and then turned and left.

CHAPTER 10

"Let me in, Angie!"

Coleman knocked on the front door and tried the key again. Everything opened, except for the hotel-style latch, which gave about an inch of clearance, then stymied entry. He could have kicked himself for having that thing installed. There had been a minor break-in on another street in the neighborhood – some landscaper, who had desperately needed to use the restroom, chose to kick in a client's door rather than sully his pants – and Coleman had arranged for additional security measures as a result. Angie thought it was a complete overreaction at the time, but Connor was young and her husband had insisted, so she went along. Now, she thought, it was perhaps one of his finest ideas.

"Who is it?" she said through the crack.

"Oh, come on." He lowered his voice and whispered through the inch-wide gap. "Let me in."

A lengthy pause, before she spoke again.

"Why would I want to do that?"

"Angie!" he raised his voice. "Stop messing around. I'm exhausted."

"Oh, and who's fault is that?"

"Look, open the door! I'm not going to stand here all night."

Another pause, and then the door slammed shut.

Coleman stood there looking at it, waiting for her to unhook the latch and pull the door open. He waited, and then waited some more. He quickly grew impatient and pounded on the door with his open palm.

"Angie!"

The dull thumping sound echoed against the elegant home's brick façade and carried across the street to the front door of a lovely white Colonial that overlooked a lush, green, finely manicured lawn. A woman in her late-forties, dressed in a smart blue pinstripe pantsuit, peeked out her front door and narrowed her eyes. Coleman could feel her stare and slowly turned toward her.

"Forgot my keys!" he yelled over. "I'll try the back!"

The woman watched him go and slowly coiled herself back inside.

Coleman jogged around the garage, quickly opened the fence and rushed across the patio to the French doors at the back of the house. Angie stood outside, blocking the doors, and waited for him.

"You're not coming in," she said.

"The hell I'm not."

"I mean it, Rob. That was big last night. You don't get to get away with that."

"What, so I'm not allowed in my own house?"

"Not tonight at least."

Coleman was quiet for a moment as he tried to process things. "What is this, Angie? You don't get to unilaterally ban me from my own home."

"I do when you're a bad influence on your son. You showed up stinking drunk last night, and we won't be a party to that."

"I wasn't stinking drunk. I had a few beers with Armstrong and Steve after our meet-and-greet with The Bank, which I crushed, by the way."

"I could smell it all over you, and you missed the entire performance. It's unacceptable."

"I'll tell you what's unacceptable..."

"What?"

"Giving me grief about running late for a silly school concert, when I'm out there literally killing myself so I can build you a beach house when I close this deal!"

Angie crossed her arms and raised her voice to match his own. "Alright, first of all, you weren't literally killing yourself. You were figuratively killing yourself, and you sound foolish when you say 'literally.' Second, and we've discussed this before, but I don't really care about a beach house, Rob! Sure it would be nice to have, but how often do we go, twice a year, tops? It seems like a complete waste of money, when we could just rent a place for a week and..."

"Waste of money? That's all you could talk about last summer!" Coleman had raised his hands to his head and squeezed his hair in a show of frustration. "And, quite frankly, I'm the one making the money, so I'll determine whether it's a waste or not."

"Whether it's a waste. Not 'whether it's a waste or not,'" she muttered under her breath.

"Who are you, the grammar police? Just let me in the house. I'm hungry."

"You're not coming in."

"Yes, I am."

"No, you're not."

"Excuse me very much," Coleman said. "It's my house. I paid for it. And I'll come and go whenever I damn well please. And if you don't like the rules, you can go and buy your own damn house!"

There was a long silence as Angie chewed her lower lip and stared at the ground. The sun was going down, and they could hear car doors slamming and dogs barking up and down the street as neighbors returned from work and their kids and pets came out to greet them. Finally, she looked up, disappointment showing in her eyes, and she spoke softly.

"What happened to you?"

"What?"

"What happened to you? Did I do something wrong? Did I screw up and push you into this character you've become?"

"What are you talking about?"

He watched as she shook her head and her face began to flush red. She pursed her lips and her throat caught when she continued.

"I never needed any of this, Rob. It's nice to have, and I'm not complaining about it. You've provided for us better than I could have ever expected. But I never needed any of it. I was just as happy, happier even, when we were in that little apartment and you were trying to play soccer for a living."

"Oh, come on," he said. "Cut the martyr routine. I didn't hear you pumping the brakes when we built this house."

"No, I know that, and I worry that I pushed you to act like this. I hope I haven't. I really hope I haven't."

"Stop this..."

"Because you're just not an attractive person when all you talk or care about is money, and the next big deal, and beach houses, and cars and whatever else you're chasing."

"Whoa, hold on there..."

"I just want you to be present. Be around. Be yourself. Not this hard-charging tycoon guy I'm looking at. I don't even know this guy. You used to care deeply about other people, your friends, your teammates, your family. Now it just seems like money, or winning, I'm not sure."

"I can't believe this," Coleman said. "I really can't. This is so typical. You see this stuff in bad movies, but I never believed I'd actually hear the words coming out of your mouth, of all people..."

"Rob, please..."

"So just to be clear, you were happier when we were broke and I was out of work? You don't give a rip about the money I make? And the nice things I buy you? And the estate home I put over your head? And all the advantages I've provided for our son??"

"Rob..."

"And the cars, the vacations, the social activities, the clothes, the gadgets, the furniture, the window treatments, the freaking drapes, the pillows, the pillow covers, the rugs, the runners, the hair appointments, the spa treatments, the doing of the nails, the wine cases, the gourmet kitchen equipment, the exercise appliances..."

"Stop it."

"Oh, I'm sorry! Did I miss anything? You know, I bet I did! I just remembered the wallpaper, the couches, the shoes, the airfare for your parents, the personalized stationery, the catering for the Christmas party, all the stupid little gifts for your stupid little friends..."

"Stop!"

"Oh, and that big expensive rock on your finger that you just loooooved to show off every time one of those stupid little friends came over. Now, I think I got everything. So, just to be clear, you were happier without all that stuff, and you just want me to be 'present?'"

"Not tonight, I don't."

"Well you're going to get your wish, you ungrateful excuse for a wife." The vein in Coleman's neck pulsed and pushed against his skin. She was silent as he turned to go, and it only made him angrier. About halfway to the fence, he turned back.

"I'll go, Angie. But you'll regret this. And I refuse to be blamed for whatever happens tonight."

She watched him rage through the gate and heard the car door open and slam shut. The engine roared and she heard the squeal as he drove off, away from their home and away from their family.

When she was sure he was gone, Angie sat gently at the patio table, rested her elbows on her knees, dropped her head into her hands, and sobbed until she had no tears left to give.

CHAPTER 11

He was early to the Oyster Bar, and he sat alone, hunched over his beer with his feet propped on the brass rail. The drinking crowd slowly arrived in pairs or small groups, and nobody had yet begun to congregate on the dance floor. Coleman had politely made chit-chat through his first three beers and a shot of cinnamon whiskey, but his lack of eye contact and slumped body language helped move the bartender down the line to a couple of livelier new arrivals.

Coleman fiddled with his wedding ring and thought about his outburst. She was right, to an extent. It hadn't always been like this.

Back in the beginning, before Connor, before the big house, before the big job, Rob and Angie Coleman hadn't ever worried about wealth accumulation, multiple properties, luxury vehicles, investment strategies, tax implications, or the like. They were just happy to occasionally afford some new furniture, or a shopping trip to the outlet malls, where $200 could refresh their wardrobes for an entire season.

They had been that young couple that made older couples fondly reminisce, but that other young couples couldn't stand. They were the couple that jogged together in the mornings, and brought each other coffee, and held hands and laughed all the time. They were the couple that could spend hours just sitting somewhere together, without some contrived activity to engage or distract them. Unlike other couples their age, they never felt the need to be doing something at all times. They turned down invitations to happy hour, they avoided the kickball league and, while they both had plenty of friends, they declined most of those forced "girl's and guy's night out" invitations, in favor of hanging with one another.

As his career prospects improved, and they departed the glow of their newlywed phase, things began to gradually change. This was nothing new, and every couple went through the same process, but when Angie got baby

49

fever, Coleman's competitive side came to the fore. He was determined to give their children the best life he could provide, and he took that to mean the accumulation of wealth, and multiple properties, and luxury vehicles, and so on. Meanwhile, Angie understood his role to be less of a financial provider and more of the protecting, benevolent, ever-present leader of their household, independent of how comfortable that household might be.

And so they began working at cross purposes. They both intuitively understood the difference in philosophies, and they both assumed that they would meet somewhere in the middle of these notions to create the perfect little family in the perfect giant house. What they hadn't factored, particularly Coleman, was how consuming each philosophy could be, and how difficult it was to depart or divert from their respective courses once charted.

Angie nested. Coleman hunted.

What Coleman made, Angie spent. That's the way he thought it was supposed to go. Earn, provide, spend.

Rinse. Repeat.

What he didn't expect was the backlash against his increased earning power. The more he made, the more time it required to make it, which meant more time out of the house, which meant more evenings alone for Angie, which meant growing distance between them, simmering resentments, an argumentative undertone and, finally, the events that had led to that evening's battle royale.

It was exhausting to think about, and part of Coleman deeply regretted his role in getting to this point. He hated seeing her like that, and his shoulders slumped as he thought about her, sitting on the couch alone, crying her eyes out and wondering what had happened between them.

He had never intended to hurt his wife.

Still, an occasional demonstration of gratitude would have been nice. Coleman worked his tail off to provide for her and their son. On a daily basis, he had to deal with the arrogance and rigidity of a Vijay Kumar and the inconsistency and spontaneous vindictiveness of a Neal Armstrong. A little show of thanks from Angie, and maybe even a little ego-stroking, would go a long way to making all the ugliness worthwhile.

Here and now, though, in the middle of a fourth beer and another dose of whiskey, Coleman wondered why he even bothered. He was sick of feeling bad, he was tired of being chastised, and he was sick and tired of being told what to do all the time. He wanted a little cheer in his life, and he wanted someone to tell him he was a good guy, that he was doing a good job, and that his efforts meant something.

More than anything, Coleman wanted a few moments of joy in his life...

"Hey you. If I sit down, you'd better not run out on me again."

And there it was.

The blonde from before.

Tonight she wore black, and this time Coleman didn't bother with modesty or decorum. He stared at her legs, lean and toned, and he inhaled a whiff of her perfume as his eyes climbed upward, stopping at her chest for a few long beats, before he met her amused gaze.

"Ashley, remember?"

She bit her lip suggestively and slowly leaned against his shoulder for support as she slid onto the stool beside him.

"I remember," he said. "I'm Rob."

"I remember, too."

"You do?"

"Definitely."

He signaled for the bartender and indicated another beer. She just smiled at him, and Coleman thought he saw the man roll his eyes as went to work fixing up her martini.

"Extra dirty?" Coleman said.

"As dirty as possible."

She leaned in close and whispered something softly in his ear, and Coleman felt a jolt rush through his body.

He forgot everything bad about the last few days, and his smile disappeared.

He looked intense.

Eager.

Hungry.

They didn't wait for their drinks. Without taking his eyes off of her, Coleman left some money on the bar.

He stood and followed her out.

CHAPTER 12

When the pain started, it was like nothing Coleman had ever felt before. He had injured his feet numerous times during his soccer career, and sustained plenty of sprained toes and ankles, but this...

This was some kind of pain.

It was far different from the bruises, welts, dents, bangs and bumps he had encountered over the years. This pain was like a stream of molten lava flowing toward the ball of his right foot, where it morphed into a swarm of switchblade-wielding hornets that stabbed and stung the joint, attacking from within, an angry gang of counter-insurgents determined to murder his foot from the inside.

The pain was so excruciating, it jarred him awake. Coleman gasped and sat up, expecting to see an anvil resting atop his foot. All he saw was the thin white hotel sheet covering him from the waist down. Yet somehow the weight was crushing, and he flung the sheet away, revealing both his naked body and that of the blonde woman sleeping beside him.

Coleman stared at his foot. It look normal, other than maybe a tinge of pink on the exterior of the ball, yet it throbbed like a beating heart and hurt so badly that he whimpered aloud.

At this, the woman stirred, but Coleman didn't notice. In a panic, he swung his legs off the bed. When his feet hit the floor, he yelped. The pressure felt like heat from a thousand suns. Instinct made him stand, and he limped tenderly away from the bed, applying all weight to his left side, but he made it no further than the opposite wall, where the television was still on, tuned to a cable news channel. Coleman collapsed beside the desk that supported the TV and turned so that he could lean his back against the wall.

He extended his leg.

Across the room he could see the red numbers of the digital alarm clock atop the bedside stand.

3:07 am.

Reaching down, he very gently touched his palm to the skin. The ball of his foot was hot, and the very touch itself was like a bolt of lightning. Coleman yelped again, then steeled himself, took a deep breath, and began to grope his foot, to massage it, and to knead it like he was a guest chef on some macabre cooking show.

It did no good.

He shrieked and then, as tears began leaking from his eyes, he wailed a one-man symphony.

The woman awakened and glared at the naked man cowering in the corner, playing with his foot.

"What the f..."

"Help me!" Coleman shouted. "Call a doctor or something!"

She covered herself with the sheet and stared, mouth agape, as he writhed on the floor, stroking his foot and loudly moaning.

"I have seen some messed up stuff before, but this is too much."

Coleman watched her climb out of bed and quickly pull on her black dress and grab her purse. Her reaction didn't register with him until she had forced her heels on and crossed the room to the chair where he had thrown his clothes.

"Wait, no!" he said. "I'm in pain. My foot! I need help!"

"You definitely need help!" she said with her back to him, as she picked up his creased khakis and rifled through the pockets.

"Wait, what are you doing?"

She continued until she had found the wallet in the back pocket of his pants. Wasting no time, she opened it, eyed the denominations, and removed three crisp $100 bills.

"Hey!" Coleman shouted, then moaned as another surge of hornet stings blasted the inside of his foot.

"This is what you owe me," she said, folding the bills and tucking them into her purse.

"For what?"

As she turned toward him, her eyes filled with pity. She stared at him there on the carpet, naked, whimpering, wiggling every which way in his desperate attempt to avoid the searing pain. She frowned and made a sad face.

"For last night, what do you think?"

"For last night?"

"Uh huh," she said, turning to leave. When she reached the door, she turned back again. "Take care of yourself, okay? I hope your...foot...feels better."

He watched her step through the doorway and into the hall. The pain, the hangover, the early hour, and growing pangs of guilt all contributed to his cloudy and deeply confused state. When the facts finally hit him, it was more than Coleman could bear.

A barbaric yet slightly girlish sound – gurgling somewhere between a howl and a shriek – exploded in the room, filtered out into the hall and disappeared into the dark, unforgiving night.

CHAPTER 13

The X-rays had come back negative, yet Coleman still looked at the doctor like he was a quack. His pants legs were hiked up above the knee so that both of his bare feet dangled from the examination table. The thin white paper crinkled beneath him as Coleman shifted his seat and leaned forward to give the doctor an even more penetrating stare of confusion.

"That's not possible. It might not be a bone, but it's definitely a torn ligament or something."

"I'm quite certain that's not what it is," the doctor said.

"No, you don't understand. I played college soccer. I know what a sprain is like. That has to be what this is."

The room was tiny, no larger than a closet really, and with no windows to filter natural light, the fluorescence from the tubes above gave the little room a bright, sanitary wash that accentuated the doctor's white coat. He removed the pen from his breast pocket and placed it along with his clipboard on the table against the wall, then sat and rolled his stool toward the exam table.

"Mister Coleman, may I ask you a few questions?"

Coleman nodded and winced as the doctor's hands reached for the offending foot. The doctor noticed his patient's discomfort and pulled his hands back, resting them finally on his lap.

"How old are you?"

"Forty."

"What did you do last evening?"

"What did I do?" The events of the previous night cycled through his memory with lightning speed, and Coleman's eyes grew wider as he recalled the hotel room. "I went out to dinner. That's all."

"Okay," the doctor said. "Was there alcohol at dinner?"

"What do you mean?"

"Did you have something to drink? Maybe a few beers?"

"Maybe, why?"

"What about your diet? Any shellfish involved? Maybe some shrimp, or some clams? Anything like that?"

"Maybe, why are you asking what I ate?"

"Mister Coleman, it's pretty early in the morning," the doctor said, glancing behind him at the clock on the wall, which read 5:30 am. "What time did you notice your foot beginning to hurt?"

"I don't know, maybe 3:00, 3:30?"

"Okay, and you said it was like a burning sensation, more than a throbbing in your foot?"

"All of the above."

"Okay." The doctor looked at Coleman's feet again. The right foot had a noticeably red hue near the big toe and appeared slightly larger than the left. He pursed his lips and nodded, as if to confirm a mental diagnosis, but reached for the X-rays anyway.

After a lengthy silence, Coleman finally asked. "So what is it?"

Placing the X-rays down, the doctor turned toward him, looked him straight in the eye, and declared his verdict quickly, professionally, and without sympathy.

"Mister Coleman, you have the gout."

For a good 15 seconds, the only sound in the little room was a dull buzzing from the fluorescent lights. Finally, Coleman spoke.

"The gout?"

"The gout."

"The gout?"

The doctor nodded.

"The gout," Coleman said, more of a statement than a question.

The doctor nodded.

Another lengthy silence, and then Coleman exploded.

"How in the world do I have the gout? Isn't that something that old, fat, lazy drunks get? I'm a 40-year-old athlete, I'm thin, and I'm definitely not lazy! Check it again! There's no way I have the gout!"

Now the doctor paused for a long moment, before speaking in a soft, professorial manner.

"Mister Coleman, forget everything you think you know about the gout. You referred to it as something for the old, fat, and drunk. Others have called it the 'Disease of Kings,' because Henry VIII had it, and he was overweight, indulged in ale and rich foods, etcetera, etcetera. But that's not at all representative of the gout's true nature."

"The gout has a true nature?"

The doctor sighed. "Forgive my clinical speech. I'll try to put this in layman's terms for you."

"I'm telling you, it's not the gout."

"Mister Coleman, first of all, it is not a disease. I would describe it as a condition. Second, lifestyle can bring about the gout, yes, but it is not the only impetus. It can also be hereditary, or connected to other medical conditions, such as hypertension, metabolic syndrome, abnormal lipid levels, things like this.

"In your case, Mister Coleman, I suspect that it's probably a combination of factors. You mentioned that your diet has included alcohol and shellfish recently. The gout also likes purines, such as turkey, your red meats and, particularly, beer."

"So, basically, everything I enjoy."

The doctor flashed a knowing frown. "Yes, but it is not nearly as bad as it sounds. You wouldn't need to remove these things from your diet. Not even beer. You would just need to moderate your intake."

Coleman shook his head. "There's no way I have the gout."

"I know it seems hard to believe. As you said, you are in fine physical condition. But I imagine someone in your family has had gout before as well."

"I have no idea."

"It's okay. Genetics play a big role in our health, and most of the time we never even know that we're predisposed to something. But combine genetics with lifestyle, diet, etcetera, and these things can creep up on us."

Coleman stared at his foot, but didn't dare move it for fear of the hornet's nest ready to explode again.

"Why does it hurt so much?" he finally asked.

"That is due to the uric acid build-up in the joint. The uric acid has crystallized around the ball of your big toe, and the white blood cells are attacking it. Hence the shooting pain."

"More like a stabbing and stinging."

"Yes, that too."

"What about this uric acid? Please don't tell me you're talking about urine?"

"Without getting too technical, yes, it is excreted from the body when you urinate, but uric acid is a compound produced by an enzyme that is filtered through the kidneys. High incidence of uric acid can also be related to kidney stones."

"So you're saying I have...piss...in my foot?"

"No, no, no, Mister Coleman. When the levels of uric acid are higher than normal in your blood, they can move toward your extremities, most often the feet, where the 'extra' uric acid that hasn't been discharged from the body can crystallize, or harden, in your joints."

"So I have hardened...piss...in my foot."

"No, Mister Coleman! It runs through the blood stream, but it is not urine. Let's not overthink this. Let's concentrate on how we can mitigate the pain and avoid future flare-ups."

Coleman nodded his consent. "How long is it going to hurt?"

"It could be a few days, or it could be a few weeks, or it could last as long as a few months. It depends upon the severity of the attack and how your body responds to it."

"A few months of this?"

"Statistically, that would be somewhat rare, especially based on your current health. But you did have quite a severe attack, so I wouldn't entirely rule it out."

Coleman's thoughts turned immediately to The Asylum and his commitment to The Bank. He could barely walk, and if his foot didn't get better fast, it could potentially torpedo the deal.

"How do I get rid of this?"

The doctor stood and stepped over to the table. He placed a hand atop Coleman's knee and slid the other hand gently beneath the calf. Slowly, he raised Coleman's leg until the gouty foot hovered in the air.

"First things first, I want you to stay off of it. Keep it elevated when you can. Use an icepack, or a bag of frozen peas even, to help with any pain or potential swelling.

"Second, I'm going to prescribe you an NSAID. It's basically a very strong ibuprofen. This will also help with the pain and swelling. You don't have any known side effects to ibuprofen, do you?"

Coleman shook his head.

"Good. Then the third thing is your lifestyle. Like I said, you don't need to quit any of the food and drink we discussed. But you do need to moderate it. Try not to place yourself in any high-pressure situations. Be sure to exercise, and try to take it easy at work and at home. Stress can certainly be a contributing factor to another attack."

"Terrific," Coleman muttered.

"Any questions about any of this?"

"Yeah, are you absolutely sure this is the gout? I mean, seriously, it just seems insane to me that I would have the gout, of all things."

"Look, Mister Coleman, you are not the first to come in here and have this reaction. The gout is wrongly viewed by society because of the whole 'Rich Man's Disease' reputation, but I assure you, it is nothing to be ashamed of, and it's not even that out-of-the-ordinary anymore. We diagnose the gout more and more frequently these days, due to common diet, longer lifespans, and so on.

"For example, I just had a 20-year-old fratty boy in here last week..."

"Fratty boy?"

"Fraternity kid. He and his buddies went on a weekend bender and he woke up on Sunday morning with his foot looking and feeling just like yours. And just like you, he insisted he had broken his foot. When I told him he had the gout, he nearly broke down and cried."

Coleman nodded his understanding.

"The only way to absolutely rule out gout is to shove a very big, very long needle into the joint and extract the fluid. Most people prefer to accept the initial diagnosis."

Coleman considered this for a brief moment, then waved the idea away with his palm extended.

"Seriously," the doctor continued, "don't get caught up in the stigma. The gout is really not a big deal, and it can be easily treated. You are going to be just fine."

"If you say so."

Coleman lowered himself from the exam table, applying all the weight to his good foot, and rolled his pants legs down. Despite his gouty foot hovering above the floor, he winced at even the slightest sensation against his skin. The doctor watched him, then spoke softly and thoughtfully.

"Mister Coleman, there is one other thing you should know."

"What's that?"

"More than half the people diagnosed with gout will suffer another attack within one year."

"Another attack?"

"I'm afraid so."

"Oh God," Coleman whispered to himself.

"In order to prevent this, just watch your diet. Like we said, moderate all your meats, your shellfish, your alcohol. Keep exercising, keep your weight down."

"Anything else?"

The doctor shrugged. "They also say that cherries can help cleanse the blood of uric acid."

"Cherries?"

"Yes."

"Terrific."

Coleman hopped his way closer to the door, being sure not to place any weight whatsoever on his right foot. Watching closely, the doctor frowned and picked up his clipboard to write something.

"Mister Coleman, I'll arrange for a set of crutches to be available when you check out at the front."

"Okay," Coleman nodded, reaching for the door. "Thanks."

Coleman looked so forlorn and downtrodden that the doctor felt compelled to reassure his patient as he exited.

"Mister Coleman?"

"Yeah?"

"Really, it's not a big deal. It's just the gout."

CHAPTER 14

Had it not been for the early hour, with little to no traffic on the roads, driving could have been a fatal event. The right foot was in such excruciating pain, and had continued to swell, to the point that Coleman could barely touch the gas pedal without whimpering. He had tried the old one-two-switcheroo maneuver, where he crossed his left foot over to operate both the gas and the brake, but that had been an unmitigated disaster. As the left toes engaged the gas and the car accelerated, the left heel kept grazing the brake, slowing the vehicle's momentum.

Coleman had jerked along like this for a while – Go! Sloooow. Go! Sloooow. Go! Sloooow – until discomfort from the whiplash exceeded the pain in his foot. He gritted his teeth and switched back to his right foot for both the gas and the brake until, thankfully, he coasted into his driveway and brought the car to a stop. Using the door as a support to haul himself from the driver's seat, he nearly slammed his fingers when it tried to swing shut, then lost balance on his good foot as he gently pulled his offending foot from the car. Coleman wobbled for a moment, then yelped when his right foot, instinctively seeking balance, touched down on the driveway, sending a fresh hornet attack through his joint.

The air was cool in the early morning, and his neighbor held her hands tight against a steaming mug of coffee as she watched from her front lawn. Her little Pomeranian, which Coleman privately referred to as "the rat dog," had stopped sniffing the dewy grass and turned its attention to the man floundering and fumbling his way around the driveway across the street. It was an interesting sight, and the dog cocked its head as it considered the meaning of the familiar man's movements, among them an awkward hopping on one foot to the trunk of his car, intermittently punctuated by audible cursing.

Coleman lifted the crutches from his trunk and exhaled as his underarms settled into their saddles. He noticed the dog and the woman out of the corner of his eye, and the accompanying irritation and embarrassment caused a hot rush of blood to his head.

"What?" he yelled across the way.

The woman said nothing, but crossed her arms against her robe and lifted the mug to her lips. The dog cocked its head the other way.

Coleman grumbled under his breath and limped along on his crutches, up the path toward his front door.

"Come on!" he shouted to the world, upon realizing that he had left his keys in the ignition. Shifting on his crutches, he turned back and stopped. The car seemed really far away, and he mentally calculated a cost-benefit analysis of the return trip against the throbbing pain of his foot and the watchful judgment of his neighbor and her dog. Fortunately for Coleman, the door swung open, and the relief was visible on his face as Angie looked him up and down.

"What now?" She pointed to the crutches and eyed his right foot, which Coleman had lifted behind him to avoid any contact with the ground.

"Don't worry about it. Please just let me in."

"What happened to your foot?"

"Nothing. I think I tore a ligament, or it might be a sprain. Can I come in?"

"From what?" Angie stood in the doorway and crossed her arms.

"From all the training stuff I have to do for The Bank deal. I told you about all that."

"So what did you do, fall or something?"

"Angie, please! I'm in a lot of pain, I've been popping ibuprofen on steroids, and all I want to do is sleep in my own bed."

"Ibuprofen on steroids?"

Coleman sighed and pleaded with his eyes. "Don't worry about it. It's extra strength. Supposed to make the swelling go down."

"Well, what doctor did you see? How long are you going to be on crutches?"

"Angie, come on!"

"Fine!" she said, stepping aside and allowing him to hobble his way across the threshold and into the foyer.

Coleman looked up at the dual staircase and groaned. He didn't even want to think about climbing those steps. Instead, he veered right, into their well-decorated but rarely-used living room, where he plopped down on the sofa and dropped the crutches onto an ornate Oriental rug of deep blue that covered nearly the entire floor. A black baby grand piano stood across the room, and Angie swept away some accumulating dust with her fingers and listened quietly as the grandfather clock in the far corner ticked the time away.

Coleman said nothing as he propped his right foot on the back of the sofa, so that it was elevated above his other foot, which rested on the cushions. His head nestled into a pillow and he shut his eyes, despite her presence in the room.

"So did they give you a cast or anything?"

"It's not that kind of sprain," he whispered.

"I thought you said ligaments?"

"One or the other, they weren't sure. They said it would heal on its own. I just have to stay off of it for a few days."

Angie considered this and wiped another spot of dust from the piano. "Well, do you want a bag of ice or anything?"

"No, I'm okay," Coleman said, his eyes beginning to dance from side to side beneath their closed lids. "I'm just gonna rest here for a little bit."

Angie walked over and sat on the cushion that supported his good left leg. Even with her slight build, and despite the distance between her and his elevated foot, vibrations from the physical act of sitting climbed the sofa and sent a blistering hornet attack through Coleman's foot. His eyes popped open and he gasped with pain. With his good leg, he pushed his wife off the couch.

"What the hell, Angie?"

"I'm sorry!" she said moving away from the sofa. "I didn't realize it hurt so much!"

"It hurts so much!"

"Sorry!"

"Please, just leave me alone for now. Please just go somewhere and don't come back for a while."

She glared down at him. "We are going somewhere. I'm taking Connor to church. We thought you might want to come."

"To church? God, no." He settled back into his sleeping position and closed his eyes. "Wait, it's not even Sunday. Why are you going to church?"

"They're having a family day, where the entire family gets together with a bunch of other families, and they put together care packages for families that might need them. You know, a really family-friendly event for the whole family."

"Sounds thrilling. Have a great time."

"Well, are you at least going to try and make his soccer game this afternoon?"

"What time is that?"

"Three."

"Maybe."

"Maybe?"

"What do you want?"

"I want you to support your son."

Coleman opened his eyes and threw his arms in the air. "If I can walk, I'll be there, Angie!"

"He's going to be crushed if you're not there."

"Fine, I'll pop some pills and try to make it. But it would be a lot easier if you'd let me sleep."

"Fine. Sleep. Sleep all you want." She left the room and turned toward the kitchen. "Try not be a jerk when you wake up."

Coleman listened to the click of her shoes against the tile. When she was gone, he adjusted his foot, winced at the pain, then shut his eyes and faded into a deep, dreamless sleep.

The nap was a short and unsatisfying one. The Pomeranian across the street had discovered a squirrel and chased it up a tree. Coleman awakened to the sound of a shrill and consistent yapping that continued for several minutes without pause. As he crossed the fuzzy line from sleep to consciousness, he swung his legs down to meet the floor.

The sounds of a wounded tiger crashed through the walls of Coleman's home. Across the street, the Pomeranian heard him roar, and it stopped barking, stared for a moment, then darted back toward its own front door.

From his spot on the couch, Coleman dug into his pants pocket and produced the small brown canister of pills. He dumped two into his open palm and threw them into his mouth. Without water, he swallowed them down dry and coughed as they passed the back of his throat.

He hoisted himself from the couch and limped his way to the kitchen, using the wall for support. There was no question that Angie would scold him later for whatever finger or handprints he left on the clean, slate-gray flat paint that coated the halls. Coleman didn't care. He would ignore the tongue-lashing like he ignored most of the others.

Reaching the kitchen at last, he pulled open the stainless steel refrigerator door and looked for something – anything – to drink. On the top shelf, he found an assorted mix of half-empty juice boxes. Connor had obviously cracked a new one each time he got thirsty, without finishing the previous box. Coleman now finished them for him. He slurped from each straw, draining the cold juice until his throat had recovered from the rough edges of the pills.

The house was quiet with the others gone, and he silently limped his way down the hall toward his first-floor home office. The door was open, and Coleman looked out the window, which faced the street and the neighbor's yard across the way. The rat dog was gone.

Coleman flopped down into his desk chair, taking care not to graze his right foot against anything. The walls looked like any other home office, with framed degrees announcing his qualifications, and Coleman also had a few of his finer moments from collegiate soccer framed and mounted. Dust had collected on the wooden frames (Angie was right – they needed to get the cleaners in there more often), but he looked past it and considered the images.

There was the penalty kick he scored to beat Virginia in the national semifinals his senior year, and a shot of the whole team celebrating at midfield when they won the conference championship. There was also a blown-up shot of Coleman, wearing a Team USA jersey, as his right foot connected with the ball – the same foot that now stung and throbbed.

Coleman winced and reached for the foot. He had removed his shoe at the doctor's office and had not put it back on. It was now covered only by a sock, and he wasn't about to remove it for fear of whatever pain might result. Slowly, ever so gently, he placed his hands on the sock and moved them toward the joint. The pressure felt good near the arch and at the heel, but when his fingertips reached the ball of his big toe, Coleman yelped. It was still a searing pain, despite the pills, and the whole thing had begun to swell to the point that it was noticeably larger than his functional left foot.

Coleman glanced at the clock on his wall. *10:30 am.* He had a few hours until he had to make an attempt at Connor's game. Spring concerts and church events were one thing, but missing a soccer game would be viewed as a treasonous offense in his household. Still, there was time for another nap, maybe a hot bath (since standing in the shower might present a problem), and some food.

But what food? It seemed like everything he enjoyed was now on the forbidden list. Except for cherries. He remembered something about cherries. Coleman reached for the laptop on his desk and opened it across his legs. The screen hidden by the slim, silver casing came to life and he quickly navigated to a search engine.

Gout.
Gout in foot.
Gout in foot of healthy male.
How to get rid of gout in foot of healthy male.
Gout food.
Gout cherries.
Misdiagnosis of gout.
Ligament damage mistaken for gout.

He cycled through various links on each topic, learning nothing much more than the doctor had already told him. Cherries could be helpful, moderation was ideal for all red meats, purines, and alcohol, and a moderate routine built around a moderate diet and moderate exercise, with a moderation of stress, was the best course of action. And, no, it was not at all likely that the doctor had inaccurately diagnosed a more severe ligament injury in his foot.

Coleman had the gout, and he would have to get over the gout as fast as he could.

The Asylum.

The Half-Marathon.

He had agreed to a rematch, and his heart sank as he looked through the online pictures of the course and the muddy participants. On the bright side, Armstrong would be happy, as there was no chance of winning now. Coleman could barely walk, however, and that was not going to be a good look for Armstrong, the executives at The Bank, Steve, Vijay, or anyone else.

Honesty.

Honesty in all things.

The memory of The Bank president's words made him ill. He couldn't tell those guys that he had the gout! He couldn't even tell his wife.

Angie.

In the wake of his health scare, Coleman had given very little thought to the events of the prior evening.

Ashley.

The guilt attacked him as hard as the gout had. He had never done anything like that before, and he began hyperventilating as he tried to rationalize things.

Honesty.

Honesty in all things.

The pills, the hangover, the fuzzy memories – some guilty, some good, some angry, some really good – collected in his head and spun through his mind like a dusty cyclone about to level a sturdy building. But instead of causing a natural disaster, the cyclone knocked Coleman back to sleep.

When his eyes flicked open, the clock read 2:12 pm. He had passed out right there in his chair, and Connor's game was at 3:00 pm. Coleman sat up straight, and gently, ever so gently, lifted his right leg so that he could reach the foot.

It was even bigger than before. Swollen. Throbbing.

Reaching into his pocket, he popped the canister and gobbled two more pills.

Where were his shoes? He couldn't remember. He had either left them at the doctor's office or in the car. Didn't matter anyway. No way could he squeeze his foot into a loafer.

He hobbled over to the closet where he kept a gym bag and some old soccer gear. There were several pairs of shoes piled on the floor. Some were cleats, but there were also indoor soccer shoes, running shoes, and shower shoes.

He tried the indoor shoes first, but the narrow toes made his foot scream. The shower shoes were a no-go because they opened his foot to the elements, and he didn't want to take any chances.

Reaching for the oldest, most broken-in pair of running shoes he could locate, Coleman slowly, ever so slowly, pushed his inflated right toes inside until the entire foot was safely seated. It hurt like nothing else, and he didn't bother to tie the shoe for support. His foot had already swollen to fill any extra space.

He limped his way to the bathroom to freshen up, before limping his way down the hall. He stopped quickly in the kitchen for a drink to wash down the pills. He patted his pockets, remembered that the keys were still in the car, and dragged his foot down the hall, out the front door, and onto the stone walkway.

Across the street, the Pomeranian had returned. When it saw the limping, cursing man, it began yipping in its annoying high-pitched tone.

Coleman gave the dog the finger and climbed into his car.

CHAPTER 15

Leaving the crutches at home, whether by accident or through some subconscious refusal to accept his limitations, was probably a mistake, and Coleman paid for it as soon as he climbed from the BMW. He had made it to the park just on time, but he had not accounted for the long walk to Connor's sideline which, of course, was all the way on the other side of the field. Coleman made a game-time decision to watch from the opposing sideline, the one nearest the parking lot.

Still, the lot was elevated above the field, which lay about 15 feet below in a small valley with two additional soccer fields and a softball diamond and backstop. The softball area was empty, but kids of all sizes and age groups mechanically drilled on the soccer fields.

Youth soccer was a fall sport in most states, but North Carolina was not most states when it came to soccer. Boasting multiple championship-caliber university programs, and serving as host to many of USA Soccer's training camps and World Cup tune-ups, North Carolina had invested heavily in the game, and the results were apparent in the kids who pursued the sport. Springtime soccer leagues were common throughout the state and often were limited to the highly skilled and those identified as having great potential.

Connor Coleman fell into the latter category. As a 6-year-old, it was difficult to determine how skilled the boy really was, but the great potential was certainly there, and represented in the flesh by the man currently hopping down the hill from the parking lot on one foot.

Coleman tried to make himself as inconspicuous as possible, but he was pretty conspicuous. Normally, he was out on the field during warm-ups helping the kids kick the ball back and forth or standing in goal while they tried to score. They had originally asked him to coach the team, but Coleman had made a big, magnanimous production about how he didn't want to make it all about him, and how he didn't want the game to be so competitive at such a young age, and how the team would be better served by a coach who stressed fun and camaraderie, and how he would be happy to help out in the background but didn't want a public role, and how he just wanted to be the team's biggest cheerleader, and on and on and on.

In reality, Coleman didn't want to take the time. He had better things to do, like close big deals and make money, and he figured he'd ride out Connor's younger years and jump in when the boy hit puberty and the game really started to matter. For now, he was more than content to preserve his status as a local legend – at least to these boys – and goof around with them before and after games.

Unfortunately for Coleman, the only thing goofy at that moment was his pathetic attempt to traverse the mild hill and make his way down to the field. Some of the kids had looked up and noticed him, and stopped with their drills while he limped down the hill.

"Mister Rob! Mister Rob!" One of Connor's teammates waved. His long-sleeve, teal blue soccer kit was already muddy. There were games every hour, and this made about the sixth or seventh match of the day, so the field was not in the best shape.

"Hi Dad!" Connor waved and then, feeling an extra burst of energy with his father watching, he took off dribbling toward the goal and booted the ball safely into the lower right corner of the netting.

Coleman waved back. "Nice shot, champ!"

Connor waved again, then rejoined his teammates as they zigzagged through a set of small orange cones, as part of their warm-up routine.

From across the field, Angie noticed him limping to a stop. Confused, she walked briskly around the field, careful not to cross the sideline chalk, passed behind the goal, and made her way to the spot where Coleman stood. He hadn't moved an inch since he had made it down the hill, and all his weight rested on his left side, to the point that he looked like he might topple over.

"Where are your crutches?"

"I accidentally forgot them."

"You're going to injure it worse if you don't use them," she said.

Coleman nodded and swallowed hard. The drive over and the short walk down the hill had left his foot screaming, and he could feel it throbbing beneath the running shoe, which looked like it had been inflated with a balloon.

"Well, do you want to try and go over to the other side and join the team?"

He shook his head and remained where he was.

"Do you want me to stay here with you?"

Shrug.

"What does that mean?"

"Do whatever you want, Angie. I'm not moving."

With a look of disdain, she walked around the field, past the goal, and over to the team's sideline, where she joined a group of the other parents. Looking back across the field, she noticed Coleman slowly lowering himself until he was seated on the grass with both legs extended.

When the game began, she watched him watching the action. Normally, Coleman was active and ebullient. He didn't yell or interject like some of the other parents. He took more of a participative role, jogging up and down the sidelines, shouting encouragement. He was also very good about reinforcing anything that Connor did well, while holding his tongue after any mistakes or bad plays. Today, however, Coleman just sat and stared, mostly at one spot in the grass, while the action carried on before him.

The game itself was nothing special, which is usually the case when 6-year-old boys are involved. It featured a whole lot of running back and forth, with pretty much everyone but the goalkeepers chasing the ball at all times. Every now and again, the teams would settle in and boot it around for three or four touches but, on average, it looked like a free-for-all, with the better players dominating the ball and playing keep-away with the defense.

Connor had a few nice chances. He sent one shot just wide of the net, and he kicked one ball directly at the goalie's chest. When the ball came to him, he tried his best to maintain control and deliver crisp passes to open teammates. For a 6-year-old, he looked pretty good out there.

Coleman hardly noticed. Busy protecting his aching foot from passersby, he rarely glanced up, and only when the air horn sounded at the end of the game did he turn his full attention to the field.

There was no real celebration, as the game had ended in a scoreless tie, and the kids buzzed around, slurping through the ceremonial post-game orange slices, attempting to arrange sleepovers with their friends' parents, and generally just acting like rambunctious kids. Connor and two of his buddies raced across the field with a ball to where Coleman was seated.

"Dad, Dad!" Connor shouted, "Juggle for us, like you do at home!"

Coleman saw them coming and slowly pushed himself up off the ground until he could rest his weight on his left leg.

"No, no, buddy, not today. My foot's not feeling great. I must have hurt it somehow."

"C'mon Dad!" Connor pointed to his friends. "I told them how you can do all these tricks and the ball never lands on the ground."

"You can do it, Mister Rob!" one of the boys added.

"Come on, Dad! Just one time."

They looked like puppies, the eager little boys. And not "rat dog" puppies – they looked like golden retrievers with all their blonde hair and bubbling enthusiasm.

Even Coleman didn't have the heart to decline their request.

Connor kicked the ball over to him, a well-placed pass with nice pace that landed firmly between Coleman's two feet. Coleman drew a deep breath and hesitated, mentally trying to figure out the best way to proceed. The boys had gathered in a semi-circle, about three feet away, and they waited impatiently for him to decide.

His right foot was utterly useless, therefore his balance was wildly questionable, but Coleman still thought that if he could get the ball up on his left knee, he could alternate between the knee, his head, and his chest. If he could pull off about five bounces, that should be enough to sufficiently impress the boys, and it shouldn't hurt too terribly, although some weight would need to be applied to the right foot. But maybe he could apply it to the heel? Sure, that could work. His toe wouldn't even need to touch the ground.

"Alright, guys. Alright. I'll give it a shot. But I'm going to need your help."

"Sure, Dad! What do you need?"

"Connor, come get the ball and stand back a few steps."

The boy did as instructed and held the ball in his hands.

"Okay, now when I say GO, I want you to toss the ball so that it lands just above my left knee. Right about here," Coleman said, indicating exactly where he wanted it. "You think you can do that?"

"I can do it!"

"Okay." Coleman took a deep, deep breath. He dug his right heel into the dirt to try and help support his weight, and to try and prevent his big toe from meeting the ground. "Are you ready?"

"Ready, Dad!"

Just before he gave the word, Coleman looked up and spotted his wife. She had noticed what they were doing, and had started jogging across the field toward them. The expression on her face was one of impending doom. Just as Angie shouted out his name, Coleman gave his son the order:

"GO!"

And then everything went horribly wrong.

Despite his best intentions, Connor's throw went to the wrong spot. Coleman probably should have let it drop to the ground and started over, but instinct took over and he couldn't stop his body from reacting.

Instead of hovering just above Coleman's left knee, the ball arrived at about mid-torso, and caused him to make a course correction so that he could get to the ball. In order to do so, he had to quickly shift a substantial amount of additional weight over to his right heel, which he had dug in tight to the ground.

This quick shift caused him to immediately lose his balance, and Coleman flailed his arms about in a futile attempt to remain upright.

He had a split-second decision to make: move weight to the ball of his gouty foot for support, or fall over hard on his right side.

In a battle of two bad choices, Coleman chose to land on his side.

He straightened, pulled his arm in tight to his side and, like a tree falling in the forest, he landed with a pronounced THUNK in the mud beside him.

Angie arrived just a few seconds too late, and kneeled down to help him.

"Whoa!" one of the boys said, pointing at him on the ground.

Connor's face flushed red, and he stared at the ground to avoid his friend's gaze.

"Your father could use some practice," the other boy said.

CHAPTER 16

The rest of the weekend had featured a rather unimpressive five-act drama at the Coleman household, highlighted by Coleman in bed, Coleman popping pills, Coleman with a bag of frozen peas on his foot, Coleman limping through the halls, and Coleman back to bed. He felt a little better by Monday morning, but not much, and he had no choice but to squeeze his still-swollen right foot back into the running shoe as he dressed for work.

He remembered to bring the crutches this time, and after a somewhat shaky commute in which he reserved his right foot for the gas, and applied his left foot to the brake, Coleman climbed from the car and gingerly stepped away from his parking spot. The strap of his laptop bag crossed his chest diagonally and the bag itself dully bounced against his lower back with each forward advance of the crutches.

There were plenty of interested looks as he made his way through the atrium to the elevators and up to his floor. The invincible Rob Coleman usually marched that course, with no regard for the banal morning pleasantries of corporate life. Today he seemed to notice every nod, every greeting, every forced smile, and he kept his head down with eyes affixed to the floor until he had safely navigated to his own corridor. He slowly clunked his way through the cubicle farm and focused on his office at the end of the row. Armstrong heard the noise and emerged from his own office. He wasn't the first to see Coleman ambling along, but he was the first to say what everyone else was thinking.

"What happened to you?"

It was an unsympathetic tone. Coleman said nothing, but motioned with his head to follow. Armstrong reluctantly obliged, though his hard expression registered growing displeasure. When they were inside the office with the door shut, and Coleman had set his crutches aside, removed his bag, and eased into his chair, he finally addressed his boss.

"It's nothing. A minor little injury from playing soccer with my kid this weekend. The crutches are purely precautionary."

Armstrong stood before the desk with his arms crossed, and interrogated Coleman with his eyes. "What kind of injury?"

"Seriously, it's nothing," Coleman said. "A little sprain. They want me to stay off of it for a little bit, and they gave me some ibuprofen for my trouble. Should be good to go in a few days."

"A few days, huh?"

"A few days, nothing more."

"They want a rematch, Robert, you are aware of that, yes?"

"Of course."

"Ducking out of the half-marathon because of a little injury is not going to be acceptable to them. You understand that, yes?"

"Yes."

"Then get healthy, and get healthy quick."

"I will."

"And use your brain, Robert. Get rid of any extracurricular activities until this deal is done. I shouldn't need to explain this to you."

"I know," Coleman said. "It won't happen again."

"Oh, I'm aware of that. Because if it does," Armstrong said, backing out of the office, "your presence here won't happen again. Understood?"

Coleman looked at him for a moment, then nodded. "Understood," he said softly.

As Armstrong left, Coleman reached into his bag for the canister of pills. Producing two, he popped them in his mouth and chased them with a swig from a bottle of water he had brought from home. With both hands, he hoisted his foot up onto the desktop, reclined in his chair, and stared up at the ceiling. He didn't notice Steve enter.

"What's with the crutches?"

"It's nothing." Coleman's voice was a soft monotone.

"What happened?"

"Foot."

"Are you alright?"

"I'll be fine."

"What'd you do?"

"Tweaked it playing soccer with my son."

"Can you run?"

"Not yet. Few days."

"Have you told Armstrong?"

"Just talked to him."

"Bummer," Steve said with a shrug. "Well, since you can't run, I guess you'll have plenty of time to focus on getting the technology right. We've got a meeting in 15 minutes."

"Kill me," Coleman exhaled.

"Gladly," Steve said, "but I'd like to get my bonus first."

"Vijay's not still here, is he?"

"Nope, he flew home. He'll be joining by phone."

"Well, thank God for tender mercies."

"Rob, you really need to try and work with him. I know you guys can't stand each other, but he really is the brains behind this thing. The network architectures he's designing for The Bank are amazing. I mean, this is disruptive stuff. He's going to have to them on the bleeding edge of the financial services industry. Firewalls, security group segmentation, interlock with the wireless platforms, mobile app integration, the identity tracker component..."

"More buzzwords, please. More jargon. I just can't get enough."

"Hey, you're supposed to know this stuff."

"That's why I have you."

"Well, it would help if you could at least articulate these services and solutions to your little running club, there."

"Steve," Coleman said, as he lifted his foot from the desk and slowly placed it on the ground, "we're all the same to those guys. Their underlings will lock themselves in a room with Vijay and the support team, and those guys will figure out all the technical details. But those guys know as well as anyone, that it's all the same. The tech is all the same, the solutions are all the same, and even the price will be roughly the same. In the end, they just want a partner they can lean on from time to time for price breaks, they want to know who to yell at when it's time to yell, and they want somebody they can feel comfortable hanging out with once a month when they have to see us."

"And that's you."

"That's me."

Steve walked over to the window and looked out over the grounds. It was a great view. The spring flowers were starting to pop, encouraged by the morning mist kicked up by the fountain in the pond. He made a mental note to ask for a better office once the deal closed.

"Just for today, can we try something?" Steve had turned around to face Coleman.

"What's that?"

"Listen to them. Don't jump in and start yelling at people. Just hear them out. Half the time they're just thinking out loud anyway, and I think you take it as insubordination. But listen to their concerns, and maybe even show a little support. I think you'll be surprised by the results you'll get."

"Are you serious?"

"Of course I'm serious."

"Steve, did you get a new management book?"

"Don't mock me. I mean it. Show some respect to these folks. They're a good team, and you're going to need them whether you believe it or not."

Coleman was tired. It was difficult to get any good sleep with his foot hurting so badly, and he wasn't eager for a Monday morning meeting anyway. A request for his silence could easily be granted.

"Tell you what," he said. "How about if you run the call? I'll be in the background and ask questions if needed. Deal?"

"Seriously?"

"Sure," Coleman said.

"You've never let anyone else run those calls. Believe me, they've all asked if someone else could. Anyone else."

"Today you get your wish, Steve. I'll be on my best behavior."

Steve considered this as he watched Coleman rub the outside of his shoe, applying slight pressure to the joint area. At the very least, it would be a change of pace. He nodded his assent, and briskly walked toward the door.

"Good," Steve said. "I'll see you in there!"

☺

Steve, in a very short amount of time, proved to be a far superior meeting host. The conversation was pleasant, respectful, and flowed naturally. The technical people had an opportunity to offer their input, concerns were expressed, issues were addressed, and timelines were agreed upon. Nobody yelled. No one got blamed. There was even some laughter on the phone, and a few smiles around the conference table.

Enjoying the attitude overhaul, Steve looked over at Coleman and gave him the thumbs-up sign. The usual host had reclined in a chair at the far end of the table. His head was propped against the wall, and his aching foot was extended and resting on the carpet. The crutches were placed horizontally in his lap, and he used them as armrests while he listened to the call.

As Steve was winding into his closing statements, replete with positive reinforcement and motivational oomph, Vijay interrupted. He had been silent for most of the call, occasionally adding a clarifying comment or asking a technical question.

"Steve, where is Rob?" Vijay's British accent was crisp and pointed. "Why is he not on the call?"

"Hi Vijay," Steve said, "we mentioned this at the top..."

"I'm right here, Vijay," Coleman raised his voice to carry across the room, but didn't move from his reclined position.

"Rob, why is Steve running this call? I was late and missed the explanation."

"It's fine, Vijay. I'm taking the day off."

"You always run this call, Rob. This leads me to believe that something is changing with the internal workings of the account."

Coleman lifted his head and stared across the table at the star-shaped speakerphone.

"Nothing has changed, Vijay." His voice hardened. "It's one freaking call."

"But why today, Rob? What is it that you are not telling us?"

"Nothing, Vijay! I'm tired, and I'm not feeling well. Steve is handling things just fine."

"Steve is handling things quite well in comparison," Vijay said. "It just strikes me as odd."

"What is your problem, Vijay?" Coleman sat up and grew animated, grabbing a crutch in each hand and pointing them both at the phone, like rifles ready to fire. "Why is everything a conspiracy with you?"

"This is highly unusual behavior, even for you, and you owe us a full accounting of any changes to our prospectus."

"Our prospectus?"

"If Steve is assuming a larger role on this deal, we need to know it, Rob. And we need to know it immediately, so that we can make the appropriate adjustments."

"What adjustments, Vijay? What are you talking about?"

Coleman stood and the weight against his foot caused him to audibly grunt from the pain.

"What was that noise?" Vijay said.

Coleman winced and planted his crutches so that he could lift his right foot. Watching him suffer, Steve granted Coleman a few extra moments of recovery time and jumped in to speak with Vijay.

"Hey, it's Steve. There really is no change, Vijay. Rob hurt his foot over the weekend and he's taking it easy today. That's all."

"What did he do to his foot?"

"What does it matter to you, Vijay?" Coleman had recovered and assumed his typical posture of hovering over the table and shouting into the phone.

"Does this deal not hinge on your athletic prowess? Your relationships with the executives? Is this not what you stressed to me during my last visit? Is this not why Neal has placed you in the lead role? Will you not need your foot for these activities?"

"My foot is fine! It's completely...OWWWW! OWWWW!! AAAAHHHHH!!!" While inching closer to the phone, Coleman had inadvertently bumped his toes up against one of the table stanchions.

A few of the engineers seated around the table snickered as Coleman fell back into his chair. His eyes watered and his face flushed red as he reached desperately for the foot. Kneading it like dough, he whimpered softly until the pain had subsided.

"What was that?" Vijay's voice pierced the awkward silence. "What was that noise? It sounded like a shrieking cat."

"Or two little girls in an argument," another engineer's voice lifted from the phone.

"Or like a cow being milked," another voice said.

"Or like..."

"Enough!" Steve yelled, grabbing the immediate attention of the room and everyone on the phone. "Come on, team, that's enough. This has been a productive call, and let's not derail it now. Thank you everyone on the phone for joining and, for those in the room, thank you for your attendance. Next week, same time, same place, and we'll be in touch with our break-out groups throughout the week."

"Steve, will you be running the call next week?" Vijay had to throw in one last barb.

Steve glanced over at Coleman, who was now hunched over with his head between his knees.

"I don't know, Vijay."

"You acquitted yourself well, and I would recommend that you assume these responsibilities moving forward."

"I'll take it under advisement, Vijay. Goodbye everyone."

Steve reached for the phone and ended the call. He waited as everyone in the room filed out, some stopping to take one more look at their leader, who now sat clutching himself around the arms and shivering. Steve shook his head and motioned for them to leave.

"Are you gonna make it?" he asked, once they were alone in the room.

Coleman looked up and nodded.

"Why don't you go home? I can handle things till you get back."

Coleman held his stare for a moment, then agreed with a shake of his head. Holding out his hand, he silently requested help getting up. Steve reached out and pulled Coleman to his feet, where he briefly wobbled, then settled into the saddles of his crutches.

"Good job with the call," Coleman said. "Maybe you should lead it from now on."

"I'd be happy to," Steve said. "Although, even I wound up yelling at the end. I think you're a bad influence."

"I'm a good influence and, trust me, yelling at Vijay will become one of your favorite parts of the job."

"I didn't like it."

"Learn to like it," Coleman said, his crutches slowly clunking their way toward the door. "Some of the people on this team need to be yelled at."

Steve watched him go and spoke under his breath when he was sure that Coleman was out of earshot.

"I can think of one in particular," he said with a grin.

CHAPTER 17

The extra sleep seemed to have helped a bit, though the swelling and redness had not subsided, and the foot still hurt to the touch. Coleman lay in bed, staring at the ceiling for a while, mentally replaying the events since his embarrassing doctor's visit. He couldn't walk, he couldn't kick a ball with his kid, he felt like his boss and his colleagues were on to his whole "injury" excuse and, despite the strong position he had placed his company in through his exploits at The Asylum, he didn't feel good at all about their next steps.

Coleman fell into a trance as he watched the ceiling fan whirl around, again and again and again. He deeply inhaled the air cascading down upon him and exhaled with a small cough. The cough reminded him that it was almost spring allergy season in North Carolina, and he would need to load up on medication. Pollen from the pines affected just about everyone, be they natives or relocated Yankees from the Northeast. The red, itchy eyes, the morning sinus headaches, and the wheezing coughs would last about two months. An allergy pill a day usually did the trick, but he would also need to change out all the air filters in the house to make sure the airflow was clean, and it wouldn't hurt to have a diagnostic check-up performed on the AC unit. Much, of this, however, would involve climbing up to the attic, or stepping on ladders, and Coleman winced at the thought of such trauma on his foot. He decided to add some heating and air technicians to Angie's punch list.

Coleman extracted himself from the bed and hobbled his way down the hall to the foot of his dual staircase. He silently cursed himself for not having an elevator installed when they built the home. Angie had fallen in love with the castle-like feeling the staircase evoked, with steps on either side curving down to the dramatic foyer. At the time, he didn't really give a rip about the romance involved – he was more concerned with the implications for resale and, at the time, the stairs seemed like a nice touch. At this time, he could have kicked himself, if it wouldn't have hurt his foot so much.

There were precisely 26 steps on each branch, and each step represented an opportunity for pain. He chose the branch to the right, so that he could support himself against the railing with his left arm and allow his right foot plenty of clearance between the railing and the wall. Slowly, slowly, and even more slowly, he stepped 26 times, using the heel of his right foot for balance and protecting the toes as much as possible. It took a few minutes, but he made it relatively unscathed and happily collected himself once he had reached the foyer.

The grandfather clock in the living room chimed five times, announcing the hour of the afternoon. At this, Coleman smiled. It felt good to be home, instead of at work, like he was getting away with something. His socked feet scooted along the tile floor, slowly and painlessly, until he emerged in the kitchen, illuminated by recessed lighting that reflected off the marble countertops and steel appliances. The white cabinetry enhanced the glow, and Coleman squinted at the brightness.

"Hey, Dad, how's your foot?"

Connor sat up on his knees on a high-backed bar stool at one side of the rectangular kitchen island. He was coloring in a book full of outlined superheroes, and half the crayons had rolled off the surface and come to rest beneath the chair.

"It's okay," Coleman said. "Getting better."

Angie worked on the other side of the island, closer to the countertops and the sink. She wore a pair of jeans with boots, a light-pink cotton long sleeve shirt, and a white fleece vest. Her sleeves were rolled up, and she washed a head of lettuce under the faucet. On a cutting board beside her, tomatoes and cucumbers had been neatly chopped. She looked up when he came in, but continued with her preparation.

"You slept awhile."

Coleman grunted.

"We were thinking we'd grill some steaks for dinner with a salad and potato," she said. "Oh, and there's beer in the fridge if you want one."

He looked down at his foot and frowned.

"Uhh, I'm okay," he said. "I'll just grab a bottle of water."

She watched him hobble over to the refrigerator and open the door. He stared expressionless at the three filets, each wrapped with bacon, that stared back at him from the shelf. He reached for a bottle of water from the side rack and took a long drink.

"Do we have any cherries?"

"What?" Angie said.

He closed the door and turned to her. "How about if I just go with a salad tonight?"

"Just a salad?"

"Yeah, I'm not feeling all that hungry."

She watched him limp past Connor to the family room, where he eased himself down onto the nearest cushion of the three-seat leather couch. Reaching for the remote control, he turned on the television, which hung flat against the wall above the fireplace, and clicked over to the sports channel. He lifted his leg and propped his right foot on top of a magazine on the coffee table before him.

Angie wiped her hands on her jeans and walked over. She stood with her arms crossed at the other side of the couch.

"What's going on?" she said.

Coleman stared at the television. "What do you mean?"

"What do I mean?"

"Yeah."

"Rob, you came home from work early, you slept all afternoon, you've been popping pills like they're M&M's, and you turned down steak and beer. What's going on?"

"Nothing! I hurt my foot."

Angie sat on the couch and faced him. There was a cushion still between them and she leaned forward to close the distance.

"I've seen you with sports injuries before. You always had plenty of energy and an appetite. But now you seem totally out of it, and what's with the cherries?"

He looked away from her and back at the TV. He started to say something, then thought better of it and shook his head.

"It's nothing."

She inched closer to him.

"What's wrong, Rob? Did the doctor find something else?" Her voice dropped to a whisper. "Oh God, please don't tell me it's cancer."

"What?" He looked at her, baffled. "I don't have cancer!"

"You can tell me," she said. "You have to tell me."

"Angie," he lowered his own voice, "I don't have cancer. What are you talking about?"

"We can work through this.

"Angie, I don't have..."

"We can get help."

"Angie..."

"You don't have to keep it to yourself."

Unable to withstand the barrage any longer, he blurted it out.

"Angie, it's not cancer. I have the gout!"

She was silent for several moments as she processed the information. When she spoke, she was incredulous.

"You have the what?"

He lowered his voice again. "The gout. I have the gout."

And then, all at once, she burst out laughing.

"Hey!" he said, growing perturbed.

"You have the gout?"

"Yes."

She laughed again. "I'm sorry, but this is too funny. I thought you were dying or something! I knew it wasn't a ligament tear or anything like that, but the gout? The gout??"

"Are you through?"

"Wait," she said, "isn't that something that hits overweight people?"

"It can be hereditary," he said defensively. "Or the result of a diet rich in purines."

"I'm sorry, purines?"

Coleman sighed and then told her everything the doctor had said. He told her all about the uric acid, all about the symptoms, all about the recovery, all about the misunderstood reputation, and all about the cherries. When he was finally done, the look of bemusement refused to leave her face. The smirk was frozen solid, and she couldn't stop shaking her head.

"What?" he said.

Angie stood and placed her hands on her hips. Looking down at him, she smiled.

"You need to make some changes."

"I know," Coleman said, resigned to the ridicule. "I know."

CHAPTER 18

Neal Armstrong was on the cusp of something great. He had joined the company in the mid-1990's, when the Internet was still just an idea to most people. A handful of brilliant university researchers had stitched their visions together to create one of the greatest inventions of the 20th century, an invention that would connect people all over the world and allow them to work, study, share, and collaborate without ever leaving the comforts of their own home. To Armstrong, the Internet was the third greatest invention of the last century, just behind the Wright Brothers biplane, and NASA's entire Apollo space program. And, though it was third in his heart, it was first in his mind because, for Armstrong, the Internet was far and away the most lucrative.

Something had to power the Internet connectivity and access that would explode in the late 90's and become globally ubiquitous as the new century dawned. There were equipment bundles to sell, solutions to propose, and services to render, and Armstrong was right there at the vanguard of a booming billion-dollar business. Through hard work, guile, and no shortage of ruthlessness, he had risen through the ranks, climbed the corporate ladder, and navigated the competitive seas to land where he was today – a top executive at a top Internet company in the top country in the world. It was heady stuff, enough to make a humbler man shudder, but Armstrong was not given to introspection. He only saw the next step, the big prize, the final destination.

The Chief Executive Officer was stepping down at the end of the year, and the Board of Directors would soon appoint a replacement. Armstrong didn't really think he would become the next CEO, but he did sense opportunity. If the Chief Operating Officer assumed the top spot, as rumored, there would be a need for a new COO. The deal with The Bank, when it closed, would place him squarely in the lead for such a role.

They had come in together, the CEO and COO, and had built a Fortune 500 company over the past two decades. Armstrong had been with them the whole way, albeit a lower-ranking salesman to start, but they knew his work ethic, they knew his drive, they knew his skills, and they were intimately familiar with his results. He had been in the room with them time and again, and they knew what he wanted.

For Armstrong, assuming a bigger chair meant an incredible life of globe-trotting to deliver lectures and keynote addresses, a veritable catalog of memberships on executive boards throughout the country, and a respected and important voice in the governmental regulatory environment. This last perk was the one that interested him most.

There was an inherent gravitas placed on the opinions of the top executives at a top Internet company, and Washington was always listening. There were already whispers that, upon his retirement, the CEO was set to join the President's administration as Chief Technology Officer. Armstrong cared nothing for this, but he could see how the puzzle pieces might one day fit together and lead him to his true love.

Space.

The technology was so incredible at NASA. They were going to new planets, they were landing on comets, they were making plans to colonize the moon...there was no limit to their imagination. And with all of these projects, there would be a vital need for communications, all powered by Internet technology and capabilities. Armstrong would be there to consult them.

He could envision it all in his mind. Get the job as COO, crush the competition, gain Washington's ear, land on NASA's doorstep, lead the space program to new frontiers.

He had brought the company's East Coast operations up from nothing, and helped to turn their little patch of North Carolina into a technology and research corridor. He had helped usher in a new era in Internet technology, presiding over the wireless gold rush, and now he was overseeing the security boom.

He had gotten very rich in the process, but he wanted more. He wanted what he wanted. It was all there before him. But, first, they would have to close with The Bank.

Armstrong had staked his reputation on this deal, and the other dominoes didn't fall without The Bank falling first. They were a quirky bunch, the people at The Bank, but Armstrong would win the business, no matter what it took.

Rob Coleman would not stand in his way.

The swelling had gone down quite a bit, but standing was still the furthest thing from Coleman's mind. It hurt way too much and, other than the pills, the only solace he could find was from elevating the foot and alternately massaging and icing it. He had slipped the old running shoe off and the heel now rested atop his desk, a yellow legal pad serving as a cushion underneath.

He had willed himself into work that morning, figuring that keeping his mind occupied was a better way to block out the pain than staring at the stupid foot all day. Instead of the usual bacon, eggs, and English muffin, Angie had prepared him a breakfast of half a grapefruit and two packets of plain instant oatmeal. It was the opposite of delicious, and left him feeling unsatisfied and slightly cranky. She had also cut him off at one little teaspoon of sugar in each mug of coffee, when he preferred it strong and sweet.

When the clock ticked past 10:30 am, where Coleman usually reached for a Snickers or some peanut butter crackers, today he found only carrot and celery sticks. No dipping sauce to be found. Angie had packed those for him, too, shoving them into his laptop bag inside of Connor's little plastic lunch baggies. Coleman registered his disgust with every bite, and only finished the raw vegetable medley because he was starving.

By the time the clock crept toward noon, he was ready to eat his own gout-filled foot. It was about this time that Armstrong decided to grace Coleman with his presence.

As he always did, the boss marched into Coleman's office without so much as a knock on the door. He usually had a joke or an enthusiastic energy about him, but today Armstrong seemed cold and determined. His eyes were small slivers above that beak of a nose, and his jaw muscles rhythmically tightened, then relaxed, tightened, then relaxed, as if he were chewing gum. When Coleman looked up and saw him standing there, he instinctively pulled his leg back and set his foot on the ground.

"What's up, Neal?" he said, forcing a smile.

"The question is, what's up with your foot?"

"It's better," Coleman said. "Much better."

"But not good enough to go this weekend?"

"This weekend?"

"The half-marathon."

Coleman looked down at the foot, tucked safely inside the old running shoe.

"I might be ready. A few more days of..."

"Stand up," Armstrong said.

"What?"

"Stand up."

Coleman reluctantly began to slowly rise out of his chair. He pressed his palms against the desk to help push himself up. When he was standing, he straightened his knees and removed his hands, supporting himself upright under his own weight. He gritted his teeth and forced another smile against the waves of pain he knew were about to arrive.

"Now I want you to walk."

"Walk?"

"Over to me. Let me see you walk." Armstrong had backed up to the doorway, leaving a course of approximately 15 feet for Coleman to traverse.

Coleman's gait was so stilted, he looked like the office version of a wooden soldier. He favored his right leg with every step, and each time it grazed the carpet, waves of pain crashed against his entire body. He was so concentrated on fighting back the grimace painted across his face, that his eyes had widened like saucers. To Armstrong, he looked like some sort of corpse dressed in khakis and a button-down.

"Alright, that's enough," Armstrong said.

Coleman had made it a total of five steps.

He walked backward, retracing his steps and, completely defeated, sunk deep into his chair. Armstrong approached. Standing before the desk, he crossed his arms, and peered down.

"I didn't think you would be ready," he said. "So I asked for a postponement."

Coleman looked up. "You did?"

"I did. You're off the hook for this weekend."

Coleman returned his gaze to the ground and exhaled a deep sigh of relief.

"I told them that you needed a little more recovery time," Armstrong continued. "That they had done a number on you at The Asylum."

Coleman looked up again, a flash of hope in his eyes.

"What did they say?"

"Oh, they ate it up," Armstrong said. "They're still stunned that you were able to hang with them."

"I beat them."

"Yes, you did. And now, because of what I told them, they think you sacrificed your own foot to do it."

"So we're still good?"

Coleman reclined, not only relieved, but now feeling some self-satisfaction. He set his elbows on the armrests and leaned back a little too much for Armstrong's liking.

"Good?" Armstrong said, raising his eyebrows.

"On track," Coleman clarified. "We're still on track?"

"Yes, we are still on track. But we are far from good, Robert."

Coleman was quiet as Armstrong leaned forward from the other side of the desk.

"You only get one screw-up on this deal," Armstrong said, each word seeming to spit forth from his thin lips. "And you have already used yours."

Coleman nodded his understanding.

"You have a prerogative to take care of your body until all that money is ours. I don't care what you have to do. I don't care what family rituals you have to miss. I don't care if your child never speaks to you again. You will get that foot healed quickly, and you will see this deal through until the signatures are on the contracts."

"I understand," Coleman said.

"I'm glad, because if you stumble again, if you do anything to sabotage this for me, you will never work in this industry again. Are we clear?"

"Crystal."

"Good. Now, I bought you at least a week. So get healthy, and have fun out there, Robert!"

Armstrong clapped and smiled at the end, then turned and walked out into the hall. Coleman sat in silence for a while, slowly recovering from the verbal assault.

It was all so absurd.

This was, by far, the biggest deal of Coleman's career. It was also, by far, the most bizarre. It was difficult to process how a group of high-powered bank executives could make such a huge financial decision based on something so stupid. The Asylum, the half-marathons, the triathlons...they were all pointless activities, at least in his mind.

But then, who knew why people did what they did? Coleman's company and Armstrong, in particular, had a reputation for creative deal-making. Coleman had watched the man hunt quail in Texas, had seen him snowmobile through the woods in Minnesota, and had been on the boat while he sailed in Lake Michigan. Armstrong was a man who could adapt to the situation. The only reason he wasn't taking this one himself was because he couldn't keep up with their athleticism.

No matter how crazy it sounded, to Coleman it had always seemed true. Among the competition, the technology was basically all the same. The terms were basically the same. The prices were practically identical. The only real difference was him.

The Bank would be won or lost on the feet of Rob Coleman.

The idea made him shiver, and he thought of Angie and Connor, their big, beautiful home, and his dreams of a big, beautiful beach house. If he didn't get better, it was all gone. So if this is what it took, this is what he would do. He would get the foot better, and get back out there on the trail. In a way, he felt like a prostitute, but he would do it.

In a way, he felt like a prostitute.

A prostitute.

Her.

Oh no. Since his episode of the gout, Coleman had successfully eliminated that portion of the evening from his brain, but now it came rushing back all at once.

The black dress. The blonde hair. Stumbling into the room. Throwing back the covers. Falling onto the sheets. Everything that came next. And then...

The money.

Three hundred bucks, directly from his wallet, while he wallowed in miserable pain up against the wall in the corner.

He had no idea. He honestly thought she had been taken by his charm and good looks. If his foot didn't hurt so much, he would have kicked himself with it. He dropped his head into his hands and quickly tried to, once again, erase the memories.

There was a knock on the door, and Coleman looked up to see Steve and two of the engineers standing there. They seemed loose and giddy.

"What's wrong with you?" Steve said. "You look like somebody just shot your dog."

"I don't have a dog."

"Well, cheer up," Steve said, pointing his thumb at the teammates, who stood behind him. "We just nailed the schematics. The architecture documentation is ready to be signed, sealed and delivered. Even got Vijay's approval."

Coleman nodded. He knew it didn't matter. It was just one more box to check. The only thing that mattered was his foot.

"Hey, we're heading out later for drinks to celebrate. You coming with us?"

"I'm sorry, Steve. I've got a lot to get done here. Armstrong has me scrambling right now."

"Alright, well, seriously, cheer up. We're hitting the home stretch. We may hit these deadlines yet."

They looked so happy, and he had worked them so hard. Coleman didn't have the heart to tell them. It just didn't matter.

"Hey guys," he said. "Incredible job. I'll catch you next time."

As they walked away, he reached for his foot and furiously massaged it.

CHAPTER 19

There was nothing Coleman loved more than a cold beer when he had the grill fired up, with a nice slab of meat slowly cooking over the flames. He would turn his face to the sun, sip on the beer and savor the smoky smells of a searing steak. Added to the strains of birds chirping and the visions of flowers in bloom, an evening with his beer and his grill was one of the great pleasures of Coleman's life.

On this evening, he sipped from a plastic bottle of water and tried not to burn a white fish filet.

He grumbled to himself as he flipped the mahi over, leaving a layer of flaky skin stuck to the grates. At least he thought it was mahi – to Coleman, it looked like rubber. He turned the knobs to lower the natural gas output on his burners and closed the lid. When he thought about it, he was actually surprised that he had never cooked a fish on this grill before, but then why would he, when there were so many great cuts of meat to enjoy instead? He would have given a leg, and certainly a right foot, for a nice filet mignon wrapped in bacon, or a delicious, dry-rubbed ribeye. Instead he got a fish that he wish would have been thrown back.

It was a cool early evening, and Coleman wore a fleece vest against the breezes that softly swayed the treetops of the property's Carolina pines. Those same pines would drop giant globules of yellow pollen in a month or so, and he grimaced at the thought of the coming headaches and sneezing fits. It was the price to pay to live in such a beautiful, temperate area, and Coleman could only hope that his rotten gouty foot would have healed by the time the pollen dropped.

Illuminated by the patio's outdoor floodlights, Connor kicked his soccer ball into a little goal, ran to retrieve it, repositioned, then kicked again. He shot from various angles and distances, and Coleman watched him repeat the process several times without interrupting. The boy hadn't really said much to him since the debacle at Connor's soccer game, and Coleman wasn't really sure how to go about explaining his current medical condition, or how to apologize for falling on his tail in the mud in front of Connor's friends. So he did what came naturally – Coleman hobbled over to the goal, did his best to stand upright, and beckoned for Connor to kick it again.

"Alright, buddy, see if you score one on me!"

Connor eyed his father warily, not sure whether this was such a good idea.

"Come on, champ," Coleman insisted. "Let's see what you've got!"

Connor shrugged and rolled the ball into place, about 10 feet away and a little bit off to the left of the goal. Coleman stretched both arms out in an overly dramatic display of goalkeeping, and then he watched haplessly as the ball skipped between his legs and nestled firmly in the back of the net.

"You got me there, buddy! Let's try it again."

Favoring his bad foot, Coleman bent over to retrieve the ball and rolled it back to Connor, who now stood in a different spot, a little off to the right. The boy was expressionless and seemed relatively unimpressed with the goalkeeper's acumen. Feeling mischievous, he scorched the next shot directly at his father's right foot.

Coleman dropped any pretense of the dynamic between a father and his young son, in which the father playfully allows the son to succeed at his own expense. He was mentally a few steps ahead, and Coleman's eyes widened as the ball careened toward him. He adjusted, set his left foot for balance, and reached down to collect the ball with his right hand before it could touch the foot. With a deep sigh of relief, he straightened and pulled the ball into his chest. When he looked up, Connor was smiling.

"I think the fish is burning," Coleman said, not exactly pleased with the boy. He lay the ball on the ground and limped back over to the grill, leaving Connor to resume his one-man game.

Angie poked her head out the French doors leading to the patio. "How are we doing?" she said.

Coleman lifted the lid and pondered his piece of fish. It didn't smell bad, but it looked like it had barely been cooked. He used the tongs to flip it again, and left a few more thin strips on the grill grates.

"I'm not sure," he said. "A few more minutes, I think."

He watched her nod and close the door behind her. Through the windows, he eyed the tight jeans she wore over an old, broken-in pair of Western boots. Her long-sleeve cotton shirt was cut just low enough to make the mind wonder, and the light-green shade brought out the emerald color of her eyes.

Coleman didn't lift his own eyes for a bit, and just watched. They had slept in the same bed, but they hadn't been together since he showed up late to Connor's spring concert. Part of that was her – she had kicked him out of the house for a night, after all – but part of that was him, too. Since then, in a pathetic show of defiance, he had resisted even the slightest physical contact with his wife. Tonight, though, his mood was a little brighter and his foot felt a little better.

His mind began to wander.

Unfortunately, it wandered immediately to the place he didn't want it to go.

Coleman had never, ever stepped out on Angie before, not during their marriage and not when they were dating. He still wasn't completely clear on what had ultimately triggered his recent stumble, and he was doing a poor job of trying to block it from both his conscious and subconscious minds. Sure, he had been furious with her for booting him from their home for a night and, of course, the alcohol had been a contributing factor. But he still had trouble believing that it was him who had left with the girl in the dress.

Maybe it was the attention. Maybe it was the novelty. Maybe it was a mid-life crisis. Or maybe he was just a complete and total jerk.

Probably all of the above.

When she returned, a shockwave of shame jolted him and he quickly stared at his grill in order to avoid her eyes. She was holding a glass of red wine in each hand, and she brought one over to him.

"Here," she said. "One's not gonna hurt."

He reached for the glass and held it in front of him. "Are you sure?" he said.

"I looked it up online. It should be fine as long as you remember to keep *all things in moderation.*"

She emphasized the last part in a tone laced with mock seriousness, and Coleman snorted. He was sick of hearing that advice, too, and he appreciated the little joke. Before he drank, though, another thought popped into his head.

"What about the pills?"

"Nope, you're fine," she said, sliding into one of the patio chairs and crossing her legs. "It's just a strong ibuprofen and you can have a glass of wine over top of that."

Coleman considered this and brought the glass closer. He swirled the wine and, placing his nose near the opening, inhaled deeply. He was no sommelier, but he caught a hint of dark cherry in the waft and inwardly grinned. Cherries were good for the gout.

"How do I know you're not trying to kill me?" he said, bringing the glass to his lips.

"Because if that were the case, you'd already be gone."

At that, they shared a little laugh and Coleman drank. It was a full-bodied red, and he savored the flavor of anything new after nearly a week of nothing but water. He wasn't sure that it was the best choice to pair with a piece of fish, and he further lamented the absence of red meat on the grill, but he kept this to himself.

Behind them, Connor blasted away at the goal. They watched quietly while he ran back and forth, kicking the ball, then retrieving it and bringing it back. Coleman turned to her and nodded approvingly.

"He's getting pretty good."

"He comes from good stock," she said playfully.

"Indeed."

"You'd better check that grill. If you burn your fish, you're stuck with salad tonight."

Coleman frowned and lifted the lid. The mahi seemed done, but he didn't really know how to judge. It had browned some and smaller pieces were beginning to flake away from the larger piece. He switched from the tongs to a hamburger flipper and slid it beneath the fish. He transferred it from the grill to a plate and, when it hit the porcelain, it fell apart into four separate pieces.

Angie had watched the culinary display and couldn't help but laugh. "Not to worry!" she said. "We can throw it on top of the salad and make it a Coleman Special."

She called for Connor to come inside and clean up, and they adjourned to the dining room to eat as a family. Angie took control, and Coleman felt like an invited guest as she led them to their chairs, dimmed the chandelier lights, lit the candles on the table, instructed Connor to ask the blessing, and served the meal. It was warm and pleasant and easy and good, and he couldn't recall feeling that way in a very long time.

Later, after Connor had showered (this was also new for Coleman – normally, the boy took a bath, but he had insisted on a hot shower) and Angie had read him a story and turned out his bedroom light, they sat together on the family room couch.

She had cleaned up and put everything away in the kitchen behind them, and Coleman had flipped through a magazine while he waited for her. Soft music played from the surround-sound speaker system. He removed his shoes and propped his right foot up on the couch and reclined against one arm. When she joined him, she lifted his leg and slid beneath it so that his calf stretched across her lap. He winced at the touch.

"I'll be gentle," she said, and she had been. Coleman didn't feel a thing.

They sat quietly for a while listening to the music, and he allowed his eyes to shut, as he fluttered in and out of a light, gentle sleep.

"I'm sorry," she said softly.

"Hmmm?" He opened his eyes and looked up at her.

"For last week," she said. "I shouldn't have kept you out of the house. That was a terrible thing to do."

He didn't respond at first. Embarrassed and feeling responsible for the events, he looked away. They were quiet again for a long moment before he spoke.

"I won't let that happen again," he said. "I shouldn't have shown up like that."

"He doesn't need to see you that way," she agreed.

"I know."

They sat quietly again, and Coleman settled in deeper into the couch. Angie straightened and smoothed the fabric of his pants and ran her hand over his leg, taking care not to come near the foot. He had begun to fade again when she whispered to him.

"Rob?"

"Hmmm?"

"Have you ever thought about having another?"

"Another what?" he mumbled.

"I think we should have another child."

"What?" Coleman's eyes popped open.

"I get so sad watching him play in the yard by himself. I think he needs a sibling."

"Where is this coming from?"

She looked straight ahead as she spoke, avoiding eye contact with him. "He's in school now, and I have nothing to do all day. I thought I'd like that, but I'm..." her voice trailed off. "I'm lonely."

"Well, I mean, there are lots of things you could do." Coleman sat up a little.

"Like what?"

"Well, you could volunteer, or even go back to work, or I don't know. What do you want to do?"

She turned and looked him straight in the eye.

"I want a little girl."

The silence lingered for a bit, as Coleman tried to wake his senses and process this unexpected information.

"Angie, I don't think that's the way it works," he said, sitting up even straighter. "Even if we did have another kid, I'm not sure I could promise you that."

Now she was the silent one. She stared off at the fireplace and bit her lower lip. As she did, both hands began to rub over his leg, and one hand crept closer and closer to him. Finally, she turned her head and Coleman was rendered breathless by the look on her face.

She was going to get what she wanted.

"Well, I guess we'll never know if we don't try," she said.

Coleman swallowed hard and drew a shaky breath. He was powerless to do anything but agree.

"I guess we'd better go try, then."

CHAPTER 20

"Let us bow our heads and pray."

Coleman waited until the rest of the congregation had bowed their heads and he took a look around. It had been quite some time since he had last been there, and the ambience and surroundings brought back good and important memories. They had been married there and Connor had been baptized right up front, where the Reverend now stood leading the prayer.

The church sat elevated on a rolling hill, overlooking the road that approached it. It was a beautiful old white structure, with an elongated rectangular sanctuary that supported the tall spire of a chapel. The big wooden double doors at the entrance were painted red and, on a nice day, the red doors set against the white chapel, set against the green hill, set against the blue sky, gave the church an idyllic pastoral feel, like something out of a Norman Rockwell painting.

Inside, the layout was traditional. The sanctuary featured rows of wooden pews, set on either side of a wide aisle, that stretched from front to back. At the front, three steps led up to a dark wooden pulpit, where the Reverend conducted his sermon. Behind him, three rows of chairs accommodated the choir, who sat silently in their deep blue robes. Off to one side was an organ box and, above the choir, the silver organ pipes stretched all the way to the ceiling.

Coleman inhaled the sanctuary air, thick with the smells of wood stain and silver polish, the old pages of pew Bibles and hymnals, and the assorted perfumes, colognes and hair products worn by the parishioners. Morning light filtered through the artistic designs of stained glass windows that stretched along the walls, illuminating the dust particles rising toward the vaulted ceiling. Suspended high from this ceiling, a giant wooden cross seemed to float above the congregation and beckon the souls below.

Coleman's soul had a few things to atone for but, on the balance, it felt better than normal.

The week had flown by, and he had made real progress. Incredible progress. Some might say *miraculous* progress. He had walked into the church that morning under his own power. No crutches. No painkillers. No limp.

It had taken about a week longer than the doctor had initially projected, but it seemed that the crystallization of the uric acid that resided in the joint of the big toe on his right foot had completely subsided.

In other words, the gout was gone.

He wiggled the toes and marveled at the absence of pain. He had been able to fit into a leather loafer without any issue and, with positively bursting energy, he had bounded up the steps before the service to hold the red door for his wife and son.

They sat about midway down the aisle on the left side and, apart from an older couple dressed in their Sunday finery, they had the pew to themselves. Angie and Connor had penitently bowed their heads and, as Coleman watched them, he wondered what prayers they were praying. He had a pretty good idea, and he wrapped an arm around his wife.

The Reverend had finished speaking and now asked the congregation to silently confess their sins and ask forgiveness. Coleman looked around first to make sure he was doing it right, then bowed his head and squeezed his eyes shut. His mind was blank and he wasn't sure where to start, but he thought back on his week and how things had improved at home and at work. He thought about Angie and he thought about Connor and he thought about the sibling (a girl?) that she wanted for him.

Then, as it often did in these moments of quiet reflection, his mind turned to food. He was starving. At Angie's behest, he'd been eating fish and lean chicken and salads all week and, besides coffee, he had skipped breakfast altogether that morning.

He wanted eggs. He wanted steak and eggs! He wanted hash browns. He wanted sausage and bacon. He wanted scrapple and grits. He wanted toast and biscuits and butter and jam. He wanted food, by God, food! Coleman squeezed his eyes tight, wrapped his arms around his mid-section and tried to fight it, but there was no stopping the thunder emerging from within.

Like a bulldozer crashing through a pasture, his stomach shook the prayerful and awakened the sleeping.

"Amen," the Reverend said, just moments too late, for most in his flock had already raised their heads and stared directly at the infrequent attendee who now sat hunched over in a feeble attempt to hide behind his wife and child.

"Sorry," Coleman finally said, raising his hand, after Angie had elbowed him in the ribs. Connor didn't know whether to laugh or hide, and the old couple beside them looked down their noses with judgmental disdain.

"Sorry," Coleman reiterated, then studied his church bulletin to avoid their stares.

Next up on the agenda was the Reverend's sermon, and Coleman was grateful that attention would be returned to the pulpit. He was grateful, that is, until he noticed the sermon's title:

When Love Goes Astray (Your Cheating Heart).

For the next 20 minutes, Coleman squirmed. It was a real stem-winder, and the Reverend spared no feelings as he blasted away at the sinful nature of lust and the existential threat to society posed by adultery. It was an Armstrong-level dressing down and, throughout the sermon, Coleman felt like the Reverend was addressing it directly to him.

He desperately avoided any eye contact with Angie, but tried to sneak a glance here and there to see if anyone else shared his discomfort. The old man seated beside him caught his gaze, and Coleman quickly looked away from the man's narrowed eyes. The Reverend poured it on thick with the stories of broken marriages and tales of children born out of wedlock. Coleman's breathing was short and quick, and his right foot began to involuntarily fidget. Finally, finally (finally!), just as Coleman thought he might stand up and confess, the Reverend concluded the sermon and they finished with another silent prayer.

This time, there was no sound from Coleman's stomach. He no longer had an appetite.

On the way out, the Reverend stood just inside the red double doors and said his farewells to the congregants. Coleman tried to take the outside lane and sneak past without being noticed, but the Reverend was making eye contact with each person, and he noticed Coleman quite quickly.

"Robert!" the Reverend said, reaching for Coleman's arm. "How long has it been?"

Coleman sheepishly smiled and looked at his shoes.

"Too long, Reverend," he said. "Terrific sermon. Really moving."

"Well, thank you, Robert." He grinned and, as he patted Coleman on the shoulder, the flowing sleeve of his purple robe fell back to reveal cuff links in the shape of soccer balls on his dress shirt. "But I trust the content of today's lesson did not apply. You have such a beautiful family."

At this, the Reverend warmly greeted Angie and reached down to tousle Connor's hair. Coleman forced another smile and shook his head.

"Good! Well I am glad we bumped into each other today," the Reverend continued. "I have a real opportunity that I think would be perfect for you."

Oh no. Coleman looked over at Angie and stared hard. This was nothing new, the Reverend and his "opportunities." There was always a fresh project that needed money, or some new group seeking members, and Coleman had done his best to avoid such opportunities since they had joined the church. Sure, he occasionally wrote out a check, but that was always after some nagging from Angie. As the Reverend had just noted, Coleman could barely drag himself to Sunday services. The thought of increasing his involvement was not something he wished to entertain.

"It's a tremendous new ministry we're developing, that will have a positive impact on our youth. We could really use your involvement, Robert."

Ugh.

Coleman began shuffling his feet and allowed the line forming behind them to push him out the door and away.

"Well, uh, I tell you what, Reverend. Things are pretty busy at work right now, and I'm not sure the time will allow me to..."

"He would love to help!" Angie said. "Please just give us a call and let us know what you need. I'll make sure he follows directions."

She smiled and pushed him along with one hand, while she pulled Connor along with the other. The Reverend returned her smile and waved, then turned to the next person leaving through the red doors.

Shaking his head, Coleman allowed her to nudge him down the steps toward the car. Reaching back, he grabbed her hand and held it.

CHAPTER 21

Steve ran the Monday meeting again, and Coleman sat happily against the far wall. He kept his participation to a minimum and only interjected when necessary. The meeting flowed well, and the technical people accomplished a great deal. There was a small problem with maintaining remote access into the proposed network, but the team had brainstormed multiple workarounds and felt they could mitigate the issue before their final proposal to The Bank.

A few of the engineers in the room had reflexively looked over when Vijay broached the topic but, instead of yelling at them to fix it, Coleman had merely crossed his arms and nodded, deferential to the team's expertise. Steve had made quick work of the problem, soliciting feedback from the experts, outlining their options, and driving toward a solution, all without the hint of an argument or the residual hurt feelings that normally followed.

Coleman was rather pleased with the tone and cadence of the meeting. Steve really did do a good job of massaging the various egos involved, particularly Vijay's, and he was operationally smooth and unflappable with the agenda and the apportionment of action items. If he was being perfectly honest, Coleman was a little ticked off at himself for not delegating sooner. It was a lot less work, his mood was vastly improved, and his replacement seemed to thrive in the role. He made a mental note to unload more of his responsibilities to Steve.

As the call wound down and Steve closed things out, Coleman sprung to his feet and clapped his hands.

"Great job, everyone. Great job. Today, lunch is on me!" He walked over to the center of the table and, hovering just above the speakerphone, spoke into it. "For those of you on the phone, thank you for your help today. Next time you're in town, lunch is on me."

There were a few smattered and cautious expressions of thanks.

"And Vijay?" Coleman said.

"Yes, Rob?" Vijay's accent was distinct and his voice direct.

"Hey, we couldn't make this happen without your expertise and guidance. Thank you for your continued help and support. I mean it."

The silence lingered for a few moments and no one spoke, as if waiting for some sort of punchline. Steve looked over, his eyes probing for motive and possibly questioning Coleman's sanity. Coleman looked back at him and shrugged.

Finally, Vijay broke the awkward silence with a simple, "Thank you, Rob."

After the pizzas were delivered and they had engaged in routine small talk and inter-office gossip, Coleman excused himself and walked briskly down the hall. He started to veer off toward his own office, but had a different idea and detoured through the cubicle farm.

Armstrong had a new welcome mat at the door to his office. It depicted the surface of the moon, with the unmistakable footprint from a NASA space boot placed squarely in the middle. The image appeared three-dimensional, so that a visitor would feel like they, too, were walking on the moon as they entered the boss's office.

Coleman rolled his eyes, gave a quick rap on the doorframe, and hopped over the mat.

Armstrong stood behind his desk. He had a tall glass of something very orange, and he looked up as he stirred the liquid.

"Please tell me that's not Tang," Coleman said.

"It's Tang. You want a glass?"

Coleman waved him off and pointed down at his shoes. He wore a pair of tan buck oxfords and shifted his weight from side to side.

"Neal, do you notice anything different?"

Armstrong took a long drink and winced at the tart flavor. He ignored Coleman's question.

"Guess who I just got off the phone with?"

"John Glenn?"

"Very funny," Armstrong said. "But I have met him before. I'll have to tell you the story sometime."

"Can't wait," Coleman replied.

"That was Vijay."

"What did he want?"

"He wanted to know if I was firing him."

"What?" Coleman said. "Why?"

"Because apparently you acted in a polite and professional manner this morning, and he seemed to take it as a signal that he will be released from his employment."

Coleman shook his head. "You can't win with this guy."

"Robert," Armstrong said, grimacing as he took another sip. "Never drink Tang after you've brushed your teeth."

"Okay."

"And, if you're going to completely change your attitude and demeanor, try to do it gradually. It throws people for a loop when you pull a 180 like that."

"Nobody else seemed to freak out. Vijay is a special case."

"Vijay certainly is a special case. I don't need him to be happy, Robert, but I do need him to be consistent. And when you're in there acting bi-polar, Vijay can't be consistent."

"I'm not acting bi-polar, Neal, I'm just...I'm just feeling pretty good right now. I'm getting some things right in my life."

"Is it the painkillers? Kindness is so out of character for you. Have you increased your dosage?"

"No! I'm off the painkillers. Seriously. My foot is feeling light-years better. Watch this."

Coleman reenacted the pseudo-sobriety test that Armstrong had given him the previous week. He walked forward, tapped his hand on Armstrong's desk, then stepped back the way he had come. His movements were fluid, full of energy, and the confident athleticism had returned. To add a final flourish, Coleman touched the fingertips of each hand to his nose, like an actual roadside sobriety test, and stood on one foot. His bad foot.

"Oh, that's very cute. Very cute, Robert."

"I thought you would like that."

"Here's what I don't like," Armstrong said, his face curling into a mean smile. "You should have been able to do that last week."

Coleman stopped showing off and dropped his hands to his sides. "I know," he said.

"You cost us a week."

"Yeah, but it was a just a week," Coleman protested. "I think I needed the recovery time anyway. Foot or no foot, my body was killing me."

"We lost a week, Robert." Armstrong had moved back behind his desk and eased into his black leather chair. It had a high back, like a throne, and he reclined slightly and pressed his fingers together to form a pointed arch. "You know who didn't lose a week?"

Armstrong didn't wait for Coleman's reply.

"Our competition. So after you exceeded expectations at The Asylum and put us into first class, your absence last week kicked us right back into steerage."

"Steerage, Neal? I think that's a little much."

"You do realize that they've run the half-marathon with everyone else? That we're the last up?"

Coleman crossed the carpeted floor and took a seat opposite his boss. The chairs for visitors were not situated as high off the ground, and Coleman had to look up a good foot at Armstrong, who appeared to revel in the optics and the subtle feeling of superiority created by looking down on his charge. Like LBJ pressuring some lowly Congressman into an unfavorable deal, Coleman thought. He figured LBJ must have had something to do with NASA.

"But, Neal, can't that sort of thing be spun in our favor? I'm the only one who beat them, so it only makes sense that I should be the last to go in the next round."

"Oh, believe me, I've been spinning. And spinning. And spinning. They don't care for your rules. They have their own rules, and they wanted to get you back right away."

"So what did you tell them?"

"I told them it wouldn't be that easy. I told them you were a princess, that you needed to be romanced, that you were playing hard to get."

"What did you really tell them?"

"I told them you were in India."

"India?"

"Sure. I told them you were in India overseeing our engineering team, and that you were making sure the technology was up to snuff."

"You lied to them."

"Sure. So what?"

"I mean, do you think that's a good idea? You remember what they said, Neal, about 'honesty in all things,' and that whole spiel."

"Well, you lied to me, Robert."

"What?"

"You lied to me. I lied to them. What's the difference?"

"When did I lie to you?"

Armstrong clenched his hands together tight in a ball and slowly set them down on the desk. He looked down at Coleman, his stare hard and cold.

"What happened to your foot, Robert?"

"Neal, I told you," Coleman stuttered. "I tweaked it playing soccer with my kid."

"So you said. Now what really happened to your foot?"

Coleman stopped and let the question simmer. A few scenarios coursed through his mind, but they were too difficult to process so quickly, and he pushed them away.

"What is this, Neal?"

"I know the boss doesn't always get the credit he is due," Armstrong said. "But I made it here for several reasons. One of those reasons is the power of observation."

"Okay," Coleman said, unsure of how to respond.

"You may not have observed it, Robert, but I am very observant."

"Okay."

"It was a clever try, I will give you that, but leaving your pills out on your desk was probably unwise. It was quite easy to read and then research your prescription."

"Neal..."

"And your diet had changed so dramatically, in just one week. You used to be cheesesteaks and three-beer lunches, and you switched to carrots, celery and water? That set off some alarm bells. So I researched that, too."

"This is crazy..."

"But the cherries were the dead giveaway. Cherries! Who eats cherries? Cherries are a garnish on a cocktail or a sundae, but I've never known anyone to snack on bags of cherries at their desk. So I looked it up."

Coleman didn't bother to respond. He knew what was coming and he dropped his chin against his chest.

"Do you know what pops up when you do a web search on 'cherries' and 'foot pain?' Do you? There are pages of entries with your real diagnosis!"

Defeated, Coleman exhaled and attempted to mutter an explanation.

"It's embarrassing, Neal..."

"You have the gout!"

"That's why..."

"The gout!"

"...I said it was a sports injury..."

"Gout!"

"...and I don't think..." Coleman's voice trailed off. Armstrong was deriving far too much glee from the episode, and there was no point in arguing the matter. He fell silent and looked up.

Armstrong's smile was now genuine, and he almost seemed sympathetic as he stared across the desk.

"Don't ever lie to me again, Robert, certainly not about something like this."

"I'm sorry." Coleman's voice was a whisper.

"This deal is too big for everyone involved."

"I understand."

"Don't ever lie to me again. Are we clear?"

"Crystal."

"Good!" Armstrong stood and clapped his hands together. He stepped around his desk and sat on the edge so that his knees were only inches from Coleman. "Now, on the bright side, it's just the gout!"

"What?"

"Sure, it's wildly embarrassing, self-inflicted and the result of gluttony and sloth."

"Well, not really sloth..."

"But, other than that, it's nothing! Had it really been a sprain or a tear or, God forbid, a break, we would have really been screwed. But you're already back on your feet and bouncing around!"

"It's definitely feeling better..."

"This weekend, Robert."

"This weekend?"

"Be ready."

"Be ready?"

"It's all set up."

"The half-marathon?"

"The half-marathon," Armstrong said. "So rest up this week. Go home and celebrate with your family. Drink lots of water. Eat lots of cherries. This weekend, we win the deal."

CHAPTER 22

Like many states, North Carolina had not been shy with its use of tax breaks and incentives as bait for major corporations to break ground within its borders. Once a big company was lured and hooked, the resulting jobs that were created led to new neighborhoods and small business growth, all of which supported the anchor company and provided a boon to the local economy. Plus, the state could then turn around and make its incentive money back by taxing the influx of new residents. Thus, a major financial institution – the third largest bank in all the country – had relocated from New York to the Tarheel State. With the relocation had come 8,000 employees, three of whom now inhabited a private room in the company gym.

The global headquarters of The Bank looked more like a college campus than a powerful seat of the financial industry. Twelve buildings, each 10 stories tall, sprawled out over a half-mile stretch in a wooded office park that had not existed before the company's arrival. Paved walking trails traced the edges of manmade ponds and crisscrossed as they led to the shiny silver structures. Near the entrance to just about every building was something fun: a beach volleyball court near Building 4, a regulation-sized blacktop basketball court beside Building 7, and an outdoor grilling area in the courtyard between Buildings 10 and 11.

Each building, too, featured its own food court, with all manner of selections from burgers to sushi, to Italian, to Chinese. This had been a major bone of contention with the local powers-that-be, as employees were staying on campus for lunch instead of spending their dollars at the variety of restaurants that grew up around the office park when The Bank had arrived. Responding to local pressures and, eager to maintain its extremely favorable tax benefits, The Bank had taken a phased approach to getting rid of some of their cafeteria locations. They were slowly transforming these spots into other enticing spaces that included viewing rooms for the latest movie releases, art galleries featuring employee works, music centers for those who wished to jam after a hard day's work and, of course, various fitness-related endeavors such as spinning centers and yoga rooms.

It sounded like an amazing place to work with every perk imaginable, but it was nothing more than the realization of countless sociological studies indicating that, the longer employees remained at the workplace, no matter what they were doing, the more productive they would be. The Bank intended to squeeze every drop of productivity out of every employee.

And so the workers, many toting backpacks and computer satchels, buzzed along the trails as they made their way through campus. A few younger employees threw a frisbee near the grilling area, and a some longer-haired young men, no doubt from the IT department, had started an impromptu game of hacky sack on the lawn outside of Building 9.

Through the windows of their private room in the company gym, the President of The Bank and his two sidekicks, the Italian and the Swede, watched the game without comment. More than likely, they were mentally calculating worker productivity.

The gym was expansive, technologically state-of-the-art, and featured a vast array of exercise equipment for the beginner to the expert. Gym workers in tight, white, sweat-wicking uniforms helped employees manage their workouts on nautilus machines, ellipticals, treadmills, free weights, rowing machines, and exercycles as the strains of house hip-hop thumped through the ceiling speakers.

Alone in their private room, off to one side of the free weights area, the three executives stood atop colored exercise balls and performed difficult calisthenics while maintaining their balance on the rolling pedestals. The balls were each about 2 ½ feet tall and made of strong reinforced rubber. Most people rested their lower backs or their core muscles atop the balls and pushed with their legs to create low-impact stretching exercises. The executives had created their own routine.

They were barefoot, and each wore a black nylon bodysuit that covered every inch of skin on their bodies, apart from their hands, feet, and anywhere from the neck up. The men alternately squatted, extended, stretched to their toes, and even hopped on the balls. It looked at any moment as if they would lose their balance and topple to the padded floor, but they never did. They looked like a male ballerina troupe, in perfect harmony, standing atop an assortment of Christmas ornaments.

They had turned their collective attention away from the hacky sack game on the other side of the studio windows and now concentrated on their individual exercises. The hip-hop music so prevalent in the common areas of the gym had been silenced in their private room, and the quietude permeated the air until the President broached a topic that had been on his mind lately.

"What are your feelings about Mister Armstrong?" he asked his charges.

The Italian shrugged and looked to the Swede.

The Swede shrugged. "What are your feelings about him?" he said, brushing back a shock of white-blonde hair from his eyes.

The President's weight shifted, and he paused as he regained balance atop his green ball. Placing his arms out beside him, like a diver on the 10-meter platform, he steadied himself and frowned.

"I believe Mister Armstrong to be a clownish and occasionally arrogant individual, prone to rash decisions. I could do without him."

The Italian and the Swede nodded in unison.

"However, he does represent a company with a strong local presence, they have reliable hardware that would likely lower our projected capital expenditures over the next 10 years, and they do have one key component that the other bids do not have."

The Italian stood on one foot atop his red ball and leaned his chest forward, never once losing balance. Turning just his neck toward the President, he raised his eyebrows. "Mister Coleman?" he said.

The President smiled. "I do rather like Mister Coleman. We will defeat him this weekend, of course, but I admire his spirit and could envision him handling our network security infrastructure for the foreseeable future."

"But?" the Italian said, filling in the silence.

"Mister Coleman is somewhat ancillary to the final decision," the President explained. "He is not the key component."

"No?" the Swede asked, as he slowly crouched on his silver-colored ball, assuming the stance of a baseball catcher.

"No," the President said.

"Then you must be speaking of..." the Italian was cut off before he could finish his thought.

"Mister Kumar," the President said.

"Mister Kumar," the Italian repeated.

"Mister Kumar," the Swede agreed.

"Vijay Kumar is the difference," the President continued. "As long as he is engaged and part of their team, they will remain the frontrunner."

"Maybe we should just hire him," the Italian said.

"Our research indicates that he is quite difficult," the President said. "It is a very common trait with highly intelligent people. I think we would be better served harnessing his technical knowledge in an outside, advisory role, and let Mister Armstrong and Mister Coleman manage his day-to-day challenges and moods."

The other two pondered this strategy for a moment. As usual, the President was a step or two ahead of them.

"Agreed," the Italian said.

"Agreed," the Swede agreed.

They quietly continued with their individual routines. They rolled their exercise balls from one end of the room to the other and back again. Like circus performers, they never stepped down or touched the floor, their balance and agility keeping them supported atop the balls. Outside, some of the younger hacky-sack players, who had never witnessed the gymnastic feats of their executives, stopped to marvel as they watched through the windows.

The men ignored their gawkers and finished the workout. The Italian and the Swede waited until the President's foot had touched the ground, and then they, too, hopped down.

"When should we tell them?" the Swede asked.

The President wiped sweat from his neck and forehead. "Why don't we keep that our secret for now."

The Italian and Swede watched as the President discarded his white towel in a hamper.

"There is no harm and no danger in allowing these entities to pursue us a little longer," the President continued. "In fact, it may be a revealing exercise."

"Revealing?" the Italian said.

"Quite revealing. We will be able to determine which teams get lazy and which teams see the deal through."

"So we should..." the Swede began.

"Continue to let them think this will all be decided based on their athletic prowess."

"That the technology doesn't matter," the Italian added.

"Correct."

"It will be an interesting exercise," the Swede said.

"Yes," the President acknowledged. "In the meantime, please make sure that Mister Kumar has all the information and access that he needs to complete the design of our network and security infrastructure. Before we award them the contract, let's see if they do the work. Agreed?"

"Agreed," the Italian said.

"Agreed," the Swede agreed.

"And let's make Mister Armstrong squirm just a bit, shall we?"

They shared a smile and then marched, single file behind the President, through the gym, up the stairs and back to their offices on the top floor.

CHAPTER 23

Neal Armstrong had been summoned to corporate headquarters and, though he flew first class, he squirmed and shifted in his seat for much of the direct flight from Raleigh to San Francisco. He only made one or two of these trips a year, and they were usually scheduled far in advance. To be summoned like this either meant something very bad – or something very good – was about to happen. Either option kept him awake from liftoff to touchdown.

A driver awaited him upon arrival at SFO, and Armstrong stared out a tinted back-seat window of the black SUV as they drove south toward Silicon Valley. His frown deepened with each mile that rolled past. This area was not his favorite. It reminded him a little of Orlando, another landscape that had been overrun by explosive growth, construction, and the sanitary architecture that came with it. The palm trees that lined some of the streets deeply bothered him, especially when they were illuminated at night. Silicon Valley did not and should not evoke a Caribbean feeling, and the contrived nature of these flourishes, along with the endless miles of concrete and pavement, stripped the area of its authenticity.

To Armstrong, it felt phony. Of course, if things went well and they moved him out to the Valley, he would have to get over that feeling pretty fast. Then again, if things went really well, he would have the power and authority to stay in North Carolina. At this thought, he smiled, and then, as they cruised down the 101 toward San Jose, his smile turned into a full-blown grin.

Just past Palo Alto, on the outskirts of Mountain View, sat the only redeeming feature of the entire Silicon Valley – NASA's Ames Research Center at Moffett Federal Airfield.

Armstrong was giddy as they drove past, and he pressed his face close to the car window and squinted for a better look at the tall white water tank, with the NASA logo emblazoned across it, and the massive hangar looming in the distance. So much history! Such incredible, ground-breaking research! What a hidden jewel, tucked away in a place that desperately didn't deserve it.

Ames had started in 1939 as a research center for Earth-based aircraft, well known for its wind tunnels and aerodynamic testing, particularly on aircraft powered by propellers. Later, it joined NASA in the 1950s, and the focus turned to space. These days, inside the gates and walls of the ARC, the nation's best and brightest turned their skills to advances in robotics, satellites, exploration of new planets and, of course, given its location in the Valley, a hearty stew of supercomputing.

Recently, one of the world's leading search engines had leased space on Moffett's grounds to help enable and accelerate a research and engineering partnership. They had also built a monstrosity of a complex on approximately 40 acres, to be used for offices, dormitories and laboratory space. When he had first read about the land grab, Armstrong was furious. How dare they intrude upon NASA's sacred terrain! But, as he considered it more and more, he had become a believer in the confluence of public and private technology.

A big believer. With big ideas. And, if all the dominoes fell the way he hoped they would, he would not only be a believer in such public/private partnerships. He would be their champion.

Armstrong was practically bouncing up and down in his leather-cushioned seat as the car whipped past and the airfield faded from sight. He would definitely make a trip to the Ames museum later and try to arrange a private tour with the Brigadier General who led the installation. He would also try to sneak a closer look at that joint research complex and see if he couldn't introduce himself to a few people while he was out on the West Coast.

Win or lose, he would be back at Moffett. But first, he had to learn his fate.

Of all the sanitary, unimaginative, utilitarian buildings that had sprouted in San Jose, this was the worst. Three buildings, each covered by dark, muted glass, stretched 10 stories into the sky. The buildings' support systems – the edges, sides, foundations and, basically, anything that wasn't a window – were colored with a dull gray concrete. The entire ensemble looked like something the NSA or CIA might prefer, rather than a titan of technology in the heart of Silicon Valley.

Armstrong hated it.

He paused a moment to collect himself, then pulled open the door and entered with his head high, an outward display of confidence to mask the uneasy churning inside. He made his way through the entrance, signed in with the lobby ambassador and received his temporary badge, and swiped it to gain access to the elevators. He rode up to the top floor alone, centered himself, and took one last deep breath before the doors opened.

Armstrong checked in with the ambassador to the executive suites, received another temporary badge specifically for that level, then was greeted by security for a few cursory questions before gaining admittance through the cherry doors that opened into something that resembled a penthouse suite at a luxury hotel.

The executive-level layout was a far cry from the other floors, or anything they had at their complex in North Carolina. Up here in this rarefied air, there were no cubicle farms, no bored and depressed employees hunched over their computers while they watched the clock until quitting time. Up here, there was very little activity at all.

Plush carpets stretched from wall to wall. The doors all had shiny finishings of brushed nickel. Flat-screen televisions mounted to the walls were tuned to business channels and stock reports. Caterers in white shirts and black pants scurried to and fro, delivering cappuccino, fruit plates and fresh-made crepes. Off to one side, behind the noise-proof glass of a conference room, men in suits motioned with their arms and pointed at presentations displayed on screens against the wall.

Armstrong soaked it all in – the sense of power and importance, the grandeur, the magnificence. This is what he wanted.

A stunning woman dressed in a conservative gray suit emerged from behind a door and walked briskly into the common space. She greeted him with a firm handshake and a warm, but rehearsed, smile.

"Mister Armstrong, it's so nice to see you again," she said, turning before he could return the salutation. "Please follow me. They're ready for you now."

"Thank you," was the best he could manage as he followed her into a massive suite with all the accoutrements of a Montana hunting lodge.

The walls were of dark wood, and the furniture mahogany. The leather was rich and oiled. Rugs of fallen animals spread over the floor. Paintings of English fox hunts decorated the walls. An electric fireplace against a far wall crackled with inviting flames, but emitted no heat. The only things missing were the stuffed heads of wild game mounted on the walls.

The brain can be swift in foreign situations, and one never knows what trail it might take. In the presence of such opulence, Armstrong found himself mentally redecorating the office into a jubilant celebration of space and a tribute to the men who had been there. Lost in his daydream, he drifted for a few moments and had to force his conscious mind back to reality, as the two men seated near the window stood to greet him.

"Neal Armstrong!" the taller man said.

"One small step for man, one giant leap for mankind!" said the shorter, stouter man.

Both men were dressed almost identically, in country-club casual style – blue blazers with gold buttons, pleated khaki pants, and shiny penny loafers. The taller of the two was clearly the man in charge, and he approached first. Armstrong grinned from ear to ear and enthusiastically pumped their hands. The shorter man, the Chief Operating Officer, placed his palm on Armstrong's back and ushered him over to their sitting area.

There were four chairs placed around a circular dark coffee table, and the three men left one chair empty as they situated themselves. The CEO and COO placed themselves across from Armstrong, and they all smiled at one another as one of the caterers brought fresh refills of coffee.

Once they were alone again, the CEO leaned back, crossed one leg over the other and rested his hands on the sturdy arms of his chair.

"Neal, how are things going?" he said.

"Things are well. Thank you for having me out here. I'd love to reciprocate the invitation and host you both in North Carolina, if your schedules would allow."

"We do need to show our faces more on the East Coast," the COO agreed. "We'll take an action to try and get that ball rolling."

The COO raised an arm and pointed off to the corner, where the attractive executive assistant sat with a legal pad on her lap, taking notes. Armstrong hadn't noticed her sit, and now he couldn't free his eyes from her. She returned his gaze with the warm and phony smile, and nodded at the COO to confirm that the item had been recorded.

"Neal," the CEO said, pulling him back to the conversation, "how are things with The Bank?"

Armstrong's eyes grew wide and color rushed to his face. "Things are looking good, gentlemen!"

"How good?"

"Things are looking very, very good!"

"Good," the CEO said. "How close are we?"

"We should know for sure in the next few weeks, but my sources tell me that we are firmly in the lead."

"Good," the COO said. "And our strategy for keeping that lead?"

"It's under control," Armstrong said, leaning forward. "I have a client executive with a unique skill set leading our charge. He's been able to really hit it off with their executives, and it is my firm belief that this relationship will lead us to victory."

"Unique skill set?" the CEO inquired.

"Yes," Armstrong said, clearing his throat. "Gentlemen, this will sound unorthodox, but please hear me out."

He proceeded to tell them all about Coleman's soccer background and The Bank team's penchant for extreme fitness activities. He gave them a play-by-play from The Asylum. He told them about the upcoming half-marathon. He explained the strategy in detail, and then waited as they digested the information. After a lengthy and uncomfortable silence, the COO spoke first.

"I will agree," he said. "It is unorthodox."

"Highly unorthodox," the CEO added.

"Bordering on strange and weird," the COO said.

"Bizarre, almost," the CEO concluded.

"Gentlemen, please allow me to..." Armstrong was cut off by a wave of the CEO's arm.

"However," the CEO said. "I am thoroughly and completely intrigued to see if this strategy will work."

"It's fascinating," the COO concurred. "Simply fascinating."

"To just assume that all the technology is equal across competitors, and to focus solely on fostering a relationship between the players involved," the CEO said, "why it's either genius or madness!"

"Ground breaking!" the COO said, staring across the table with a look that resembled admiration. "Mister Armstrong has leveraged the business model from one of those online dating websites and applied it to our company."

"Let's hope it's a love connection!" the CEO laughed.

Much of the color had faded from Armstrong's face during the back and forth. He was up, then he was down, then right back up again. He was deeply confused, and holding his breath for renewed affirmation from his two superiors.

Instead, they both grew very serious at approximately the exact same moment.

"Neal," the CEO said, uncrossing his legs and leaning forward. He paused as he fixed his eyes on Armstrong and lowered his voice to barely above a whisper. "Are we sure that we have the technology right? That we have the right people in place? That this method, as interesting as it sounds, will actually work?"

"Sir," Armstrong said. "I am absolutely sure that this will work."

"You know what it means for us, right?" the COO said.

Armstrong nodded. "Yes, I believe I do."

"In the grand scheme of things, this is a small deal. $100 million over a few years, that's a decent number, but nothing earth-shaking. But the money is not why it's so important to us."

"Neal, if we win this deal, it will be like a gateway drug for the other major global financial institutions," the CEO explained. "If we can own the network security infrastructure for all the big banks, exchanges, investment firms, and so on..."

"We can set our own price," the COO finished the boss's sentence. "Your deal would be the first domino to fall in what would become a decade or more of guaranteed profitability."

"The shareholders would be very pleased," the CEO said with a grin.

"As would the Board of Directors," the COO said.

"It would let me go out on a high note," the CEO continued, motioning to his right-hand man, "and it would give instant momentum to the next generation of leadership in this company."

"Whoever that might be," the COO said, winking at Armstrong.

"Neal, all this could be yours." The CEO spread both arms wide to indicate the expanse of the executive suites, and then nodded over in the direction of the gorgeous assistant, who smiled her forced smile back in their direction.

Armstrong's eyes grew wide and he swallowed hard.

"Don't worry, gentlemen. Victory will be ours."

"Good!" the CEO said, clapping his hands together. "Because we don't wish to even entertain the flipside, do we?"

"The flipside?" Armstrong said.

"The dark side," the COO explained.

"The ugly side," the CEO said.

"Ugly?" Armstrong asked.

"Hideous," the COO said.

Armstrong looked over at the assistant in the corner, her face now framed by a pitying frown. The two men before him registered no pity.

"Neal," the CEO said, "If the deal goes sideways, if The Bank looks elsewhere..."

"If victory is not ours," the COO added.

"Then things could be very dark for you..."

"Very ugly," the COO added.

"Things could be hideous," the CEO said.

The silence in the air had a hint of discomfort, but it was brief and quickly dissipated as Armstrong, on the receiving end of the warning, smiled broadly and clapped his own hands together.

"Things are going to be beautiful, gentlemen. Just beautiful."

The CEO and the COO laughed and slapped him on the back several times as they escorted him toward the door. The assistant shook his hand warmly, and her smile was not nearly as forced. Armstrong thought he even detected the hint of a sparkle in her eye.

His confidence had won them over and, in the end, not even the dark side, as they called it, could erase the implicit promise that had been made. If he closed The Bank, he would get what he wanted, and there was no doubt in his mind – he would close The Bank.

Armstrong's energy was apparent as he burst forth from the elevators and strode through the lobby. He gave the lobby attendants a thumbs up sign and threw open the glass doors. Stopping on the sidewalk out front, he turned and cocked his head to look upward. The drab buildings and the dark windows didn't seem so bad anymore. Perhaps the concrete jungle had a charm that he hadn't recognized. Even the palm trees lining the streets now had a breezy appeal.

As he hopped into the waiting SUV and they drove out of San Jose and through Silicon Valley, the place seemed pretty nice after all.

Armstrong relaxed in the back seat and smiled, his change of heart complete. He loved the place.

CHAPTER 24

Steve had dropped out early in the workout, and watched from a bench as Coleman sprinted around the pond outside of their offices. They were running modified "pops," a brutal training routine from Coleman's soccer days that involved sprinting at top speed around the pond, followed by about a minute of rest, and then doing it all again. Steve had quit after six of these pops and, while watching Coleman, had spent the next 15 minutes spitting globules of phlegm onto the ground and trying to contain his heaving chest.

Coleman crossed the imaginary finish line near Steve's bench and threw his head back to gasp for air. He placed his hands on his hips and walked a few steps forward, then turned back, and repeated the process until his breathing and heart had slowed to a manageable pace.

"Are you alright?"

Steve leaned over and hocked another loogie into the grass.

"No. Are you done yet?"

"Thirteen more to go," Coleman said, swinging his arms in circles to stretch them out.

"Are you serious?" Steve said. "How?"

"This is nothing. We used to do 50 pops at a time back in college."

"Fifty?"

"Yeah," Coleman said, "except we did them on a steep hill."

Steve spit again and watched as Coleman took off in a dead sprint. His red long-sleeve athletic shirt streaked by as he rounded the edges of the pond, disappeared briefly behind the plumes of the fountain, then reemerged like a rocket on the other side. Within a minute, he was back where he started, gulping air and walking short steps in tight circles.

"Twelve more."

"I don't get it," Steve said. "It's a half-marathon. Shouldn't you be training for distance? Like, shouldn't you be running 20 miles or some obscene number so that 13.1 doesn't feel so long?"

"Huh uh," Coleman grunted. "Those guys are good. Only way I'm gonna beat them is on the kick at the end. You saw what happened last time."

"You sure you want to beat them this time?"

"Uh huh."

"So you're practicing your kick."

"Yep. As long as I can hang with them until about mile 12, I should be able to bring it home and cross before them."

"You guys are nuts."

"Be right back," Coleman said with a grin, as he dashed away.

"Insane!" Steve yelled after him.

He watched for five more laps, then dragged his tired and stiffening legs back to the office, where he cleaned up in the bathroom and climbed back into his work attire, in which he felt far more comfortable. Peering out the window of the conference room, he watched as the red streak whipped around the pond and Coleman finished his final lap with both fists thrust upward to the sky.

"Insane," Steve muttered under his breath.

They had gone out to eat, and Steve was pleasantly surprised that Goodie's had not been one of the options. Coleman had selected a nearby bistro that was half-full with the lunch crowd, and they grabbed a small booth at the back, away from most of the other diners. Coleman ordered the blackened tilapia with a side of steamed vegetables, and Steve watched him take a bite as he waited for his grilled chicken panini to cool.

"Here's the thing that worries me," Steve said. "I'm not sure you should be running so hard so soon after your injury. I mean, I'm no orthopedist, but wouldn't you want the tendons, or ligaments, or whatever, to heal completely before you started pounding on them again? It was only a week ago that you were still hobbling around, right?"

Coleman dismissed the question with a wave of his left hand. With his right hand, he used his fork to cut another piece of fish and brought it to his mouth.

"It's not like that," he said, when he had finished chewing. "It was a minor sprain that looked worse than it really was."

Steve considered this, and then shrugged. He reached for a bite of his panini, and washed it down with a drink of sparkling water and lemon.

"Well, just don't overdo it, okay? We don't want you getting hurt again, obviously."

"I won't," Coleman said. "It's fine, really. The time off was actually good for me. It was like a taper."

"A taper?"

"Before big races, runners and swimmers will halt their training or just do a bare minimum to keep their blood flowing and their muscles loose. It gives your body time to rest, and when you get to race day, you feel lighter than air. You feel explosive."

"Is that how you felt today?"

"A little bit. I'll probably dial it back in the next few days, but it was good to get the work in."

Steve shook his head and took another bite. "You people are insane," he said, through a mouthful of food.

Coleman motioned to the waitress and requested another glass of sweet tea with a lemon. They ate quietly until she brought the refill, and he quickly sipped half of it through a straw. As Steve devoured his meal, Coleman watched from across the booth and considered his colleague.

Steve Wellman was a puppy dog. *A golden retriever puppy.* Loyal, eager to please, friendly, resourceful, responsible, reliable, and just slightly annoying due to the other traits. He was a guy who could keep a secret, he didn't have an enemy in the world, and Coleman couldn't think of anyone who didn't like him. Steve didn't share the ambition of an Armstrong or a Coleman, and he wasn't a noted expert like Vijay, but he was the most likeable guy in any room he entered. Armstrong and Coleman loved him. Even Vijay, who didn't like anyone, had a certain fondness for Steve.

He had come to them out of the same college as Coleman, but their paths had never really crossed on campus, and Coleman hadn't remembered him at all. While Coleman was the ubiquitous soccer star, Steve had quietly distinguished himself as a leader in student government. Not *the* leader, exactly, but a member of the executive board, where he had been instrumental in getting an old, asbestos-riddled dormitory torn down, and a brand new, state-of-the-art, technologically advanced dormitory built. The dorm, and all the forward-thinking technology built into it, had become the standard at the school since then. Coleman had even donated money to the building campaign one year, but he had no idea that Steve orchestrated the movement until he interviewed him for his current job.

While his program management skills and understanding of technology had moved his resume to the top of the pile, his soft skills had won him the job. Armstrong had absolutely loved the guy, in large part because Steve seemed to show a genuine interest in all that NASA garbage strewn throughout his office. And, while Vijay loved no one but himself, he recommended Steve for the position, because Steve had been deferential, non-combative, and respectful during their interview process.

As he watched Steve from across the booth, Coleman almost felt bad, like he didn't appreciate the guy enough. He didn't go out of his way to encourage or congratulate or thank him, and it began to creep into his mind what a loss Steve would be if he ever decided to jump ship and go somewhere else. Steve Wellman was just about the perfect Number Two. The problem that Coleman was having trouble getting past, was that maybe Steve was too good. Whose Number Two was he?

His? Vijay's? Or was he Armstrong's right-hand man?

And so Coleman very gingerly articulated his next thoughts and tiptoed into the conversation.

"Anything from Armstrong?"

"California," Steve said, his mouth full again.

"For what?"

Steve shrugged. "Routine meet and greet with the execs, I think. Nothing special. Why?"

"I don't know," Coleman said. "The timing just seems strange, being so close to the finish line here."

"I'm sure they talked about it."

"And I'm sure he gave them a bunch of bluster about having it in the bag."

"You're probably right."

Coleman wiped his mouth and stared out the window as traffic passed on the street outside.

"Steve, do you think we're all nuts?"

"Absolutely," Steve said, not skipping a beat.

"The way we're going about this," Coleman continued, ignoring the comment. "This is so much money to be decided over something so stupid."

"No kidding. I believe we had this conversation."

"I know."

"And you gave me the 'all things being equal' speech. How the technology didn't matter. How the hardware is all the same. How the differentiator is the relationship between you and their team."

"I know."

"So what's wrong?"

"I was just repeating Armstrong's party line."

"And now you don't believe it?"

"I don't know," Coleman said. "Maybe it's just because we're getting closer to a decision. I'm worried we haven't checked all the boxes, done everything we can."

"Well, don't worry. Other than the hiccup with your foot, you've done your part just fine. And Vijay has gone above and beyond."

"Yeah?"

"Rob, if they don't choose us, they're going to regret it. Vijay is a genius. A certified genius."

"Certifiable."

"No, he really is, Rob." Steve wiped his hands on a napkin and pushed the plate toward the center of the table. He had a look of seriousness on his face and his hands began punctuating his words as he spoke.

"Look, two major retailers have had massive online security breaches within the past six months. Credit card data was stolen, bank account numbers, social security numbers. You know what happened. It was all over the news."

"I remember it well."

"They estimated a $500 million impact to the business between the two companies. Not to mention the loss of trust from consumers."

"What does this have to do with Vijay?"

"Rob, he showed me how they did it."

"What do you mean?"

"He showed me how they did it. He created a dummy site with all of their protocols built in, and then he hacked into it. Right there in the conference room on his laptop. It was crazy."

"Great, so he has a future as a hacker if we lose the deal."

"No, Rob," Steve said, leaning forward. "Because then he showed me how to stop it."

"Right there on his laptop?"

"Yep. And he didn't have access to their technologies. He was just going off what he read or saw on the news, and then played around on their e-commerce sites for a few days. The guy is a wizard."

"Do you think they know at The Bank?"

"They have to," Steve said. "Vijay wrote a whitepaper on it. It got a bunch of visibility on the tech blogs. I'm sure somebody there saw it."

Coleman looked out the window again and thought for a moment.

"Do you think Armstrong knows?"

"No," Steve said, shaking his head. "You didn't know. Why would he?"

Coleman nodded. "So what are you suggesting we do?"

"I'm suggesting that you do your thing and win the relationship part, just like Armstrong wants."

"But?"

"But I'm also suggesting that you turn Vijay loose."

"Turn him loose?"

"With all respect, Rob, he's the closer. Not you."

The immediate blow to Coleman's ego subsided as he considered what Steve had just told him. If Vijay was the closer, then he was the warm-up act, and that left Armstrong as the master of ceremonies or the man making the introductions. Either way, at this point, Armstrong was practically irrelevant to the conversation.

Coleman considered this, too, until he was distracted by an incoming text message on his phone. Glancing down, he thumbed through the message, shut his eyes and exhaled.

"What's wrong?" Steve said, noticing Coleman's look of resignation.

"I'm gonna have to drop you back at the office. There's something I forgot to do."

"Something important?" Steve said.

"Something for my wife."

CHAPTER 25

The grounds of the church were far more extensive than Coleman had ever realized. Atop the hill, a vast field stretched out from the sanctuary and chapel to the edge of a wooded area. It must have been five or six acres, and Coleman shook his head as the Reverend walked him through the tall grass.

"I never knew this was here," he said. "Don't know how I missed it."

"Most people don't know that we have this land," the Reverend said. "It sits on the opposite side of our entrance and, let's be honest, other than coming and going on a Sunday morning, most people have no idea what the rest of the church really looks like."

Out of his robes, he looked like a normal guy. He wore jeans and boat shoes, and his blue button-down shirt was untucked. His sleeves were rolled up to the elbows, and he had a small pad of paper and two pens stuffed inside the breast pocket of his shirt.

"It's amazing how much we miss because we don't really see," the Reverend said.

He stopped for just a moment to jot this idea down and, smiling, returned the pad of paper to his pocket.

"So, Robert, what do you think?"

Both arms were outstretched, and Coleman followed them with his line of vision as the Reverend completed a slow half-circle.

"Well, yeah, I think this would work. You could fit one on here, sure. This is a pretty big piece of land."

The Reverend had called him out of the blue, and Coleman felt obliged to take the meeting. If he hadn't, Angie would have most certainly heard about it, which would have added an argument and a minor shaming to the meeting she would make him take anyway.

The man had an overflowing enthusiasm, but it wasn't necessarily infectious. Coleman always felt like a 10-year-old around the Reverend, like he didn't want to disappoint or let the man down. Even at 40, with a family and a successful career, he felt a childlike eagerness to please the man, and so he found himself agreeing with much of the Reverend's big plans.

He wanted to build a soccer field. Maybe a softball field, if space allowed. A multi-purpose field, and maybe a playground.

He had a vision to transform the church beyond simply a meeting place on Sundays, into a place that families, and especially youngsters, could enjoy throughout the week. He envisioned toddlers and little kids on the playground, while older kids practiced on the ballfields. He talked about adult co-ed softball leagues. Sunrise services. Concerts. Church picnics.

"Robert," he said, "the church should be a safe place for families. We have an incredible opportunity here to expand our children's ministry, and if we can encourage them to use the church throughout the week, they'll be that much more likely to use it on Sundays."

Coleman nodded, and swatted at a bug buzzing near his ear. The grass had not yet been cut that spring, and there were all manner of bugs and weeds making their homes throughout the grounds. He was sure there must be snakes hiding among the tall patches of fescue, and he stepped carefully as the Reverend showed him around.

"So what do you need from me?"

"I'm glad you asked," the Reverend said, with a beaming smile. "The first thing we need is your advice and guidance on building these fields. You are our resident soccer legend. Now, I was no slouch myself, but if we can get the buy-in of the great Robert Coleman, I think we can get real traction with the rest of the congregation."

He forced a smile. The Reverend was a huge soccer fan, and never missed the chance to prove his bona fides where Coleman was concerned. Each year, he received an invitation to watch the Champions League finale and, each year, Coleman had declined. Some years he hadn't even replied. He felt bad now, but the Reverend thankfully didn't mention the slight.

"Okay," Coleman said. "That shouldn't be a problem at all. I think Connor would really enjoy a place like this."

"I know he would," the Reverend said, suddenly turning serious, almost solemn. "And, Robert, there is something else."

He knew this was coming. He instinctively shoved his hands deep into his pockets, as if the money might fly from them upon hearing the Reverend's words.

"Something else?" he said.

"Robert, there is a financial component to my request. I want to be very clear about that. I know that I've asked you here today to help vouch for the project, but we also would love to get the ball rolling with a healthy donation. I think it would really help set the tone with the others."

"How much?" Coleman said, setting his jaw.

The Reverend hesitated, then spoke in a hushed tone.

"$50,000," he said.

Coleman coughed as the breath rushed from his lungs. "Fifty thousand?" he said. "Is that for the whole thing?"

"Well, no," the Reverend said, turning away and surveying the grounds. "We estimate about $100,000 for the entire project, from start to finish. And we'd like to get half of that up front."

"$100,000?"

"To be honest, we'd like to get all of it up front if we could, and have it paid off before work begins."

"Wow," Coleman said.

"I know it's a big thing to ask," the Reverend said. "But, Robert, you have been blessed with a beautiful family and a tremendous career, and I want you to consider giving back."

"Giving back?"

"To the church."

"To the church?"

"To God. After all, it is His money in the end," the Reverend said. "Robert, have you thought about your relationship with God lately?"

"God, no," Coleman blurted out, then immediately wished he could take it back. "I mean, no, not lately."

"Well perhaps it's time to do so. And this certainly couldn't hurt."

They walked for a bit without saying anything, the Reverend allowing for a few moments of reflection, but when Coleman reflected, he was short and irritable.

"Reverend, I'm sorry, but what kind of money do you think I make?"

The Reverend stopped and scratched a bug away from his arm. The sun had slipped lower over the trees, and golden light peeked through the branches and leafy trees and cast tall shadows over the field where they stood.

"I only know what I can see, Robert, and I can see your beautiful home, and the car you drive, and the clothes you wear. Now, you should feel no guilt whatsoever for having these things. You've earned them."

"Yes," Coleman said. "I have earned them."

"Yes, you have," the Reverend said. "But, remember, these are all blessings that have come from God, and it is right to give back to He who has bestowed them upon you."

"$50,000? You think I can just write a check for that?"

"I don't know, Robert, that's for you to decide," the Reverend said, shoving his hands into his pockets and slowly moving back toward the church. "Are you living beyond your means, son?"

"Living beyond my means? No, no."

"Well, then, it's up to you. Only you can decide in your heart what would be appropriate. The decision is entirely yours. But I just thought I would ask."

Coleman stood there in the field and watched as the Reverend walked away. He had gotten about 10 steps before realizing that Coleman was not with him, and he stopped and turned back.

"Robert?"

Coleman didn't respond. He had his own hands shoved in his pockets and he looked down at his shoes, which were half-covered by the wild grass. The Reverend took a few steps back and raised one hand to block the sun from his eyes.

"Son, are you okay?"

Coleman nodded a sort of half-nod, half-shrug, as if he wasn't sure himself.

"I don't know, Reverend. It's just...I don't know."

"Robert, we're not Catholics. You don't have to confess anything to me. But I'm right here if you want to talk about anything."

"Things at home have been...interesting...lately."

"Interesting?"

"Yeah," Coleman said. "Different. Not the same as they used to be. Maybe I'm working too much. I don't know."

The Reverend was quiet as he let Coleman think things through in his head, and then he spoke gently.

"You've been married awhile now?"

Coleman nodded.

"You've got a growing boy?"

"Yes."

"A stressful job?"

"That's a good word for it."

"Well, Robert, do you want the good news or the bad news first?"

"Good news."

"The good news is, this is completely normal. Every marriage – yes, even that of your humble pastor – goes through these periods."

"Okay, so what's the bad news?"

"The bad news is, you're going to have to work through it. It won't just fix itself."

Coleman nodded his understanding, and joined the Reverend. They walked back together in silence and, when they were almost back to the church, the Reverend stopped and clapped Coleman on the shoulder.

"Son, you want my best advice?"

"Sure."

"Go spend some time with your wife."

CHAPTER 26

The lights in Giovanni's were dim, and two white candles atop each table offered an ambience of privacy and romance. White linens dressed the tables, and tuxedoed waiters floated through the dining room, toting fresh, hot bread, refilling wine glasses, and serving heaping pasta dishes that steamed from the plate long after they had disappeared to another table. Couples wearing suits and black glittery dresses sipped wine and talked quietly and sparingly, seeming to enjoy the peacefulness and tranquility that permeated the room. Not a kid was in sight.

"How much did you offer the babysitter?" Coleman asked.

He wore a conservative navy blue suit with no tie and the collar of his white shirt open. He took a good drink from his glass of red wine, and wiped balsamic vinaigrette dressing from the corner of his mouth.

"Who cares?" Angie said, with a little giggle. "It's completely worth it. Listen."

An Italian opera played softly in the background over the beat of softly clinking glasses and silverware. Conversations were soft and understated. The waiters practically whispered as they read the specials, explained the wine list, and took entrée orders.

They paused to soak in the quiet, and Coleman smiled at his wife.

"You're right," he said. "This is pretty nice."

"It's perfect," she said. "We should do this every night."

"If we did this every night, I wouldn't have anything left to give our mutual friend. Guess who I went to see today?"

He recounted the afternoon for her and spared no detail when he got to the part about the Reverend's solicitation. The only part he left out was when the conversation had turned to her. Still, he had probably given that away, too, when he spontaneously hired the neighborhood sitter and told

Angie to throw on a nice dress. She knew that something must be up but eagerly obliged, as it meant a night out of the house.

"Wow, look at you, Mister Mover and Shaker," she said, over a fork twisted with angel hair pasta. "So what does that make this, a celebration dinner, or the last supper?"

"Last supper," Coleman said, grinning.

The waiter moved in again and replaced their bread basket, stealthy as a cat burglar. They hardly noticed as they savored their meals and drained their wine glasses. Just as quickly as he had vanished, the waiter reappeared to fill them again.

"Well, I don't care what the excuse is. We should do this more often."

Angie pointed at Coleman with her fork, then indicated the side of her mouth with one finger. He was halfway into a bowl of spaghetti and meatballs, and some of it had found its way to his face.

"Agreed," he said, wiping the sauce away. "This is delicious, by the way."

"I don't know why you always order that. You can get spaghetti at home."

"I can eat dinner with you at home, too. But isn't it better when we go out?"

"It is pretty nice," she said, and drank some more wine.

She wore a tasteful sleeveless black dress cut just above the knee, and her heels made her as tall as her husband. Her hair was down and she wore makeup, which was rare, and her lipstick was a deep, muted red that kept attracting his eyes. He only ever saw her in workout clothes or jeans, her hair was almost always pulled back and, after a day of caring for their son and tending to the house, she often looked harried and exhausted. Tonight, she looked terrific.

"So do you think we can afford that?" she asked, getting back to the conversation.

"Maybe," he said. "I mean, we could afford it now, but it would take some creative financing. If he wants to make a splash and get it all in one lump sum, it may need to wait till I close this deal with The Bank."

"The Bank," she said in a deep voice, giving it added importance. "You'd better close the deal, because I'm sick of hearing about it."

"You know what else we can get, right?"

"Does it rhyme with 'peach blouse?'"

Coleman laughed. "It does rhyme with peach blouse. I'll get you one of those, too, but I think you'll like the beach house better."

They ate like that for a while, sharing occasional thoughts or common memories, but mostly they enjoyed the quiet. No work, no stress, no spreadsheets, no profit and loss implications, no responsibilities at home, no balls bouncing through the house, no cartoons blaring way too loud from the TV, no teacher meetings and, best of all, no people. It was just them. Just like it used to be.

The wine had brought out a glow in Angie's face, and she smiled at nothing in particular as she worked her way through the bowl of pasta. An older gentleman dressed in a charcoal pinstripe suit had wound his way through the maze of tables and passed close by them, as he followed the maitre d' out of the dining room. He was a larger fellow whose haunches seemed to sway from side to side with his gait and, when he walked by their table, he left a very light breeze in his wake. Angie hardly noticed the man, but the cool air against her bare arms made her shiver slightly. Coleman noticed as she set her fork down and rubbed her shoulders.

"Do you want my jacket?" he said.

"No, I'm okay. It's just a chill." She took a sip of wine and smiled at him over the glass. "I'm proud of you."

"For what?"

"I don't know. You're just doing really well lately."

"Well, let's not get ahead of ourselves until the deal is done. We could still..."

"Not with that," she said. "With everything else."

"Everything else?"

"With the donation at church. With Connor's activities. With me."

Coleman stifled a satisfied grin and narrowed his eyes as Angie brought the wine glass back to her lips. "Speaking of you, are you sure you should be drinking?"

"Positive," she said. "Let's not get ahead of ourselves until the deal is done. Know what I mean?"

"Yes, I think I do know what you mean," Coleman said, raising a toast to her. "I suppose we should try and seal that deal as soon as we get home."

"We should definitely consider it." Angie bit her lower lip and smiled across the table at him, her eyes looking directly into his and dancing in the candlelight.

Coleman smiled and drank deeply as he held her gaze. A yellow halo created by the flame seemed to hang above her head and, coupled with the wine, left him feeling warm and light and good. He had never been the most affectionate person and did not often express his feelings to his wife. But tonight, surrounded by the glow of the candles, filled with the spirit of the wine, and swept away by the operatic voices overhead, Coleman had the urge to tell Angie just how much he loved and adored her.

Taking another deep drink, he set the glass down on the white linen tablecloth and wiped red droplets from his lips. He leaned forward and reached both hands out across the table.

"I know I don't say this enough..."

She returned his smile and reached her hands out to meet his in the middle of the table.

"But I am deeply, deeply in..."

Just as their fingertips were about to touch, Coleman caught a bright shock of blonde hair in his peripheral vision and was interrupted by a shrill voice.

"Robby? Is that you?"

Coleman recoiled, defensively drawing his arms in and pressing his back to his chair. He looked up, eyes wide, afraid, and pleading.

She wore a dark red cocktail dress with spaghetti straps that was dangerously low cut across the bust and fell mid-thigh against her artificially tan legs. A cream-colored cashmere scarf fell from her shoulders and supported her flowing bleached hair. Her lips were slick and glossy and painted the same shade as her dress, and she wore black heels that accentuated her lower legs. Her perfume was overdone and it wafted from her chest and neck and invaded the small space between them over the table.

"How is your foot?" she said. "That was a total freak-out. I've never seen anything like that before!"

Coleman had stopped breathing and no noises could reach his throat. He sat there in stunned silence, trying to think.

Think.

Think!

Angie had no such issues. She leaned on an elbow and her words were sharp and direct.

"Rob, who is this?" she said, not making eye contact with the woman.

"I'm Ashley!" the woman said, far too enthusiastically. "You look amazing. Oh my God, your hair is gorgeous. Who does your coloring?"

"It's not colored," Angie said. Her tone couldn't yet be classified as an official snap, but it was firm, even, and just slightly threatening.

"I've got to tell you," the woman continued, not picking up the signals from either of them. "Did you see this guy I'm with tonight? The big guy who just walked by? Ugh, this is the worst part of my job."

"Your job," Angie said, as much a statement as a probing question.

"Yeah, sometimes you get a good one," she said, reaching out to touch Coleman's shoulder, "and sometimes you have to shut your eyes."

Angie shut her eyes.

Coleman finally recovered his faculties and jumped into the fray.

"Angie, dear, this is Ashley, as she said..."

"Hi," Ashley said with a wave.

"Ashley was my...nurse...on duty...when I got my diagnosis."

"Your nurse?" Angie said.

"Well, no, a lot of people's nurse, to be exact. There were many, many patients that night. How is the doctor anyway?" Coleman said, turning to the woman and now begging with his eyes.

"A nurse!" Ashley said. "Well, you are just full of surprises. But we can definitely do that. It would be fun."

"Oh God," Coleman said under his breath.

"Rob, what is this..."

"Listen," she said, reaching into her purse and pulling out a pink fine-point marker. "You two are so cute. Why don't you take my number and we can set something up."

Angie watched, mortified, as the woman reached down and wrote the digits across the back of Coleman's hand. Coleman, unable to move, watched Angie watching him.

She popped the top back on the pen, dropped it into her purse, and started to walk in the direction of the large man, who now waited impatiently by the front entrance. Stopping after a few steps, she turned back and addressed Coleman, but pointed at Angie.

"I don't normally do this," she said, winking at Coleman, her lips moist and her chest heaving. "But definitely bring her with you next time, okay?"

CHAPTER 27

How he had gotten her out of the restaurant and into the car was nothing short of a miracle. It had to be a miracle, because first he had to settle the bill with the waiter, suffer an excruciating farewell from the maitre d', and await the valet driver running out to the parking lot to bring his car back to the curb. All the while, he had Angie standing beside him, saying nothing, just staring forward in what appeared to be a catatonic state. And maybe that's what it was – not so much a miracle as a clinical state of shock.

She had climbed into the car, Coleman haphazardly tipping the valet while he held Angie's door, and then dashing to the driver's side, thinking somewhere in the back of his mind that she might switch seats and drive off without him.

She had stayed, but only stared straight out the windshield, never taking her eyes off the road ahead. Although he drove, and sat only inches away from her, he really wasn't there at all.

Normally he would turn up the radio a little bit, maybe to some '90s alternative that they listened to in college, or to the country music she currently enjoyed, but he kept the cabin silent. The only noises came from the hum of the engine as it smoothly shifted in and out of gears and the soft expulsion of cool air from the forward vents. Coleman noticed her lightly rubbing her upper arms and switched off the air. He flicked a button for the passenger seat warmer but, if she noticed, she gave no indication.

They drove like this for a few miles, the widely spaced street lights alternately illuminating the inside of the vehicle, then fading off until the car reached the next interval. The strength sapped from his body, he drove slowly and carefully. There were very few cars on the road at that hour, which only added to the isolation they felt as they rolled along.

Coleman commonly drove with his left hand at the 10 o'clock position on the steering wheel, but his left hand had been emblazoned with the hot pink telephone number of the blonde woman from the restaurant, and so he had switched to his right hand at 2 o'clock and kept his left hand hidden beside his left thigh.

The blonde woman!

What in the world was she thinking?

In what universe was it good business to blow the cover of your clientele?

Why, oh why, had she been there on the same night as them? Why had she stopped at their table? Why had she said his name?

What was she thinking?!

"What were you thinking?"

Angie finally broke the silence. Her words were bullets, each one sharp, forceful, and quick, shooting from her lips, each slug rocking him, tearing at him, wounding him.

"Angie, I..."

"What were you thinking?" she repeated.

He said nothing, and only drove.

"You have a 6-year-old child," she said, her voice even and cutting.

He didn't respond, and he didn't know why it happened, but his hands shifted against his better judgment. He brought his left hand up to the steering wheel, while he extended his right hand over the center console and reached for her leg.

She recoiled, drawing her legs together against the door. At the same time, she slapped at his hand and sent it reeling back to the steering wheel.

"Don't even," she spit, finally turning her head and looking at him with pure disgust.

"What?" he said, doing nothing more than filling space as his mind futilely attempted to locate the correct path out of the situation.

"What? Are you serious?"

"Angie, come on, this isn't..."

"That's your question? What??"

"No, it's not what you..."

"It's not what I think it is?" she said, coming to life. Her eyes were wide and she had moved back to her position in the seat and had even begun leaning toward him. "Is that what you're going with? It's not what I think it is?"

"It really isn't! She was..."

"Your nurse? Your nurse?! Oh yeah, she looked like a nurse, alright."

"She was a lot of people's nurse! My foot! I was in pain, and she..."

"There is no way on God's green earth that that...person...is a nurse, okay?"

"Angie..."

"No," she said, pointing her finger at the side of his face, her nail nearly touching the skin. "Do not lie to me. Do not insult me. Do not tell me that that...person...is your nurse."

"Okay," Coleman said, his eyes now facing forward, and his head leaning slightly away from her renegade nail. "But it's different now. I swear to you."

"Oh, you'd better believe it's different now."

"You kicked me out of the house! I had nowhere to go. It was a moment of weakness, that's all it was. It meant nothing! I swear!"

They drove on in silence for another few blocks, and Coleman could feel the steam coming from the other seat. He moved his head just a touch in her direction and tried to catch a glimpse out the corner of his eye. She was seething. Her jaw was clenched, and her fists were held in little balls on either leg. He thought about saying something, but then decided against it and let the silence simmer until Angie shattered it, as if her two fists had broken through a pane of glass.

"Ashley? Of all the names in the world, that...thing's...name was Ashley?"

"Why does that matter?" Coleman said.

"Oh God, I don't even know who you are!"

"What do you mean? Who cares what her name is?"

"That's practically my name, you idiot!"

"What are you talking about?"

"Never mind. You're too stupid for words."

Another minute or two of silence passed, and Coleman thought he sensed a calmer atmosphere coming from the general area surrounding his wife. He chose not to look for verification and, instead, spoke straight ahead, softly and evenly.

"It's over. I've completely changed my behavior, just like you said at dinner. I'm spending more time with you and Connor. I've changed my diet. I'm helping out at church."

Angie said nothing, so Coleman continued.

"Don't discount those things over one incident. It's over. It's not going to happen again. Ever. You have my word. My solemn vow. You're all I care about. You're all I've ever cared about. And this is over. Completely and entirely done. Over. Finished. Done."

She still said nothing.

His eyes were trained forward, and he drove on like this for another mile, until they had reached the Silver Creek neighborhood. The grand entrance was immaculately landscaped, and decorative lighting shined from thick mulch beds below the stonework signage that announced Silver Creek's name to passersby. An impressive water feature sat just in front of the black gate that separated residents from the rest of society, and

Coleman watched as sheets of water fell down its ridges until they rippled into a collecting basin. He paused for a moment, saying nothing, hoping that some of the ambient peacefulness might transfer itself through the vents and into the cabin of his car.

Coleman lowered his window, and slowly reached out to type in the key code, then waited while the gate opened. As it was in motion, opening a pathway for his car, he took a deep breath, and slowly, apprehensively, yet full of hope and expectation, turned his head to look at his wife.

She was already looking back at him.

Her eyes were cold, her lips pressed tight, her nostrils flared, and her hair had frizzed and seemed to float above her shoulders. She carried the aura of ferocious anger, a lioness stalking her prey.

Coleman unwisely thought it appropriate to return her wild look with a smile. It was a sad smile, and one that begged forgiveness, but it was still a smile. When she saw it from across the console, it registered condescension and pity, and it filled her with the feeling that he was about to take advantage of her, all over again.

Angie clenched her right fist and reared back. And then, right there in the car, at the entrance to their neighborhood, she let it fly.

Her knuckles landed with a dull crack and knocked him back into the seat. He crumpled at once, doubling over himself, and crashed against the driver's side door. Pulling her fist back, she returned his little smile with one of her own.

She had punched him in the nose.

CHAPTER 28

"You punched me in the nose!"

As soon as the gate was open, Angie jumped out of the car. She removed her heels and began walking briskly up the street. She walked along the right shoulder of the expansive, wooded drive with her shoes dangling from her left hand and her purse clutched tight under her arm. She shook the sting from her other hand and opened and closed her fist. Crossing her arms against the cool air, she walked on as the car inched along beside her.

"I'm bleeding!"

Unable to resist, she turned her head to the left and saw him through the open window. He was bleeding alright, a steady red trickle from one nostril that had traveled over his lips and reached the bottom of his chin. He dabbed at it with the sleeve of his blue jacket and stared back at her, searching for some sort of reaction.

"Good!" was the only reaction he would get.

Coleman eased along beside her for a few more steps, but she had turned her eyes forward again, ignoring him, and so he accelerated up the street to the turn-off for their driveway. He pulled in, parked the car in its normal spot, threw the door open, climbed out, and leaned against the trunk with his arms crossed as he waited. He stood there alone for about a minute, which gave him time to try and stanch the bleeding. Still, his nose was raw and tender and spots of blood had dribbled down and stained his white shirt. When she caught up, she cut across the front lawn and walked directly for the front door.

"Angie," Coleman said, walking after her.

Angie said nothing, as she dug the key from her purse and unlocked the door. He was about 10 steps away, and gaining speed up the paved walkway, but he wasn't quick enough.

She pushed the door open, barely enough to slide through sideways, and then she slammed it just as he reached the front steps. He heard the deadbolt engage, then the hotel-style lock slide into place.

"Angie!" he yelled, pounding on the door with a closed fist.

When she didn't respond, he rang the doorbell repeatedly but, again, there was no answer. Shaking his head, he stepped down from the stoop and walked along the bushes to the right of the front door. Three windows fronted the living room, and he could just see inside the darkened space by the light of the hallway. Stepping up into the mulch bed, he reached the first window and removed the screen. Just as his palms touched the glass and pushed up on the window, Angie appeared.

She made sure the window was properly locked, then swiftly moved to the other two windows, and confirmed that they were locked, too. Coleman raised his arms in a questioning gesture, but she ignored him, and he could see her moving down the hallway toward the back of the house.

He figured out her next move a moment too late and took off in a dead sprint around the side. When he reached the fence, he grabbed the top for leverage and launched himself over it, landing on both feet in the damp grass of the backyard. Stumbling forward, he dashed across the lawn, past Connor's soccer goal, and over the stones of the patio to the French doors.

Angie was already there and, this time, she mocked him through the glass, her mouth slipping into a fake frown, feigning sadness that he couldn't get in.

He tried anyway, grabbing the handles and rattling them, pushing and pulling in a futile attempt to swing the door open. It wouldn't budge, so Coleman raced around the other side of the house, checking each window and door, but she had beat him to every one.

Finally, he found himself back in the driveway, standing beside his car. An idea popped into his head at almost the exact same time as the lights in the garage flickered on. Coleman opened his car door and reached for a button on the sun visor. When he pressed it, nothing happened. He pressed it again, and still nothing. He pressed in rapid succession, but the garage door remained closed. Coleman ran up to the door and stood on his toes to get a look through the small, square windows.

He saw Angie climbing down from a stepladder. She had disabled the mechanical drive of the garage door opener.

"Come on!" Coleman yelled, pounding on the glass.

Angie ignored him and he watched as she moved through the breezeway and back into the house.

"Angie!"

When he turned around, the babysitter stood on the front walkway, watching him with wide eyes. She was one of the high school kids who lived in the neighborhood and she had her smartphone out and looked like she was prepared to use it. Coleman tried to relax and play it cool.

"Hey," he said. "Didn't see you there. I was just, uh, checking the locks here. Can never be too careful."

"Right," the girl said.

"Do you need a ride home?" He tried to affect a casual manner as he strolled back toward the car.

"Uh, no thanks. I'm good," the girl said. "I'll hoof it."

"Good deal," Coleman said, and stood stationary as the girl took a wide berth around the car, never diverting her eyes from him.

"Hey, Mister Coleman?" she said, as she reached the end of the driveway. "You're bleeding, like, a lot."

He dabbed at his nose and looked at his sleeve. There was a dark wet spot evident, and he dabbed repeatedly until he felt like the fresh trickle of blood had stopped. When he looked up, the babysitter was gone.

He darted back to the front door and tried again, pounding on the door, ringing the doorbell and shouting Angie's name. When that didn't work, he tried the windows again. When those didn't work, he ran to the back of the house.

Unsuccessful, he emerged again in the driveway. The garage door lights were now turned off, and he could see through the windows as she switched off the upstairs lights inside.

"Angie, please!" he yelled up at the windows. He would receive no response.

He stomped back over to his car and opened the door. As he did, he noticed the neighbor across the street. She had her dog on a leash by the big oak tree in her front lawn – that stupid little rat dog – and she appeared to have witnessed the entire scene unfold.

"Shut up!" Coleman yelled across the street at her, then climbed into his car and drove away.

CHAPTER 29

Coleman drove.

When he had left the neighborhood, he accelerated and drove fast down the side streets. The clock was sliding past 9:00 pm, and it was a work and a school night in a suburban area of the Research Triangle, so traffic was at a bare minimum. He passed only one car as he reached 80 mph on the county road and split off for the ramp to the highway.

The Route 540 bypass around the city of Raleigh was a relatively new creation, brought to the taxpayers by the State of North Carolina. It was a nice, freshly paved, eight-lane highway that ran south to the countryside and connected with the commuter corridor on the north side of Raleigh. The new southern stretch of the bypass had been tolled, and the engineers had graciously installed automatic toll readers, so that cars could maintain their speed through the plaza, instead of suffering through toll booth bottlenecks.

Stretching across the lanes high above the flow of traffic, the toll sensors read a sticker or little box affixed to the windshield in each vehicle as it crossed below. At night, the sensors flashed a bright light to record each toll and, among many fleeting thoughts, Coleman quietly cursed the imposition of this new expense as his BMW raced through the installation. Government officials had assured taxpayers that, once the tolls had paid for construction of the bypass, the tolls would then disappear and passage along the route would be free of charge.

Coleman knew better. Once the spicket had been opened, the government never, ever turned it off. If anything, tolls would only increase in the coming years – they certainly wouldn't go away. Sneering, he pressed harder on the accelerator and reached 100 mph as he sped through the toll. In his rearview mirror he saw the flash of light and, for a brief moment, hoped the sensors were too slow to record his passage.

He was the only car on that stretch of highway, so he gunned it harder. He got up to 118 mph, a lone BMW driver on his own private Autobahn, before he saw the highbeams from a distant car heading toward him on the other side of the highway. He slowed down and stared straight ahead, listening to the sound of his own breathing above the hum of the engine and the rolling pressure of rubber on concrete beneath him.

Why?
Why had she been there?
Why had she stopped and talked to them?
Why hadn't she left them alone?
Didn't she know it was bad for business to expose a client to his wife?
Was she nuts?
Was she insane?
Was business so good that she didn't care about losing a client?
Business? Why was he worried about her business?
What was wrong with him?
Really, what was wrong with him?
Angie.
Oh dear God, Angie.
What must she think of him?
She kicked him out of the house. That's what she thought.
What would he do now?
Where would he go?
What would he wear?
Was he still bleeding?
Why did this person still have his highbeams on?
How much farther to the bar?
He needed a drink.
Now.

It was a slow night at the Carolina Oyster Bar. There was no band and, therefore, no gaggle of college kids, groupies and hangers-on that would normally be in attendance. There was only a smattering of couples sharing quiet conversations and lonely businessmen working their way through private dramas. Coleman sat at the bar and raised his shot glass to the businessman's collective.

He had gone straight for whiskey, and chased it with a pint of beer, a domestic light beer so he could drink it fast and easy. Motioning for the bartender, he ordered up another round before he was finished with the current slate.

"Hey, what's that on your shirt? Are you okay?" the bartender said, indicating the red stains near the collar and top buttons of Coleman's white shirt.

"Spaghetti sauce," Coleman said between gulps of his beer. "I made a royal mess of things."

"Huh," the bartender said skeptically, then turned to get the refills.

A royal mess of things.

No kidding.

Coleman silently toasted the businessmen again, threw back the shot of whiskey, and narrowed his eyes at the romantic couples as he drained the next beer. His belly was full, so he slowed things down and ordered a vodka and tonic with a lime.

"Rough day?" the bartender said.

Coleman just nodded and kept his head down. His hands were wrapped around the glass, and his eyes wandered to the hot pink writing on his hand. The alcohol had quelled his anger some, and his brain began to work at cross purposes. On one hand, he was livid about the encounter at the Italian restaurant. On the other hand, he was drunk. Slowly, the other hand – the hand with the pink digits – exerted its will on the situation.

He reached into his pocket and pulled out his phone. The text message was short, and it wasn't making any requests. It stated his name, his location, and the word "Now."

It only took two more vodka and tonics before she arrived, and she was all full of vim and vigor as she approached him from behind.

"I am so glad you texted me," she said, sidling up beside him and looking down as he continued to stare at the glass in his hands. "You would not believe what happened with that guy! He didn't want to pay. He said that dinner was payment enough, and that I owed him! Can you believe that? As if it were a real date! So I just ditched him. Left him right there in the parking lot of the hotel, before we could even go inside. Now, the good news is, I've still got the room. He paid for it, but guess who has the key?"

Coleman finished his drink and wiped his lips on the back of his hand. He still had not looked at her and, when he finally did, his eyes were fiery and determined. She noticed and her mouth opened involuntarily, seeming to welcome his intensity. She bit her lower lip and raised her eyebrows, beckoning, encouraging him.

He stared at her, directly into her eyes, working things out in his head. When he spoke at last, his words were forceful, commanding, and left no room for interpretation.

"Let's go," was all he said.

CHAPTER 30

The hotel stood in downtown Raleigh, and their room was on a high floor, overlooking the city. It was a tall hotel with windows that broadened the view, and they had gone to bed with the curtains still open. Streetlights from below reflected upward and the waning lights from distant buildings offered their luminescence through the dark night.

They had arrived in a cab – the bartender had insisted – and the coming and going was dark and fuzzy in his memory. She had led the way, his friend in the dark red dress, and he had compliantly followed. He didn't remember much beyond that, but he could feel her presence in the bed beside him.

He was on his back, sunken into the mattress. He was parched, his mouth dry and thick, and he could hear the electric buzz from the air unit on the wall. The air smelled of perfume and stale liquor. It was murky there, deep inside his personal fog, and it took a few moments to emerge from the cocoon of gauze and cotton enveloping his head.

As Coleman's eyes flicked open, he reached for his nose. He could feel it throbbing and swollen, but could sense no blood trickling from the nostrils as he touched his fingers to his upper lip. His eyes watered from the beating pain but, as he felt around the bridge of his tender nose, he realized that its source was lower.

Lower, yet familiar.

Familiar, yet slightly different.

As the synapses fired into place and ushered in a dose of stark clarity, Coleman shot up at the waist and threw back the thin white bedsheet.

It was his foot.

Dear God, his *other* foot.

Coleman yelped like a dog and swung his legs to the floor. His mind raced back to the previous episode, to the other hotel room, to a night just like this one, and he repeated his motions almost exactly, only in mirror reverse.

He hopped across the carpet, this time on his right foot, and crumpled into a ball in the corner near the window. There was a lightstand there, and Coleman shoved it out of the way as he leaned his back into the wall and reached for his left foot.

The pain was terrific.

It coursed through his big toe and nested firmly in the joint, where the hornets were released. They skewered his foot, a brutal onslaught of merciless stabbing that left him wailing in the corner.

"No, no, no, no..." he whimpered, as he rocked back and forth, both hands covering the foot, kneading and massaging against the pain.

She had awakened from the commotion, and she sat up, squinting to see through the dim lights coming through the window. Her blonde hair was everywhere, and she pushed it back from her forehead and eyes. When she realized what was happening, she backed up into the headboard and pulled the sheet up over her body.

"No, no, no, no!" she yelled at him across the room.

Coleman looked up at her, his expression pleading, begging for her help. All the while, his hands continued working on the foot, squeezing, rubbing, and stroking the skin.

"You sick freak!" she yelled.

She reached for a pillow behind her and covered herself before jumping out of the bed.

"Are you serious? This again?" She rooted around on the floor for her dress. "What is wrong with you?"

"Please help me," Coleman whispered, reaching out for her.

"I helped you last night," she said. "And I'll do a lot of things, but this is like the weirdest thing ever. You can play that game by yourself, buddy."

"I need help," he said, moaning in the corner as he stroked the foot.

"Oh, you definitely need help!"

She found her dress and quickly pulled it on. As soon as she was clothed, she found the switch on the wall and turned on the lights. She looked around for her heels and found them under the bed. Squatting to retrieve them, she glanced over at him. A thin trickle of blood now dribbled from his nose.

"Oh, gross!" she said. "Listen, don't contact me anymore, okay?"

Coleman moaned.

She strapped her feet into the heels and went looking for his clothes. She found them in a loose pile on the other side of the bed, and reached for the pants. His wallet was in a back pocket, and she sat on the bed as she looked through it.

"That's it?" she said, holding it up to him. "You only have $80?"

"Wait, don't take that..." Coleman moaned.

"Oh, I'm taking it," she said, neatly folding the money and placing it inside of her purse.

"Please," he said. "I need a ride."

"I gave you a ride."

"No, my car, it's not here. I need a ride. I need a doctor."

"You need a shrink!"

"Please..." Coleman begged, reaching out for her.

She backed away from his outstretched hand and crossed the room. When she got to the door, she grabbed the handle, but then stopped and slowly looked back at him.

He was a mess, lying there naked in the corner, bleeding from his nose, rocking back and forth against the wall, with his hands clutching his left foot and his face frozen in a grimace full of agony and suffering.

Just for a moment, she took pity on him, and she reached inside her purse. She pulled out a $10 bill and crumpled it into a ball.

"Here," she said, throwing it across the room at him. It landed on the carpet near the bed. "That should get you back to your car, at least."

Coleman looked at the little green paper ball and then looked up and thanked her with his eyes.

"Now, seriously, don't ever contact me again."

She opened the door, stepped into the hall, and she was gone.

Coleman watched as the door closed on its own. He leaned his head back against the wall and took several deep breaths. He removed his hands from his left foot, and winced. With one hand, he wiped the blood away from his nose.

With the other hand, he wiped a tear from each eye.

CHAPTER 31

Her charity had gotten him back to his BMW, which was one of a handful of cars still parked in the Carolina Oyster Bar's parking lot, though he did have to stiff the cabbie on a tip. The drive had been painful, if slightly more pleasant than last time, simply because his left foot had no responsibility. The car had an automatic shift, so Coleman rested the throbbing foot against the floorboard and navigated as quickly as he could to the hospital. This time, after he had parked in the emergency room lot and limped his way through the sliding glass doors, he approached the front desk and requested the same doctor by name.

It was about a 30-minute wait, which Coleman spent reclined in a cheap plastic-molded chair, with the back of his head resting against the wall. He had taken another identical chair and elevated his left foot on it, then shut his eyes and tried to pass the time through sleep, though sleep was tough to accomplish among the bright lights and constant motion of the ER. When they called his name, he limped down the hallway, using the wall as a support, until he reached the tiny space where he waited another 15 minutes for the doctor to arrive.

Same room. Same white walls. Same bright lights.

Coleman had no doubt it would be the same result.

When the doctor entered, there was a brief moment of recognition for the patient seated on the edge of the examination table and, before the doctor could speak, the patient had self-diagnosed.

"It's the gout," Coleman said. "Other foot."

The doctor frowned and sat on a stool. On his clipboard, he jotted a few notes, and then rolled over to the exam table, where he stared silently at Coleman's foot for a good half-minute.

"Alcohol?" the doctor said, looking up.

"Lots." The thin strip of paper covering the exam table crinkled as Coleman shifted his weight.

The doctor nodded, and jotted a few more notes.

"Well, Mister Coleman," he said, setting the clipboard down on the small desk against the wall, "this is somewhat rare and a bit unusual for it to happen so soon after the first episode but, yes, you are correct in your diagnosis. It's the gout. In the other foot."

"Yeah," Coleman said.

"I think we discussed this during your last visit, but more than half of those diagnosed with gout will suffer another episode within a year. Usually it doesn't happen so soon after the first attack, but it's nothing to fear. The timing is somewhat rare, but the reemergence of the gout itself is rather common."

"So why did it happen so soon for me?"

"Well, you said it yourself, Mister Coleman. Lots of alcohol. That's probably the main reason. Have you been attentive to your diet?"

"Yeah, I cut out all the purines, and I've been eating a bunch of cherries. Do you know how disgusting cherry juice tastes?"

The doctor ignored the question and seemed to be concentrating on Coleman's face.

"Any added stress in your life right now? At work, maybe?"

"That's all I have at work. It's part of the job description."

"What do you do?"

"I'm not sure lately, but it used to be considered sales," Coleman said.

The doctor nodded and pursed his lips. "You need to try and manage your stress. I know it's easier said than done, but anything you can do to relax and leave your work at work is going to be helpful. Is everything okay at home?"

"Perfect," Coleman said. "Never better."

"You're married?"

"I think so."

"Kids?"

"One."

"What happened to your nose?" the doctor said, rolling closer to the table and peering in at the injury.

"Oh, uh, that's nothing," Coleman said, bringing his hand to his face and feeling around at the bridge of his nose. "Playing soccer with my son. Caught one in the face."

"Mister Coleman, hold still for a second. This might hurt just a touch."

The doctor stood and placed his thumb and forefinger against the bridge of the nose, where Coleman's own hand had just been, and he lightly wiggled. A lightning bolt of pain exploded in the nasal cavity. A high-pitched squeal came out of his mouth, and his eyes filled with water.

"Sorry about that," the doctor said, pulling his hand back. "Well, it's not broken, but you did take a pretty good shot there. Looks like there's some residual blood build-up in the nostrils. Let's go ahead and get that cleaned up and stabilize the bridge."

"How do you do that?" Coleman said, wiping at his eyes.

"Just a strip of heavy tape. Nothing too intrusive."

"Great."

"We'll go ahead and write another prescription for the NSAID. That should help with your foot and your nose. Any side effects last time?"

Coleman shook his head, no.

"Good. Do you still have your crutches from before?"

He nodded, yes.

"Use them. Stay off that foot. Make sure it heals. With the exception of the alcohol, it sounds like your diet is on the right track. Keep away from the purines for a while, and Mister Coleman?"

"Yeah?"

"You really do need to shy away from the alcohol. We normally suggest moderation but, in your case, with the frequency of these attacks, it's probably your best bet to just avoid it altogether until things get back to normal."

"Okay," Coleman said. "I understand."

The doctor jotted some more notes – quite a few notes, Coleman thought – before clicking his pen and sliding it into his breast pocket. He clutched the clipboard under his arm, pushed his white coat back with his free hand, and buried the hand in his pants pocket.

"Any other questions for me, Mister Coleman?"

"How long? For my left foot to be okay?"

The doctor frowned.

"Probably a little longer than it took the right foot. You'll want to make sure that your foot has completely recovered before you get back to your normal routines."

Coleman's shoulders slumped. He ran his hands through his hair and propped his elbows on his knees. The doctor noticed the sense of defeat in his body language and tried to place a positive spin on matters.

"Don't worry," the doctor said. "If it happens again, we can regulate your uric acid through medicine, but let's see how things play out first."

Coleman didn't look up.

"The nurse will be in to tend to your nose. That should feel better in no time."

No response.

It wasn't a mental health visit, so the doctor didn't make much more of an effort to encourage him. On his way out the door, though, he did have a flash of empathy, and he turned back before exiting.

"Hey, listen. It's not the end of the world," he said. "It's just the gout."

CHAPTER 32

Coleman had fallen asleep in the parking lot. After his appointment with the doctor, he had limped out of the hospital and struggled his way to the car, where he turned on the radio and stared straight ahead for a good 20 minutes. The volume was low and, at that hour, as the morning light crept in and began to take over from the evening darkness, his eyes slowly began to shut. The deep voices and smooth, even tones of the news reporters hummed through the speakers and lulled him into a hushed and calm state, until he was reclined in his seat, dead to the world – just another suburban jerk who had been kicked out of his house, contracted the gout, and fallen asleep in the car.

An ambulance had been his alarm clock. It rounded the corner and stopped just in front of the entrance to the emergency room. When he opened his eyes, he could see the flashing red lights reflected from his windshield, and he stared at them for a few long moments, suspended in a warm and easy haze. Then his eyes drifted to the digital clock on the console above the radio.

8:32 am.

Coleman shot up and grabbed the steering wheel. He was already two minutes late for his meeting. He quickly fished around for his phone in his pocket and pressed down on the direct-dial key he had assigned to Steve. The phone was connected wirelessly to the sound system, and the voices of the news reporters stopped abruptly and yielded to the ringing tone. He rubbed his eyes and waited as it rang three times, four times, five times and, finally, connected.

Voicemail.

"Answer your phone!" Coleman shouted upon hearing Steve's message. Instead of leaving one, he disconnected the call and cranked the ignition. The engine came to life and the reporters greeted him anew.

It was a quick 15-minute trip to the office that Coleman made quicker by taking back roads and ignoring speed limits. He drew a few threatening looks from sleepy parents manning the bus stops beside their kids but, otherwise, he had an uneventful trip. He parked as close as he could to the entrance, and he climbed from the car, swinging his legs wide and applying the weight to his right foot as he stood. He checked his pockets for gum or a mint or something, but there was none, so he scraped an index finger across his teeth, rubbed his palms over the parts of his face that didn't hurt, and attempted with his hands to generate some sort of hairstyle.

With no bag and nothing to hang on to, he instead straightened his clothes as much as possible and limped forward, moving toward the lobby.

Upstairs in the conference room overlooking the office pond, where the fountain was in full morning bloom, the engineering team laughed at some inside joke related to the technology behind their project. Steve understood most of it, and he laughed along with them, if not as boisterously. He had silenced his phone, as he always did before meetings, and shoved it deep in his pocket. A few times he had glanced at the clock and wondered, but really thought nothing of Coleman's absence. Since he had been running the Monday meetings lately, he figured it was just another subtle handoff, and he privately welcomed the added responsibility.

Things were going well.

Things were going very well.

Vijay had challenged the team members, most of whom he had hand-selected for the project, to a hack-a-thon. He had created a dummy shell of The Bank's web portal to their online banking site, and he had mimicked the security architecture, functionality, and encryption that powered the site. He had created two mock-ups, one for The Bank's current configuration, and one designed in his own image, with Vijay's proposed enhancements.

The team had made quick work of The Bank's mock portal, but over a 24-hour period, they had no success breaking into Vijay's solution.

Empty pizza boxes and 2-liter bottles of soda were strewn about the room and piled up on the table. The engineers were giddy from the all-nighter, fueled by lack of sleep and the sense of achievement.

As the team joked about knocking over the bank and transferring funds to their own accounts, Steve could sense the satisfaction and pride pouring forth from the speakerphone. Even though Vijay sat at his desk on the other side of the world, he was right there in the room, celebrating with his team.

It was a banner day. In a sense, it was the final breakthrough the team needed. There was still some back-end functionality to clean up and refine, but that was all academic at this point. The engineers could tinker with the details in their sleep. What they had before them, though, thanks to Vijay and his team, was the solution they would implement at The Bank.

All they needed now was a signed contract.

Steve was just about to dismiss the team and let them go home for the day, when he looked up and saw what could only be described as a homeless, albeit well-dressed, man who appeared to have been beaten in a street fight.

"Rob, what happened to you?"

Steve jumped out of his chair and was beside the door in a split second, offering his hands in assistance. The engineers had stopped joking and the phone went silent, as those in the room stared at the wraith in the doorway, while those who had patched in remotely wondered what the others were seeing.

Coleman stood before them, ashen and nearly catatonic, like a brain-eating zombie, and stared off into the distance, to where the fountain sprayed its plumes of water onto the placid pond.

"Oh my," someone said out loud.

"What's happening?" Vijay said, his voice coming from the speakerphone. "Steve, is everything okay?"

Coleman's blue suit pants were creased in odd places and hung loosely from his thighs, while clinging tightly to his lower legs, where they bunched above the socks. He wore only one shoe, on his right foot, where he supported all of his weight. His left foot was covered by a sock, and the only part he would allow to touch the ground was the heel.

His suit jacket had a combination of dirt and lint and what looked like glitter caked to the sleeves. He was missing his belt, and his white shirt was coming untucked at the sides, so that his midsection appeared airy and puffed like a marshmallow. There were deep, dried stains of red just below his collar that looked like an amateur rendering of the Rorschach test.

There was a heavy and wide strip of white tape across the bridge of his nose, and the last vestiges of dried blood were caked inside his nostrils, so that he breathed heavily through his mouth. Coleman's eyes were sleepy and hungover slits, and dark bruises had begun to form beneath the lids.

"I'm okay," Coleman said softly, as Steve rushed to support his weight. "I'm okay. I'm okay. I'm okay. I'm okay."

Coleman repeated the line to each person in the room, and then fell into the chair that Steve had grabbed for him.

Down the hall, Armstrong rocked in his high-backed office chair and grinned, practically bursting with glee, as he looked out the window and watched the fountain spray its rainbow-tinted mist over the pond. He had hardly been able to sleep the previous night, but there was no sense of somnolence. On the contrary, it seemed like the man had been injected with liquid energy.

When the CEO had called him the evening before, Armstrong was at home, relaxing in his study, thumbing through an awful book rife with conspiracy theories about faked Apollo moon landings, unreported alien invasions, and the truly bizarre NASA cover-up of a "face" carved into the rocky Mars landscape by indigenous planetary laborers. He had mostly laughed at the absurdity of it all, though his mind did wander a few times to the dark, conspiratorial side of governmental affairs, and it only strengthened his resolve to become a NASA insider, to join the ranks of those in the know. For Armstrong, the CEO's call proved to a step in the right direction.

They had mapped out a succession plan, and Armstrong would be the third vertex in their power triangle. The plan was for the reigning COO to take over for the outgoing CEO for two years only, to serve as a glorified placeholder for the sake of consistency during the leadership transition. It would also give the COO ample time to teach Armstrong the tricks of his trade, and provide a warm hand-off when the time came for Armstrong to ascend to the top spot.

The CEO himself had been tapped as the government's Chief Technology Officer which, to hear the boss describe it, sounded like one of the greatest accomplishments one could achieve in a lifetime. To most of the Silicon Valley executives who had been considered for the role, however, it represented a massive paycut, an unwelcome move across the country to Washington D.C., and a host of new bosses in the White House, Senate, and the House of Representatives, most of whom were more incompetent than the stockholders they currently served. Rumors in the tech rags and gossip circles indicated that five people had passed on the position, including one of the President's top fundraisers during the last campaign, and that the White House had gotten desperate. They were seeking someone – anyone – to take the position, ostensibly to bolster public perception that they were a hip, savvy outfit, plugged into the latest technology advances and trends. In reality, they wanted someone with their ear to the ground, who had the respect of their peers, but who was pliant enough to enact the administration's agenda without any major hang-ups about minor quibbles such as "privacy" and "spying."

Armstrong's boss was a perfect fit.

And so the wheels had been set in motion. The flight plan had been logged. Mission control had given the okay for lift-off. Neal Armstrong was set to become the second most powerful man for one of the most well-known technology companies in the world.

Now, the CEO had spared no feelings when he informed Armstrong that there were other aspirants, as well, but he clearly articulated that these were merely show ponies for the Board of Directors, who would want to see at least three candidates before making a final decision. But, for all intents and purposes, the decision had been made, and only one important detail stood as a potential roadblock.

The Bank.

Armstrong leaned back in his chair and made no effort to stifle a giggle. The Bank was so close, he could taste it.

He would close The Bank, quite possibly within the next two weeks and, by the end of the month, they might be announcing his transition to COO and a nice move out to San Jose.

For the CEO, it meant leaving on a high note. To knock over that first domino would be a huge victory and set the company up for domination in the banking and financial services industry. As he assumed his new role, it also meant a rolling start for Armstrong.

Once they reached a certain level of growth and success, major corporations in most industries became little more than copycats. Since The Bank was such a major player, there was little doubt in Armstrong's mind that, once they chose their security solution, other institutions would quickly follow. And once they gained market share within the financial vertical, entire industries would come calling. Healthcare, retail, energy, manufacturing, and the biggest cash cow of them all, the federal government. And, lo and behold, when that happened, they would have an extremely well-placed advocate already sitting in Washington.

Armstrong would have the potential to oversee a very lucrative growth period, and all that stood in his way was the completion of a deal that was nearly done.

Kinetic and crackling, the energy and enthusiasm emanating from every pore, Armstrong spun around in his chair, slapped the top of his desk with both hands and charged out into the hallway. His smile was big and wide, and he clapped his palms together as he strode long strides toward the conference room.

As he approached the doorway, he stopped and the breath whooshed from his lungs. The color flushed from his face and the eyes, perched just above that beak of a nose, widened into astonished saucers.

Coleman limped out of the conference room. His left arm was wrapped around Steve's shoulders, and he used Steve as support for his left foot. He only wore one shoe, and his nose was taped and red, and dark bags drooped below his eyes. He looked like he hadn't slept, showered, or shaved, and he appeared to be mumbling to himself.

"What is this?!" Armstrong said.

"I'm okay, I'm okay, I'm okay, I'm okay..."

At once, the color returned to Armstrong's face, starting out splotchy, then growing increasingly red, until it was one uniform shade of crimson.

"This had better be a practical joke," he said through gritted teeth.

"I'm okay, I'm okay, I'm okay, I'm okay..." Coleman mumbled, his eyes fixed on the ground.

Armstrong looked at Steve. Steve looked at Armstrong. The looks they gave each other said all that needed to be said.

Armstrong stomped one shoe on the ground and pointed at Coleman's foot.

"Outside!" he yelled. "Right now!"

CHAPTER 33

It had started to drizzle, big intermittent drops of rain that plopped into the pond, creating deep divots that rippled outward in mild waves. Steve stood on the path and watched the raindrops, not wishing to make eye contact with Armstrong, who stomped back and forth in tight, angry steps, a temper tantrum worthy of a 2-year-old.

Coleman had slumped into a seated position on one of the benches. He stared off into the distance, looking out over the pond toward the trees on the other side.

Steve turned to him, pleading with his eyes to do something, to channel some energy, to make the nightmare go away, but Coleman didn't respond. He just looked off into the distance. For a moment, his eyes traced the flight of a bird, and Steve thought he saw the corners of Coleman's mouth rise into the smallest of smiles.

Steve shook his head in disbelief. His eyes wandered past Coleman, across the parking lot, and up the building to the conference room windows. They had an audience. The engineers stood shoulder to shoulder, staring back at them, watching events unfold on the ground. He had no doubt that Vijay was receiving a running commentary through the phone.

"Get up!"

Armstrong ignored the raindrops, which were growing smaller and increasing in frequency, and pointed down at the bench. Coleman slowly turned his head and looked up at him. Steve closed his eyes and his chin dropped to his chest.

Coleman had a full-blown smile on his face.

"Get up!" Armstrong shouted.

Coleman took his time.

It had been a real struggle making his way to the elevator and out to the pond. Steve had abandoned him about halfway, obviously torn between supporting Coleman and hurrying along to catch up with the boss. Coleman was exhausted, still hungover, and in tremendous pain – he hadn't been able to fill his prescription yet, and his foot absolutely throbbed. The storm of physical suffering and subconscious understanding that he was majorly screwed swirled together and made him laugh.

It was a little laugh through pursed lips that grew into a bigger laugh, until he had thrown his head back and emitted a big, guttural guffaw that sent Armstrong into a state of apoplectic fury.

Armstrong charged the bench, reached over, and grabbed Coleman, pulling him up by the lapels of his suit jacket. Coleman's body was heavy, and he kept on laughing as Armstrong struggled to pull him upright.

"What did you do?" Armstrong spat at him. "What did you do?"

Coleman laughed.

Armstrong released him and turned away, walking a few steps along the path, one hand on his hip and the other tracing the thin hair over his ear. He shook his head and silently muttered to himself. When he was about 10 feet away, he abruptly turned back and pointed at Coleman. His words were direct and his tone laced with disgust.

"Run," he said.

Coleman furrowed his brow, narrowed his eyes, and wrinkled his face, as if to question the general point of the exercise.

Steve jumped in and questioned it verbally.

"Mister Armstrong, he can't do this..."

"Be quiet, Steven!" Armstrong pointed at him, then moved his long, bony finger back toward Coleman. "I said to run."

"I'm only wearing one shoe, Neal," Coleman said, balancing on his right foot, the foot that had a shoe on it.

"Do I look I like care?" Armstrong yelled. "Run!"

The rain had picked up, and Coleman's hair was wet and clinging to his head in clumps. The tape across his nose had started to curl at the edges. He gently matted down the tape, and slicked his hair back with both hands.

"You want me to run, Neal?"

"Show me you can."

"You want me to run?"

"You have 13.1 miles to run in a few days. A half-marathon. Now show me!"

Steve could hardly look. He covered his face with one hand and watched through parted fingers. The engineering team, spectators from above, had collectively leaned forward against the glass for a better glimpse.

Coleman removed his jacket and tossed it on the bench. His white dress shirt had come completely untucked at one side, and he pulled out the other side so that it fell uniformly over his pants. The rain quickly dampened the white fabric, revealing the outline of the v-neck undershirt beneath. His stray sock, navy blue to match his pants, had bunched up at the ankle on his left foot. Resting his weight on the heel, Coleman reached down and pulled the sock up, straightening it over his calf, wincing the entire time.

He stood up straight and took a deep breath. Armstrong wasn't standing very far away. He could make it. It was a few steps, nothing more. It would hurt, but he could make it. He could make it. He could make it.

He could make it!

He made it three steps.

With his weight still on the heel of his left foot, he started with the right shoe, planting it on the pavement and driving his left foot forward. When it hit the ground, the hornets raged through his toes, and his whole body buckled. The right foot fell forward and his shoe touched the ground, but that was the last step he would take.

Coleman fell to the ground, slamming his left side, landing squarely on his hip and shoulder.

Steve rushed over to help him.

Upstairs, the mouths of the engineers stood open, and a British accent piped through the phone, saying, "What happened? What happened?"

Armstrong stared at the man on the ground for several long moments, lost in thought, then turned and walked back toward the building. The engineers all scurried back away from the window before he could spot them.

Squatting down, Steve watched Armstrong walk away, then turned to Coleman and shook his head.

Coleman had rolled onto his back and looked up at the sky. He turned to Steve with a look of incredible pain painted across his wet and bruised face.

"How'd I do?" he said.

CHAPTER 34

Armstrong stood at his office window for a long while, gazing out at the spot where he had left them. The rain continued in diagonal sheets, popping against the glass and drenching the pathways and parking lots below. He had removed his blazer, damp with the rain, and he had a white towel draped over his shoulder.

Dark shadows crept across the office. The blinds were pulled all the way back, but the grayness outside held back the sun, and the desk lamp was the only artificial light shining in Armstrong's space.

Several minutes passed before Coleman limped in, supported by Steve, who had an arm wrapped around his waist and assumed the natural weight of Coleman's left side. They didn't knock, but neither did they interrupt the pensive air they had entered.

Armstrong heard them, but said nothing. He just stared out the window.

Steve stood off to the side as Coleman sunk into the office sofa. He removed the wet sock from his left foot and tucked it into a suit pocket. The joint was red and raw, and Coleman straightened his knee until the foot was fully extended beneath the coffee table before him.

The silence lingered, each man lost in his own thoughts. The two interlopers awaited an opening salvo, but Armstrong did not speak. Unable to bear the silence any longer, Steve opened his mouth first.

"I'm sure we can get another delay, Mister Armstrong. They can't be that bent out of shape about a stupid half-marathon, can they? Maybe we can invite them here, walk them through the mock-ups, explain some of the functionality behind it. These are things they have to sign off on eventually anyway, right? So let's just reverse the order a little bit until Rob is healed. I'm sure he'll be ready to go in no time."

Coleman's shoulders were slouched and his head was down. He stared at his foot, but offered neither agreement nor dissent. Like Armstrong, who had his arms crossed and his back to them, Coleman simply stared and stared.

Steve couldn't take the silence.

"Mister Armstrong, please, I'm sure they'll understand if we tell them that his injury hasn't fully healed yet. They don't want to beat him at half-strength! They want the full Rob Coleman. This kind of thing happens to elite athletes, right? So let's just talk to them and see. I'm happy to do it. I know I can convince them that..."

"It's not an injury," Armstrong said, barely above a whisper. His back was still to them and he stared out into the gray sky, his eyes unblinking.

"What?" Steve said, confused.

"It's not an injury," Armstrong said louder.

"What do you mean?" Steve looked over at Coleman, who didn't respond at all.

Armstrong slowly turned around. He wiped the edge of the towel over his forehead and took a step toward them.

"Injury is a sign of weakness," Armstrong said. He stepped over to his desk and supported himself on his fingertips as he leaned closer to them. "We are selling security to them, and injury is not security. Injury is weakness. But that's not what this is."

"I don't follow," Steve said.

"You haven't told him, have you?" Armstrong looked at Coleman, who still didn't respond. "That doesn't surprise me in the least."

"Told me what?" Steve said.

"Your friend here doesn't have a foot injury, Steven."

"What do you mean?"

"He has the gout."

"The what?"

"The gout," Armstrong repeated with disgust.

"I'm sorry," Steve said, confused and looking back and forth between the two men. "What does that even mean, the gout? Isn't that a big lump on your neck?"

"That's a goiter," Coleman whispered. "I have the gout."

"You have the gout?"

"He has the gout," Armstrong said, his tone dripping with sarcasm as he continued. "The 'Rich Man's Disease,' the 'Disease of Kings!' You don't look like much of a king to me, Robert."

"You have the gout?" Steve was incredulous.

"It really hurts," Coleman said.

"How do you even get that?"

"It is a self-inflicted disease of decadence, sloth, and gluttony," Armstrong said. "You get it by being undisciplined and unaccountable."

Coleman smiled to himself and turned to look at Steve.

"Not entirely true. It can also be hereditary. It's actually a build-up of uric acid in the blood, which then travels to your lower extremities, where it crystallizes and..."

"You get it by being selfish!" Armstrong interrupted, slamming a fist down onto the table. "I've asked you for one thing throughout this deal. One thing! And you couldn't even take care of your body long enough to follow through."

"What do you want me to say?" Coleman shrugged. "I'll be fine in a week, and then I can prance around at your little sporting events with these guys. By the way, I don't see you volunteering for the job."

"I've had a hip replaced, you know that," Armstrong said, growing angrier.

"I'm sorry, is that not a sign of weakness?" Coleman snapped back. "I mean, they are purchasing security from us, and hip replacements are pretty weak, if you ask me."

"Rob, don't..." Steve said.

Coleman lifted a hand to stop him.

"Yeah, let's see you get out there, Neal. You do The Asylum. You run the half-marathon."

"Rob..." Steve tried to stop him from continuing, to no avail.

"You wouldn't even be in this position without me, Neal," Coleman said, "and you and I both know it."

Armstrong dropped his head and thought for a moment. When he lifted it, he looked at Steve with sorrow, and then his anger returned as he made eye contact with Coleman.

"You are not fit for this deal," Armstrong said. "And I'm no longer sure that you're fit for this company. Get out of my office."

Armstrong pointed at the door. This time, Steve didn't stop to help Coleman up. He just turned and left.

CHAPTER 35

They had reconvened in the conference room at Armstrong's request. He had sent a message to the group and asked that Vijay and the India team patch in, as well. It was later in the day – several hours had passed – but there was very little productivity. They had seen the drama unfold outside, and they all had an inkling of the unorthodox approach the account team was taking on this particular deal. They also rarely, if ever, had a meeting called by Armstrong himself, so they all knew that it probably wasn't going to be a celebration.

Steve was particularly confused. He had left Coleman in there, had gone to dry off and throw on a change of clothes, and he had not seen him since. Armstrong's office had been dark and empty. Coleman's office, which was normally arranged in a neat, orderly fashion, seemed especially clean and tidy. He looked everywhere they might be but, if they were still at the office, Steve couldn't find them. He retreated to his own smaller office, the one with the lesser view of the parking lot, the one he wished he could upgrade, and busied himself with administrative tasks: scheduling, timecard reporting, vacation approvals, meeting confirmations, and anything he could to keep his mind from drifting to the scene that had played out in Armstrong's office.

He knew it wasn't good. Armstrong joined meetings occasionally, but when he wanted to get a point across, he ran information through Steve and Coleman to disseminate to the team. Steve couldn't recall the last "All Hands" meeting that Armstrong had called.

Steve sat at the head of the table, swiveling his seat from side to side, and stared at the speakerphone. Vijay and others were listening on the other end, but they were muted. The engineers in the room, the same ones who had watched Coleman's fall outside, now sat around the table, each buried inside the world inhabited by their phone, tablet, or some other sort of gadget.

Armstrong came in quickly and without fanfare.

He chose not to sit, but found an unoccupied chair, rolled it back against the wall, and stood there with his arms crossed and looking slowly from person to person. After taking a mental inventory, he placed his fingertips on the table and leaned forward slightly.

"As of this morning, Mister Coleman has been relieved of his responsibilities here."

Silence.

Steve turned his head to make eye contact with Armstrong, but the look was not returned.

"Mister Coleman failed to meet the standards that we had mutually set for him, and The Bank is too important to this company to leave in the hands of someone who falls short of our goals."

Nobody in the room made a sound. Rather than catch the gaze of the boss, they all seemed to be staring at the speakerphone, which still remained silent, but made a convenient landing area for their eyes.

"We will develop a transition plan, and it will move quickly. I will need to see each of your resumes, and I would like for each of you to highlight any hobbies or areas of interest, especially if you are a fitness enthusiast or a former athlete. That sort of thing."

The engineers looked at one another, bewildered. Most wore loose fitting t-shirts and jeans, and there was not a whole lot of muscle to go around. Feats of athleticism did not seem like a plausible option.

Steve ignored the confusion in the room and turned his energies toward Armstrong.

"You seriously fired him? Just for that?"

"Just for that?" Armstrong fired back. "Steven, he was insubordinate and unprofessional. I won't let anything stand in the way of this deal, certainly not someone as easily replaceable as Mister Coleman."

"Replaceable? He's the only one who could do all the stuff you wanted him to do. Without Rob, we'd already be out of this thing," Steve said.

"I hardly think that's true, Steven."

"You wanted him to lose!" Steve had risen from the chair, and now stood opposite Armstrong. "Those guys at The Bank, they love Rob, because he was insubordinate. Remember all that talk about honesty, Neal?"

"Neal?" Armstrong said, glaring at Steve. "Who's being insubordinate now? Let's not get too big for our britches there, Steven."

"You can't fire him," Steve said. "I'll grant you, he might be a jerk and he can be extremely difficult sometimes, but he is our leader."

Steve looked around the room at the team of engineers, prodding, cajoling any of them to jump in and support his contention. One guy, with a scraggly beard and a Yoda t-shirt, half-heartedly agreed.

"He does keep us on track," the guy said.

Armstrong ignored him. "I'm your leader, and you'd be wise to remember it."

"This is not leadership, Neal."

"My name is 'Mister Armstrong.' Do not cross a line you can't uncross, Steven."

"This is not leadership."

"Where are your loyalties? Don't waste them on someone who has probably already forgotten about you."

A lot of thoughts flashed before Steve's eyes in that moment, pinging him with memories of his time spent with Coleman. He thought about the initial interview when they had met, all the lunches over the years, the road trips, and even the unfortunate visits to Goodies, where he had been Coleman's wingman. He had been a guest in Coleman's home, he had driven his car more often than he would have liked, and he was the one guy Coleman would call whenever he needed to talk.

Steve reached into his pocket and pulled out his phone, as if moved by some unseeable force. He looked down and glanced at the screen. There was a missed call and a voicemail from earlier that morning. They were from Coleman. Steve smiled to himself, a little nod to the cosmic confirmation his friend was sending him, and he looked back to Armstrong.

"No, I don't think he's forgotten me," Steve said. "I don't think he'll forget you either."

Armstrong was taken aback by the unexpected boldness. He liked Steve. Steve was mild. Steve was easily influenced. This was not the Steve he knew. But it was a Steve who had just challenged him in front of a room full of underlings, and it was a Steve who would now need to be taught a lesson. It was a Steve he hoped would land on his feet.

"Congratulations!" Armstrong said. "You get to join him. Quickly gather your personal effects and be gone. Security is on standby, should you wish to dispute matters."

Several of the engineers gasped. The guy in the Yoda shirt leaned forward and threw his arms up in the air.

"What? You can't fire Steve! You guys may have the title, but he's our real leader."

"Congratulations, you get to join him!" Armstrong said.

Armstrong must have warned Security that this outcome was a possibility, because two uniformed guards stood in the hallway, waiting for instructions. The room went completely silent as Steve and the Yoda guy angrily filed out. The Yoda guy turned back and yelled toward the phone.

"He just fired us, Vijay!"

There was no response.

Armstrong watched them go, then turned back to the others. "Anyone else?"

The remaining engineers once again buried their noses in their gadgets and tried to avoid eye contact with anyone in the room.

"Vijay?" Armstrong prodded.

Silence.

"Anyone else have an opinion?" he said to the phone and the room, offering one final opportunity to get pink-slipped.

The silence was even more silent.

"Good. Now, I have a very serious question..." Armstrong looked around the room.

"Can any of you run?"

CHAPTER 36

Coleman drove. He took the long route – a very long route. Along the way, he stopped at a drive-in pharmacy to fill his prescription and gobbled four of the pills there in the parking lot. Thirty minutes later, still driving around, he felt no better.

It was dusk when he pulled up to the gate at Silver Creek. The rain had stopped finally, and the last remnants of raindrops squeaked away in streaks from his windshield, beneath the blades of the rubber wipers. A small stream of rainwater runoff slowly wound down the road's shoulder, passing beneath the gate, before feeding into the lower basin of the waterfall at the neighborhood entrance. His headlights created little rainbows at the periphery as they shined against the moving water.

Coleman reached out through the open window and entered his number. The gates opened, a promising development. At least she hadn't changed their private security code, he thought.

He drove slowly through the neighborhood and made his way into their driveway. He parked in his usual place and sat there for a few moments, rehearsing what he thought he might say. It was little use. The words kept escaping him and his mind wandered all over the place, to the pond, the office, the hotel room, the doctor, to his aching, pounding, pulsating foot. He glanced in the rearview mirror. The lady wasn't there, and neither was her rotten dog.

Coleman opened the door and climbed out of the car.

Straightening his suit the best he could, he limped along the sidewalk. He had removed his blood-stained shirt and now wore his suit jacket over a white v-neck undershirt. His hair was still slicked back tight against his head from the earlier rain showers. The tape over his nose had curled again at the edges and was darker with accumulated dirt from a full day of use, accentuating the bruises beneath his eyes.

Catching a quick reflection of himself in one of the first-floor windows, he thought he looked like a drug dealer in Miami or a mobster in New Jersey – if they had decided to wear only one shoe. He took a deep breath and hobbled up the steps to the front door, where he rang the bell. As he waited, he played with his hands, clasping them first behind his back, then in front, before shoving them deep into his pockets.

Angie peered through one of the thin glass panels framing the door, and pulled back when she saw him. It was a long hesitation, and nothing happened for a while. He was just about to reach for the bell again, when she very slowly opened the door.

She said nothing and just looked him up and down. He couldn't tell if it was a look of amusement or sympathy. Maybe a little of each.

"Very nice," she said at last.

"Hi," he said, softly.

"Hi."

The speech he had semi-prepared escaped him. All he could remember were stanzas from dreadful song lyrics and romantic comedies, so he defaulted to his best alternative.

"Can I come in?"

"No, you may not," she replied, as quickly as he had asked the question.

He nodded, figuring as much, and changed course.

"Can I sit down?"

"Sure."

She watched as he eased his way onto the stoop, and narrowed her eyes as he gently extended his bare left foot and set the heel down on the sidewalk.

"The gout?" She pointed at the foot.

"Yeah," he nodded, "in the other foot. Feels worse this time."

"Good," she said, with little hesitation.

"Will you sit with me?"

"I'll stand," she said, closing the door behind her and moving slowly out to the stone path.

She crossed her arms and stared down at him, a very neutral look on her face. She wore a broken-in pair of jeans and a white peasant top. Her hair was pulled back, no makeup, and her feet were bare, her toenails painted a glossy off-white color that nearly matched her top.

Coleman looked up at her and tried to smile.

"How's Connor?"

"He's fine," she said. "I told him you had a business trip."

He nodded. That made sense. It would buy them some time before he returned to the house, or before a difficult explanation became necessary.

"I have to tell you something," he said.

"I don't want to hear anything about that. Ever."

"No, it's not that. It's something else."

"Something else?"

A light breeze rustled the leaves of the tall oak across the street. Coleman stared past her and watched until the breeze had subsided. When he told her, he was still staring at the tree.

"Angie, I got fired," he said. "This afternoon. Effective immediately."

She didn't respond at first. She followed his eyes to the tree across the street, then looked back at him.

"What does that mean? Why?"

Now he didn't respond. He looked at her directly and pursed his lips. She knew why.

"Did you get a severance?"

Coleman shook his head, no.

"So that's it?" she said. "We have no money."

"Angie, we have money. There's our savings and our investments..."

"I was talking about me and Connor. Not you."

"Oh."

"Unbelievable," she said, now pacing back and forth on bare feet. "Unbelievable!"

"Angie..."

"Boy, when you screw something up, you really screw it up. You leave no stone unturned!"

"Please, Angie..."

"Anything else you need to tell me? Did you rob a bank? Did you kill a man? Are you dealing drugs? You look a drug dealer, you know."

"No, Angie, there's nothing else," he said, his arms open toward her, pleading. "And this is not as bad as it sounds. I'm good at what I do. I can get another job in no time. But we need to work together on this."

"Together? We're not working together on anything."

"Angie, I need a place to stay. Just until I can figure things out and get back on my feet."

"Your feet?"

"Bad choice of words."

Angie paced some more, biting her lip and playing with her ponytail. "Unbelievable," she repeated several times.

Coleman had risen, pushing himself up off the steps with his hands. He tried to approach her, but she took a wide berth around him into the damp grass.

"Come on," he said. "I just need a place to stay for the night and we can figure this out."

"Not a chance." She avoided his reach and leapt up the front steps to the door.

"Where are you going?" he said. "What do we do now?"

Angie turned back at the door.

"I really don't care what you do," she said. "But I have to go work on my resume."

Coleman watched as she slammed the door shut, and he heard her close the locks on the other side.

Across the street, the woman looked on and her little dog barked through the breeze and falling leaves.

CHAPTER 37

The room had been cleared out and the three executives were high above the floor, supporting themselves on tiny colored grips and footholds.

The lofted space had been hollowed out to erect the climbing wall, and the faux rock façade stood three stories tall and stretched along two of the room's four sides. The angular wall jutted out in places, then receded, simulating the uneven rock faces and categorical ascents known intimately to outdoorsmen and experienced rock climbers. Gymnasium lights dangled from girders on the ceiling and cast a yellowish hue over the wall that harkened dusk and canyon sunsets. Red support ropes were attached to the top of the wall and stretched vertically to the ground, where they were coiled like snakes on the blue cushioned floor below.

The men on the wall did not use the ropes.

For anyone else at The Bank, it was necessary to wear a protective harness that attached to the support ropes. It was a legal requirement covered by no fewer than three paragraphs of the waiver they had to sign, and nobody had ever complained. This was quite a perk, the rock-climbing wall.

For the executives, however, it was another leg of their never-ending competition, and the support ropes only detracted from their contest to determine the most extreme sportsman.

They wore little rock-climbing shoes, the synthetic fabric clinging to their feet like socks, and cautiously placed their thin rubber soles atop red, yellow, blue, and green urethane knobs affixed to the wall. Their bare hands clung to the crimps, incuts, and pinches that were spread out along the façade in sections, separated by degrees of difficulty. Naturally, they had chosen the most difficult path.

The President was perched slightly above his two companions. The Italian and the Swede were about even on the climb upward and gave a wide berth to either side, so that the three men formed a spearhead. They wore matching black tanktops and short red shorts that clung to their thighs and highlighted the outline and strain of each muscle. Despite their experience, they moved slowly. Without helmets, without ropes, they each made sure that the next step would be firm, secure, and not lead them into a careening fall to the floor below.

Little beads of sweat glistened from the top of the President's forehead as he reached out for a blue grip and shifted his weight to accommodate the change in position. His shoulder pulsated and his bicep flexed as he moved a leg and placed a foot on a yellow protrusion, not releasing the tension from his arm until he was certain that the leg had enough support. He breathed lightly and deliberately, almost mechanically, controlling each inhalation and exhalation to match the movements of his extremities. Through it all, he spoke evenly, his tone never rising to excitement, nor falling into a dispirited state.

"I received an interesting call from Mister Armstrong earlier today."

"Oh?" the Italian said, directing his response upward, as he navigated his left fingers over a green crimp.

"Yes, it seems that they have had a slight change in plans for this weekend's event."

"What change?" the Swede said, flicking his head to move a shock of blonde hair from his eyes, as his hands were occupied, clutching at two grips on the wall.

"It seems that our friend Mister Coleman has been – reassigned – as Mister Armstrong put it, and will not be available to run with us."

"Reassigned?" the Swede said.

"That sounds odd," the Italian added.

"Quite odd," the President said. "And quite unfortunate. I was rather looking forward to getting another crack at Mister Coleman."

"Indeed," the Italian said.

"Agreed," the Swede agreed. "Did he give a reason for Mister Coleman's reassignment?"

"He did not. He apologized profusely and said that they had an urgent and immediate need for Mister Coleman's skill set elsewhere."

"Odd."

"Very odd."

"They already postponed our rematch once," the Italian said.

"And now this," the President agreed.

"We were promised another shot at him," the Swede added. "This hardly seems like a fair outcome."

Following the President's lead, they each pulled themselves up another foot, moving fluidly and nearly in unison. The President was only about five feet from the top of the wall, and his companions hovered on either side of him, level with his ankles.

"Do you get the impression," the Italian said, pausing for a moment and looking up toward his boss, "that Mister Armstrong is not being entirely truthful with us?"

"I do get that impression," the President said. "And I get the impression that we have been dealing in half-truths from Mister Armstrong since the beginning."

"You did indicate your desire for honesty," the Swede said, rising another foot as he pulled himself up and to the right.

"I believe I did," the President said. "Honesty in all things."

"I heard it with my own ears," the Italian said.

The President reached the top and threw his arms over a black piece of piping that helped connect the wall to the girders above. He waited until his cohorts had joined him, and they stood there together, their feet supported by the climbing knobs, while they caught their breath.

The Swede looked down at the sea of blue cushioned flooring below. It was a long way down, and he looked back at his companions and smiled.

"So it's just the three of us for the half?" he said.

"Not exactly," the President replied, turning toward him. "Mister Armstrong indicated that he would be sending a replacement."

"A replacement?" the Italian said. "They have someone else who can keep pace?"

"Highly doubtful," the President said. "But he insisted. He said he felt so bad about the change that he wanted to 'kill two birds with one stone.'"

"What does that mean?" the Italian said.

"Apparently, he intends to send someone who can cover the technical aspects of the project while running alongside of us for 13.1 miles."

"That sounds highly unlikely," the Swede said.

"Very questionable," the Italian concurred. "Who could possibly do that?"

"And why wouldn't he have introduced this person to us in the first place?"

The President shrugged and took his first step down the wall, back the way they had climbed.

The Swede and the Italian frowned at one another as they considered the information, then slowly followed behind their leader.

CHAPTER 38

It was a new hotel, closer to home, and one that many visitors used during their travels to the Research Triangle Park. One of the studio hotel chains, it offered customers two rooms, a bedroom suite and a separate sitting area with a couch, a clean desk, a flat-screen television, and a kitchenette with a small sink, refrigerator, and a microwave oven. The walls were painted a tonal gray with bright white trim, and had been decorated with framed prints of unremarkable wildflowers and wheat fields.

It was supposed to be an upgrade from the economy chains nearer to the airport, but the flat, darker gray carpet still felt cheap and worn, and Coleman wore a pair of socks as he unpacked and limped through the two rooms. The entire space smelled faintly of cigarette smoke, so he had placed the hotel's complimentary bag of popcorn into the microwave, and he breathed deeply as the oven emitted a buttery smell.

After Angie had prevented him from entering the house, he had returned to the office, parked his car right in front of the lobby, and laid on the horn until Security had come to see him. Following a brief and unpleasant conversation, Security had delivered his remaining belongings in a plastic mail bin, which they had placed on the pavement beside his car, and then returned to the office without another word. There wasn't much in the bin – mostly photos, books, and awards – but there had been a few articles of clothing that Coleman kept in his office, along with a pair of running shoes. He had been thankful for these, and he wore them, untied, over a pair of socks from the bin.

With his foot still in pain, it had been a difficult trip to the mall, but he had successfully navigated his way to a discount retailer, where he had supplemented his wardrobe with about $200 worth of underwear, socks, t-shirts, jeans, polos, cotton button-downs, and gym attire. He had then gone to the grocery store for coffee, milk, snacks, two giant bottles of water, and toiletries – razors, shaving cream, toothpaste, a toothbrush, and deodorant. From there, he went through the drive-thru of a fast food joint and ordered a grilled chicken sandwich, fries, and sweet tea, before checking in at the hotel.

He sat on the couch and spread everything out on the coffee table before him – the chicken, the fries, the tea, and the bag of popcorn – and devoured it all. As he scarfed the food down, his eyes wandered over to the desk. Security had confiscated his laptop, and he would need a new one. It was not an expense he wished to incur just yet; they had the desktop computer at home, and he hoped it was only a matter of time before she relented and let him back in. In the meantime, he at least had his smartphone.

Coleman reached into his pocket and pulled it out, setting the phone on the table beside the red box of fries. He hadn't bothered to look at it for a while, and he pressed and swiped at the screen while licking mayonnaise and salt off the fingers of his free hand.

There were two new messages, a text and a voicemail. He checked the text message first.

Steve Wellman: He fired me too. Thanks!!

"Oh, no," Coleman said aloud, dropping the last remnants of his chicken sandwich onto its white wrapper. He picked up the phone in both hands and scrolled to his voicemail.

It was Angie.

"Hey genius, in case you haven't heard, you got Steve fired, too. He came by the house. I think he wanted to fight you, and I don't blame him. You can do whatever you want from now on with your disgusting personal life, but you'd better fix this. Steve deserves better."

And that was the message. Terse, direct, and unsweetened.

Coleman sat there for some time, his head in his hands, and stared at the floor. He thought about calling Steve, but Steve needed time to simmer. He thought about calling Angie, but the tone of her voicemail suggested otherwise. He thought about calling Armstrong, but that didn't seem like a great idea, either. He thought about showing up at Armstrong's house, but that sounded even worse, though the idea and all its possible scenarios did give him one fleeting moment of pleasure.

He finished the meal in silence and crumpled up the trash, placing it into the fast food bag. Then he crumpled the bag and shot it like a basketball into the waste basket beside the desk. He crossed the thin carpet to the bathroom, where he flicked on the overhead lights and the fan and turned on the bath water, as hot as it would go. The bathroom was small and cramped, and he had to shut the door to create enough space for his legs as he sat down atop the toilet seat, still wearing his suit pants.

Steam from the hot water began to fill the small room, and Coleman breathed it in as he gently peeled his socks off. His left foot was a little better. Not great, but the pills had helped and it no longer hurt to the touch. He started out by testing it with just his fingertips, then slowly added his palms and thumbs until he was lightly massaging the joint and big toe. He winced once or twice, but kept going, trying to help the healing process along. When he was done, the foot was red and had swelled some from the pressure, but it felt better and he was able to apply weight to it as he stood.

Steam had begun to cover the mirror, and Coleman wiped it away with one of the coarse white washcloths hanging from the bathroom rack. He wet his face several times with warm water from the sink, and proceeded to slowly peel away the strip of hospital tape from his nose. The skin beneath was rubbed raw and a rectangular outline from the tape remained. He washed his face with soap and softly probed the area with his fingers. His nose felt a little better, too, and the dark bruises beneath his eyes had subsided a bit.

Coleman still looked terrible, but he could feel a slight improvement in his health, and he clung to the hope that things would get better from here.

His mind wandered as he listened to the water filling the tub and he looked himself over in the foggy mirror. As he brainstormed, and hoped, and planned, and pondered different scenarios, the flicker of an idea popped into his head.

It was a crazy idea, akin to something Armstrong might conjure. And, yet, Coleman couldn't shake it.

The idea had some potential.

CHAPTER 39

Rays of bright sunlight poked their way through the tall branches and leaves that provided a canopy over the wooded path. He turned his head to let the light wash over his face, and the warmth filled him with a momentary joy. It was a weird and somewhat exhilarating feeling to be walking around the park in the middle of morning. Everybody else was at work, and Coleman felt like he was getting away with something.

The park was one of the many green spaces that the county had purchased for public use. Developers had salivated at the thought of building condos and mixed-use strip malls on this same property, and supporters had argued that tax revenue from the businesses and new residents would more than compensate for the grinding traffic that was sure to follow. Along with the private enterprise, there were even discussions about constructing a new elementary school on the same site.

Coleman rarely used the park and, while he wasn't keen on extra traffic impacting his daily commute, he hadn't really cared too much at the time about preserving the acreage. As he walked the trail on this cool morning, however, he was gaining a new perspective.

It was quiet, peaceful, and not many others seemed to be playing hooky. He could hear birds chirping in the high branches above, and critters rustling through the woods on either side of him. The dirt path was narrow and worn, punctuated sporadically by gnarled tree roots and smoothed stones. Coleman cautiously stepped around and over the trail's blemishes. He passed an older retired couple and a few stay-at-home moms, and returned their morning pleasantries with a nod, but he seemed to be the lone male from his age group walking the trail.

He wore one of his new long-sleeve athletic shirts, untucked over a pair of matching blue shorts, and his running shoes fit snugly over white ankle socks. He favored his left leg and still applied most of his weight to the heel, but his overall gait had improved and the limp was not nearly as noticeable as the day before. The doctor had said that a normal gout attack might last an average of three to five days, so maybe this was a normal episode.

Normal.

Coleman shook his head. Normalcy was a concept that currently escaped him: in the past 36 hours he had been kicked out of his house, after being caught consorting with a lady of the night; he had suffered his second gout attack, this time in the opposite foot; he had been fired from his job, along with his second in command; he was living quite humbly in an economy hotel; and his wife had punched him in the nose and would probably never speak to him again.

He walked the path, tenderly attempting to add weight to his gouty foot as he went along. It was in no shape to run or jog, even, but the exercise and fresh air made him feel better and helped divert his immediate attention from his many, many problems. He followed the trail as it wound through the forest, then used hanging branches to help pull himself up an incline that leveled off at the top of a hill and opened onto a small grassy clearing.

It was about the size of an average neighborhood cul-de-sac, and Coleman limped his way to the middle of the space. The grass was wet with dew, and smallish tree limbs were scattered about, blown into the clearing by the recent storm. The wood crunched and crackled beneath his footsteps as he made his way nearer to the edge, where the clearing fell off into a gradual slope that led down to a wide, flat basin surrounded by ridges on three sides.

Coleman followed the slope with his eyes. A huge landscape stretched out below him. It was green and flat and sectioned off in large rectangles, defined by white chalk lines. At the open end of the basin stood a row of metal bleachers that looked out over the complex. At intervals along the edges, the unmistakable white nets stretched out from their piping.

They were goals on either end of a network of soccer fields.

"Huh," Coleman said, staring down at the fields, as another idea popped into his head.

When he arrived at the church, he had to wait for 20 minutes. The Reverend was wrapping up a pre-marital counseling session that two eager millenials had tried to squeeze in during their lunch breaks. Coleman used the time to walk the grounds and tried to mentally pace off the dimensions he had seen at the park that morning. The space was smaller, but it was flat, and they didn't need as many fields as the park provided. It would definitely work.

The sun was warmer now and Coleman stopped walking for a minute to raise his face and bask in the glow. He didn't hear the Reverend sneak up behind him.

"Some day, isn't it?"

Coleman opened his eyes, squinting in the sunlight, and turned around when he heard the man's voice. The Reverend looked a lot different from their last meeting. He wore pleated khaki slacks, a pinstripe dress shirt with an open collar, and a blue blazer with gold buttons. He had glossy pennies in his loafers that shined like little balls as they caught the sun's reflection. His smile was wide and he clapped Coleman's shoulder with a wide palm, then did a double-take.

"Robert, you look terrible!" he said. "Is everything okay?"

"Oh, I'm fine, just having a rough week." Coleman returned the Reverend's handshake. "How did your counseling go?"

The Reverend shoved his hands into his pockets, exhaled deeply through his nose, and frowned.

"By the grace of God, perhaps," he said. "Otherwise, there is no way those two will make it."

"Oh," Coleman said, not sure how to respond. "Sorry?"

"Nope, nothing to be sorry about. They just need prayer," the Reverend said. "How about you, Robert? What do you need? How can I help you?"

Coleman didn't immediately answer him. He turned and quietly surveyed the grounds. The Reverend followed Coleman's eyes with his own. The sun was high above the treetops, and he shielded his eyes with one of his meaty palms. As he waited, the Reverend furrowed his brow, puzzled.

"Well," Coleman finally said, "instead of helping me, I was thinking that I might be able to help you."

"Help me?"

Coleman smiled at him and simply nodded.

"Well," the Reverend said. "This is turning out to be a nice day after all."

CHAPTER 40

"I'm having a terrible day, Rob! Why don't you go away and leave me alone?"

Steve Wellman stood in the front doorway of his house and waved his arms about. He was unshaven, and the strawberry facial hair grew up in haphazard patches, leaving his face looking splotchy and unwell. He wore a terrycloth robe of faded red that was tied in a bow at the waist. His white tube socks were scrunched down on his ankles, his feet shoved inside a pair of fuzzy moccasins. His hair was matted and greasy, his teeth were unbrushed, and Coleman thought he smelled like a man lost in the jungle for a week.

"Steve, can I come in? Please?"

"Absolutely not. I don't want your Coleman voodoo anywhere near my home."

Coleman stood on the grass in the middle of Steve's front yard. He had driven straight over after meeting with the Reverend, and his phone call had gone unanswered and unreturned. So he just showed up and found Steve in all his post-layoff splendor.

"Well, if I can't come in, then you come out here," Coleman said.

"No, thanks. I'm staying right here."

"Fine."

"Hang on, I'm gonna get a beer," Steve said, turning back when he was halfway down his front hall. "You want one?"

"I'm okay," Coleman said, watching through the shadows as Steve disappeared, then reappeared holding two green bottles.

"I didn't want one," Coleman said.

"They're both for me."

Coleman nodded. He had been there not too many hours earlier. "Well, just remember to take it easy. You don't want to do anything you might regret."

"What, like get the gout?"

"Yes, among other things."

"The gout!" Steve began to laugh. "I can't believe you got the freaking gout. The 'Rich Man's Disease!'"

Coleman stood there and took it. He nodded along as Steve, wild-eyed, laughed and sneered at Coleman's podiatric misfortunes.

"You don't look like a rich man, buddy!"

"I don't feel like one, either."

"Good! Now you know what it's like for the rest of us."

Steve drained the first bottle and set it on the ground by his feet. He pulled a bottle opener from his robe pocket and popped the top on the second bottle. Coleman shifted back and forth, still favoring the left foot, while Steve took a nice, long tug from the fresh bottle.

"Go easy, Steve."

"Shut up."

"Steve..."

"I stood up for you, Rob. I told that old fool that you were our leader. Our leader! And he took one look at me and gave me my papers."

"Steve, I'm sorry..."

"Canned me. Right there on the spot."

"I can't begin to tell you..."

"Fired me, in front of the whole team."

"Steve..."

"I've never been fired before, Rob. From anything! You know what this feels like?"

"Well, yeah, I do. He fired me first."

"And you deserved it!" Steve said through a mouthful of beer. He pulled the bottle from his lips and pointed it at Coleman. "But I didn't deserve it!"

"No, you definitely didn't deserve it."

Coleman took two steps toward the door and crossed his arms. The house was nice, a green Craftsman style with a wide front porch that stood out from the other homes on Steve's street. The lawn was flat in front, and the Bermuda grass had begun to green in the early spring, covering over the yellowish dead blades left over from winter. On either side of the house, the lawn abruptly sloped downward, descending another level and, from his vantage point, Coleman could see a wooded area fanning out from the backyard.

Another idea popped into his head.

"Hey, do you have a basement?"

"What?" Already irate with Coleman, Steve now looked at him like he was utterly mad.

"Do you have a basement?"

"Yes, I have a basement. What does that have to do with anything?"

"Huh," Coleman said.

They didn't build that many basements in this part of North Carolina. The soil was too porous and tended to shift over time. At best, most homes 10 years or older showed movement and, at worst, they needed a complete foundation overhaul. If a builder did add a basement, it was almost always a walk-out style, buried in the front, and opening to the backyard. Steve had himself a basement. Coleman was impressed.

"Oh, don't tell me you need a place to live," Steve said. "You can't live in my basement, Rob! My house is off limits!"

"No, no, nothing like that," Coleman said. "I just had a thought, that's all."

"Well, keep your thoughts to yourself. Nobody here cares."

Coleman watched as Steve finished off the second bottle of beer. He reached down to collect the first bottle, and placed both into his robe pocket. As he was turning, presumably to get another refill, Coleman hollered at him to stop.

"Steve, wait," he said. "Why don't you go get cleaned up."

"You go get cleaned up!"

"Steve, come on. Let me take you to lunch. Your choice."

Steve stopped in his hallway and walked back to the door.

"My choice?"

"Wherever you want," Coleman said, grimacing as Steve moved closer. "On one condition."

"What's that?"

"You have to shower first."

They sat across from one another in a booth, and each grabbed a slice of the greasy pepperoni pizza from its silver tray. Off in the opposite corner, a bell rang and red lights flashed. Other than the pack of little kids running around, it sounded just like a fire station.

"Of all the places you could have picked, you chose this?"

"What?" Steve said. "I like it here."

Coleman had waited in his car while Steve got ready. Whether by routine or some ingenious passive-aggressive ploy, he had taken a full 30 minutes to clean himself up. When he emerged from the house, Steve wore a pair of jeans, flip-flops, and an old gray t-shirt. Not the most professional attire, but at least he had combed his hair and shaved his face.

For Coleman, the wait was irritating, but it had given him plenty of time to think things through and formalize a plan. He was second-guessing his inclusion of Steve in those plans, however, when they arrived at his preferred lunch venue.

"You're like a 6-year-old," Coleman said, taking a bite of pizza and sipping root beer through a straw from his red plastic cup.

"What? This place is awesome. I bring the family here every week."

Johnnie's Playland was the mini-mart version of an amusement park. Outside, they had walked past batting cages, a miniature golf course, and a go-kart track, and made their way inside of a dressed-up warehouse, where bright lights flashed from all corners, and the bustling sounds of children at play mingled with the jingles and jangles of arcade games and pinball machines. A row of skee-ball ramps lined the wall beside a small pizza parlor, where they had grabbed a booth and ordered the day's special from a young lady with tattoos and a nose ring, who was either home from college on spring break or had dropped out of school altogether.

"I don't know," Coleman said, watching through the glass doors as their waitress stepped outside and lit a cigarette. "Just an interesting place for a business meeting."

"This is a business meeting?"

Coleman looked across the table at Steve and set his slice down on a paper plate.

"This could be a business meeting."

"What do you mean, 'could be?'"

"I've got an idea, Steve. I think it's a good idea, an idea that could actually work, but a lot of it hinges on you. And here's why."

Coleman proceeded, over the next 10 minutes, to lay out his plan in detail. Steve was dispassionate. He merely stared across the table at Coleman, expressionless throughout, and ate his pizza.

The waitress returned at one point, reeking of smoke, and Coleman clammed up until she had walked away. Despite the clientele of preschoolers and their mothers, his eyes darted around the room while he spoke, taking extra care to reveal the plan to Steve and Steve alone.

When he had finished, slapping his palms on the table and completing his pitch with a flourish, he looked at Steve with hope and anticipation.

Steve just chewed his pizza, and it felt like eons before he finally spoke.

"That's gonna take some money," he said, wiping his fingers on a paper napkin. "If you brought me here to ask for money, I'm going to jump across the table, I'm going to beat you down, and then I'm going to tie you up in one of those batting cages outside. I'm going to set the speed to 'fast pitch,' and I'm going to feed the machine $100 in quarters. Then I'm going to stand back and watch."

"I'm not asking you for money."

"Don't ask me for money."

"I'm not. I promise."

"Then what are you asking me for?"

Coleman sipped through his straw, slurping at the bottom of his cup, and reached for the pitcher of root beer.

"Do you think it could work?"

"Maybe. If you had the money to get started."

"Don't worry about the money. I'll take care of that. But if money weren't an issue, do you think it could work?"

"Well, it's risky," Steve said thoughtfully, "but, yeah, it's possible, I suppose."

"I think it could work," Coleman said. "I know it could. I've got it all mapped out. There's just one thing we're missing."

"What's that?" Steve said.

Coleman pushed his pizza and drink off to the side. He glanced around to make sure no one would overhear him, and he leaned across the table.

"We need Vijay," he said.

CHAPTER 41

The starting area swelled with participants.

It was located at the neck of a narrow entry road that wound through the mall parking lot. A huge rectangular banner flapped above them in the breeze. Tied to trees on either side of the road, it marked the starting line and announced a whole host of sponsors for the race. The crowd that had formed beneath the banner stretched back along the road a good way and seemed to shift randomly as the runners individually warmed up. There were varying choices in wardrobe – some sported professional race kits, while others had opted for simple t-shirts and gym shorts – but each runner wore a common white square of paper with red numbers pinned somewhere to their uniform.

Armstrong stood off to the side, in the parking lot, away from the action. He paced behind a row of cars, alternately glancing at the starting line and his wristwatch.

"Come on, come on," he muttered to himself, fidgeting with the phone in his pocket, checking it for messages.

He wore a cream-colored cashmere sweater over his dress shirt to ward off a chill in the morning breeze. It was early, not yet 7:30 am, and the sun was still rising from the east. The glare was strong and bounced off the cars. Armstrong had both hands pressed to his brow, a makeshift visor, as he scanned the parking lot.

Three rows from where he stood, a blue four-door sedan with tags from another state pulled into a parking spot. Armstrong marched toward it, unsure but hopeful. The door swung open and, half-blinded from the shining sun, he could only see a dark shock of hair bouncing above the car roofs. With his back to the sun, the driver had no problem seeing Armstrong, and he yelled out for his attention.

"Neal, there you are! Did I make it?"

The voice was unmistakable – direct, slightly condescending, somewhat accusatory, and distinctly British.

"Vijay!" Armstrong shouted, not wasting any time. "Come on! It's about to start."

Vijay Kumar snaked his way through the cars. Armstrong's eyes went wide and he took a step back when Vijay reached his side. He did not look like the other runners.

Vijay wore a tight tank top of emerald green that clung to his skin and did little to contain the fields of dark chest and underarm hair flowing from his upper body. The shorts were a matching green, and far too short for Armstrong's liking. They showed off his equally hairy upper thighs and barely covered over his buttocks in the rear.

His shoes did not look like running shoes at all. They looked like some European hipster version of casual footwear, made from brown leather, with thin rubber soles and tan stripes that licked the sides. And the socks – the socks! – reminded Armstrong of the white gym socks he had worn nearly four decades earlier. They were tall white tube socks, ringed at the top by three multi-colored stripes, and Vijay had them pulled up all the way to his knees.

"Are you sure you know how to run?" Armstrong said.

Vijay looked insulted.

"Well, of course, I do. I play a great deal of tennis and cricket back home, and I am one of the fittest among my circle. And, quite frankly, Neal, how dare you question my abilities when you've made me fly all this way for such a preposterous and common exercise."

Armstrong looked him over once more, and then motioned toward the starting line.

"Come on," he said. "We don't have time to talk about it. They're waiting for you, and they're itching to go."

Armstrong grabbed Vijay under one arm and began pulling him through the lot. Vijay slapped at Armstrong's hand.

"I am not your child, Neal. I'm perfectly capable of handling this on my own."

"Look, just don't screw it up, okay? Let them take the lead, try to hang with them as best you can, and just don't embarrass us. In fact, why don't you pull your socks down a little?"

"What is wrong with my socks? If anyone should be worried about embarrassment, it is them. I am quite swift of foot."

"Never mind, Vijay, come on."

They made their way through the parking lot and down into the growing sea of runners, some of whom were stretching, shaking their arms out, and jogging in place. Vijay warmed his bare arms with his hands as he followed Armstrong through the crowd.

His eyes were a bit bloodshot, and he reached up to rub them and smooth back his hair. It was a brutally long flight from Bangalore, and Vijay felt dehydrated, stiff, and sort of like he was walking through a hazy daydream. Armstrong had given him no time whatsoever to prepare. When he had heard from the team members that Vijay was a sports enthusiast in his home country, Armstrong had instructed – no, demanded – that he get on the next plane. Armstrong had not even afforded him time to stop and greet friends during the layover in London, and Vijay was perturbed by the chaotic and slipshod manner in which the entire event had been planned. Fortunately, Vijay could recite the specifics behind a network security implementation in his sleep, and he intended to focus on the technological, rather than the athletic, commonalities between them.

"Okay, here they are," Armstrong said. "Now just let them do the talking, and you smile and play along. Understood?"

Vijay raised a brow at him. Armstrong closed his eyes for a moment, as if he was saying a quick prayer, and turned to greet the three men.

Like Vijay, they stood out from the rest of the runners bunched up toward the front of the crowd. They wore matching outfits, strange full-body suits of lycra that covered nearly every inch of skin on their bodies. The black suits were fastened to their feet with stirrups, and reached all the way to their wrists, leaving only their hands exposed. The suits featured hoods that covered their heads, and Vijay could only see their faces from the forehead down to the chin. They wore wrap-around razor-style sunglasses, and large neon yellow watches on their wrists. Their micro-fiber shoes matched the yellow watches and looked like they weighed next to nothing. Other than their body types, the three men were nearly indistinguishable, and the only way Armstrong and Vijay could tell them apart was from the race bibs pinned to their chests.

The President wore the number "1," the Italian "2," and the Swede, whose blonde hair peeked out of the hood just around the sides, wore number "3."

"Mister Kumar!" the President said, extending his hand. "What a pleasant surprise."

As Vijay shook hands with the others, they looked at him with as much bewilderment as he was channeling right back toward them.

"I told you we'd have a ringer for you," Armstrong laughed, as he greeted the men with another round of handshakes.

"I did not know you were a runner, Mister Kumar," the President said.

"Well, it's something I do not normally discuss," Vijay said, glancing over at Armstrong. "What I would like to discuss, however, is a small piece of your internal wireless architecture that I think will prove critical to the overall security deployment. You see, your border protection may be compromised without an identity tracker program in place, and..."

"RUNNERS TO YOUR MARK!"

A loud voice rang out through a megaphone and, all at once, the crowd of runners surged forward to the starting line.

The Bank executives turned away from Vijay and went with the flow of the crowd, sidestepping and angling their way toward the front of the pack.

"It's about to start," the Italian called behind him. "Follow us!"

Armstrong held his ground for a moment and grabbed Vijay by both shoulders.

"Just don't screw this up!" he shouted above the din of clomping feet. "Now, go!"

With a shove in the back, Armstrong sent Vijay careening forward in pursuit of the three men, who had swiftly navigated the crowd and stood at the ready, each fiddling with their watches as they awaited the starter's gun.

Vijay looked back, but he had lost sight of Armstrong. Turning forward, he had to jostle and elbow his way to the little space they had created, and he fell in between them.

"Gentlemen, as I was saying," Vijay continued his previous thought, "an identity tracker deployment that spans the breadth of your physical buildings and bank branches will prevent interlopers from surreptitiously gaining access to your private tunnels and, therefore, accessing your private data..."

"It's about to start!" the Swede said, his adrenalin for the race pouring forth in a vitriolic sneer, as his eyes warned Vijay to keep quiet.

Vijay returned the Swede's look with one of amused superiority, as if his child had just instructed him to mow the lawn.

"Why, I wasn't quite through, and this is something that you gentlemen quite certainly need to hear..."

"There is a time and place for it, Mister Kumar," the President said briskly.

"And this isn't it!" the Italian added.

"Excuse me, gentlemen, but I flew a long way to meet with you at Mister Armstrong's behest, and I expect the same courtesy extended as I would, of course, extend to you..."

"RUNNERS SET!"

To a person, every runner entered in the half-marathon simultaneously leaned forward in a finely choreographed starting crouch.

All except for Vijay.

He stood there looking around, still attempting to opine on the issues of his choosing. When the gun went off, he was nearly trampled in the opening stampede.

The crowd flowed forward, a gentle trot at first, as they each tried to create their own space. The pace quickly increased to a healthy canter, and then a muscular gallop. Vijay got turned around in the onslaught, and he lost track of his group. Alarmed and slightly panicked by their disappearance, he took off in a dead sprint.

Vijay was a squirrelly runner. He took short, staccato steps, yet thrust his knees high, so that his stride looked more like that of a drum major in the marching band than that of a marathon runner. He held his arms akimbo, with elbows out, and his hands pressed tight to his hips. His style drew the astonished looks of his fellow competitors, and their lull in cadence helped him sweep forward.

By the time he had reached them, Vijay was breathing heavily and beginning to show signs of fatigue.

"Gentlemen," he said, his chest heaving, "I was not quite through."

They ran in formation, shoulder to shoulder, with the President just a step ahead of the other two. Their strides were long and controlled, fluid and economic, devouring large stretches of pavement with very little impact to their feet, ankles, or shins. The Swede, who ran closest to Vijay, flashed his fiery look again, imploring him to stop.

Vijay ignored him.

"Imagine a scenario where one of your competitors, or a common bank thief, for that matter, walked into your headquarters with only his laptop and tremendous guile."

Every word became more difficult as they ran. Vijay had finally begun pumping his arms in order to keep up.

"This criminal mastermind sits down in your lobby, opens his computer and, with little more than a keystroke, is able to join your guest wireless network," Vijay said, now pantomiming with his arms, typing in mid-air, to punctuate his point. "Before you know it, he has hacked into your password database, he is crawling around inside your VPN, and he soon has access to the numbers and personal information attached to all of your customer accounts. Now, that sounds like something you wish to prevent, does it not?"

"Mister Kumar," the President said wispily, trying to control his breathing.

"Yes?" Vijay said, exhausted and now struggling to maintain pace.

"SHUT UP."

The edge in the President's voice caught Vijay by surprise and momentarily made him pause. This was all the opening that the men needed. They took off in a thunder of pounding feet, leaving Vijay to struggle behind them. For three or four grinding steps, he tried to catch up but they were long gone, and he slowed as he watched them go.

Other runners raced by, jostling him as they passed. Vijay held his arms up against his head, like a boxer in a protective clinch, and came to a complete stop. When the last runner in the race had blown by him, Vijay looked around.

He had made it about a quarter-mile.

Looking back toward the starting line, he could faintly see Armstrong in the distance. Vijay couldn't tell for sure, but he appeared to be waving his arms and jumping up and down.

Vijay took his time walking back and, by the time he crossed under the banner marking the start, his breathing had returned to normal. The area was as empty and quiet as it had been crowded and bustling just minutes earlier. All that was needed were a few stray bales of hay rolling past and it would have resembled a Western ghost town. Armstrong awaited him, red-faced and coiled tight like a cobra, but Vijay either didn't notice or didn't care.

"Those men need a lesson in courtesy," Vijay said. "I have never been met with such rudeness in all my life. To travel all this way, and then to have my ideas ignored? Well, I shall tell you, Neal, that I do not care a whit for these gentlemen and they are more than welcome to develop their own security measures!"

Armstrong pounced.

"You arrogant donkey!" he yelled, grabbing Vijay by the tank top. Their noses were only centimeters apart.

"Take your hands off of me, Neal!" Vijay slapped at Armstrong's hands until he was free of the grip.

"What did you do? What did you just do?"

"Those men told me to shut up, and I refuse to be spoken to in that manner! You may find yourself another stalking horse, Neal, for I am through with this nonsensical strategy."

Vijay stepped wide and went around Armstrong, making his way back toward the parking lot and his rental car.

Armstrong had his palms pressed flat on the top of his head, and he had lost the color from his face. His mind was churning, and he no longer looked so ferocious.

"Vijay, wait!" he called after him. "We need you. Let's talk about this!"

Vijay turned back and stared for a moment before speaking. Armstrong looked feeble, defeated. He looked scared. Vijay measured his words as they looked at one another and, when he finally did speak, he twisted the knife.

"You don't need me for this," he said. "You need Rob Coleman."

CHAPTER 42

Steve agreed to hold the meeting in his basement on one condition – Coleman couldn't be anywhere near his wife. This was for Coleman's own protection.

Apparently, Mrs. Wellman was a mildly serious to almost guaranteed threat of violence if Coleman was foolish enough to show his face again. She had heard from Steve about the prior visit and their pizza lunch and she had told her husband, in no uncertain terms, that he was not to consort with such an individual. She also made it known that Coleman would be missing a particular and quite important part of his anatomy if she should happen to run into him.

To prevent the encounter, Steve had sent her out on a mani-pedi spa day, followed by lunch with her girlfriends, where they would, no doubt, hear all about how he had lost his job and now bummed around the house in his bathrobe. He groaned aloud at the thought, then groaned again when Coleman rapped on the basement door.

"Is it clear?" Peering through the door's pane glass windows, Coleman mouthed the words, so as not to disturb the viper upstairs, should she still be at home.

Steve nodded and slowly pulled the door open from the inside.

Coleman looked him up and down. Steve had showered and shaved again and, thankfully, he had dispensed with the robe. He was dressed down, in a pair of jeans and boat shoes, but it was a solid improvement from before.

As Coleman stepped inside, Steve greeted him with his arm extended, palm upturned. Coleman stared at it for a moment, then fished out his wallet and handed over five crisp $20 bills.

"Will that cover it?"

"That should keep you alive for the afternoon," Steve said, accepting the payment for Mrs. Wellman's outing.

Coleman surveyed his surroundings, and then flashed Steve a questioning look, with a dash of disappointment.

"What?" Steve said, responding with his own look of disgust. "I was gonna use my bonus money to finish it off, but I guess that won't be happening now, will it?"

The basement was not only unfinished, it seemed to celebrate its spartan décor. Three bright bulbs, hanging naked from their ceiling receptacles, lit the broad space and cast shadows toward the corners, where little mounds of dust and rock had accumulated. The floor was hard concrete, gray and cold, and the Wellmans had made no effort to provide temporary carpeting or cover, so any noise seemed to bounce from the ground and echo throughout the basement. The walls were tall and had 2x4 wood studs spaced 16 inches apart across each surface, some of the prep work for the future renovations already complete.

Steve had indiscriminately dragged some old furniture into a makeshift conference area. It was presumably the furniture that Mrs. Wellman had banished from the upper floors, as most of it featured rips in the fabric, interesting stains of some sort, and what appeared to be dog scratches on the legs. A two-person loveseat in a color best described as "once was white" faced two matching reclining chairs with a paisley print. A brown beanbag chair sat at another end, and an ocean blue drum kit, without the cymbals, completed the rectangle. In the center of the space, serving as the conference table, Steve had overturned four empty paint buckets and pushed them together.

"Could be worse," Coleman said, patting Steve on the shoulder and opting for one of the chairs, though he sat on the edge and declined to recline.

"Here they come," Steve said. "Look alive...and try not to say anything stupid. They're not real thrilled with you, either."

Coleman nodded and shifted in the chair. Steve went to the open door and greeted them with a wave.

"Hey guys, you find it okay?"

"Steve!"

"Steve-O!"

"What's up, buddy?"

The greetings and cheers went up as the team traipsed together down the hill and arrived at the basement door. It was a weekend, so their attire was even more casual than normal. There were plenty of flip-flops, t-shirts of questionable cleanliness, and baggy jeans to go around. One of the engineers, a tall, slim woman with her long hair tied in pigtails, carried two pizzas, and the guy who had worn the Yoda shirt – the same one who had been fired along with Steve – carried a case of domestic beer under his arm.

As they filed through the door, and each of them spotted Coleman, it was like the needle had stopped on the record player. Suspended in animation, there was a pregnant pause, and then they all began yelling.

The Yoda guy, who now wore a brown shirt that just said "WOOKIE" across the chest, pointed at Coleman, but yelled at Steve.

"What the hell, Steve? Get him out of my sight, man!"

"Yeah, what's he doing here?" the woman yelled.

"Dude!"

"Come on!"

The others grumbled, while Steve tried to regain their attention.

Coleman stood and held his hands out apologetically. He had gone with more of a business look, his new creased khakis and a dress shirt, and he stuck out from the group.

"Guys, please, just hear me out," Coleman said.

The guy in the brown shirt waddled over and set the beer down on Steve's paint bucket table. He didn't even bat an eye at the furnishings.

"Do you even know my name, man?"

"Of course," Coleman said, emphatically. "It's...Brian."

"It's Mark!" the guy said.

"Sorry."

"Yeah, right," Mark said, holding out his hand. Coleman misread his body language and reached out to shake the hand.

"Don't touch me, man!"

"I don't understand."

"You owe me $20 for the beer," Mark said, extending his hand again.

"Oh, okay. Sure, why not." Coleman reached for his wallet.

"And $20 for the pizza," the woman added, setting the boxes down beside the beer and extending her hand.

"Okay, yeah, that's fine." Coleman fished out two more $20 bills and handed them over.

"I'm Jennifer, by the way," she said with a sneer.

"Hi, Jennifer."

"Jerk," she said, walking away and rejoining her teammates closer to the door.

Steve closed the door and tried, somewhat unsuccessfully at first, to corral the group and push them toward the furniture. He placed a hand on one engineer's back and grabbed another by the shoulder and gently moved them forward. Reluctantly, they all shuffled over to the meeting area and slowly began to grab seats. There weren't enough for everybody, so two sat on the arms of the loveseat, and two others stood back behind them. Mark tossed out fresh beers to everyone, except for Coleman, and then assumed his position on the stool of the drum kit.

"Okay!" Steve said, cracking open his beer. "Now that the introductions are through, why don't we get down to business?"

"Sounds great, Steve!" Mark said sarcastically, punctuating each word by stepping on the bass drum pedal. The deep thumps reverberated throughout the basement and drew bemused laughter from the others.

"Hey, Rob, why don't you get the ball rolling," Steve said, directing his words to the engineers, rather than Coleman. "And if you want my unsolicited advice, I'd start with an apology."

Coleman complied.

He paced around, recounting everything that had occurred in their pursuit of The Bank deal. He left no detail unmentioned. He lauded the group for their accomplishments and diligence. He praised their technical skill, for which he had little understanding. He explained his relationship with Armstrong. He speculated about Armstrong's motivations. He handed out fresh beers and passed a pizza box around.

Then, he told them his plan. He explained how each of them helped to complete the puzzle. He went through the pros and cons, discussed the challenges and outlined the potential roadblocks. He talked about his role, he talked about Steve's role, and he talked about the changes they could make together if everyone was on board.

He closed with an impassioned plea to maximize their potential, to challenge themselves, to take a risk, to go the extra mile, to throw caution to the wind, to fight the good fight, and to be all that they could be. When he was finished, out of breath and with sweat glistening from his forehead, he slumped down into his chair and exhaled.

There was a lengthy silence, with a lot of looking around at each other, before Mark spoke for the group.

"Dude, you got the gout?"

"Twice?" Jennifer added.

Coleman closed his eyes and sunk deeper into the chair. He simply nodded.

"Well, no wonder you couldn't run the other day, man!"

"Why didn't you tell Armstrong?" Jennifer said.

Coleman squeezed his eyelids tighter, a pained expression written all over his face. Steve noticed and, feeling bad about the derailed speech, attempted to come to Coleman's aid.

"Guys, I think what's important here is that Rob is recovering and now that he's a free agent, he might be able to use the condition to his benefit."

"Our benefit," Coleman said softly.

"Right. Our benefit." Steve drank slowly and looked around at the others. They were drinking, too, and seemed to be lost in thought. Steve hoped they were thinking about Coleman's proposal.

Mark beat on the bass drum in 4/4 time, an easy tapping sound that started softly and then crescendoed into a throbbing thump. All of a sudden, at the height of his jam, he stopped and stood up.

"I mean, I'd be okay with it," he said, moving out from behind the drums to grab another slice from the second pizza box. "But I don't have a gig right now. Living off my severance, Rob!"

Coleman pressed his chin to his chest, avoiding his eye contact. Mark took a bite and turned to the others while he chewed.

"Jenny, you and the other guys still have a good thing going. I don't know if I'd jump over in your case."

"I wouldn't call it a good thing," Jennifer said, playing with the tab on her beer can. "He's given us no direction whatsoever since he sent you guys packing. He only talks to Vijay now. We have no idea what's going on."

"At least you're still getting paid, right?" Mark said.

"I'd rather get the severance," she joked. Her buddies laughed along with her, but it was a nervous laughter and a few of them stole glances at Mark and Steve, wondering how long they could make it on dwindling resources.

Coleman had sat up in his chair, and was looking right at Jennifer, suddenly very interested.

"He's been talking to Vijay? He never talks to Vijay."

"I know it," she said.

"He always went through me to get to Vijay."

"And you always went through me," Steve reminded him.

"Right," Coleman said. "Neither of us had time for Vijay's attitude, but especially not Armstrong."

"Well, he flew him in," Jennifer said.

"For what?" Coleman stood up and crossed his arms.

"I dunno. Like I said, he doesn't talk to us, and we didn't get a chance to see Vijay."

"Tell them what you've been doing since we got canned," Mark said with a grin.

"Tetris tournament," Jennifer said. "I'm winning."

A round of protests went up from the others, and they argued among themselves while Coleman stood there, lost in thought. He caught Steve's eye and silently questioned him. Steve just shrugged.

"So no meetings with Vijay," Coleman clarified. "No updates, no plan of attack now that we're gone."

"Nope," Jennifer said. "Just Tetris."

"Huh." Coleman began pacing around the rectangle. Each of the engineers paid special attention to his feet as he shuffled by, but the limp was no longer noticeable. They seemed somewhat disappointed.

Steve, who had been standing, walked over and sat in Coleman's chair. He popped open another beer, took a long draw and looked over at Mark.

"Hey, tell him what you told me."

"What?" Mark said. "About how we were gonna mess with his car?"

"No, the other thing."

"What about my car?" Coleman said.

"Don't worry about it," Steve waved off the question. "Mark, tell him about the NCA."

Mark set his beer can down on one of the snare drums and straightened his WOOKIE t-shirt. He smiled broadly when he spoke, imbued with a sense of deep pride.

"Guess who never had to sign a non-compete?"

Coleman stopped pacing abruptly. Mark was grinning at him.

"You never had to sign a non-compete agreement?"

"Nope."

"Huh," Coleman said. "You know, neither did I, for some reason. When I joined the team, it was just never mentioned. Did anyone sign one?"

He was met with a bunch of shaking heads.

"You know why, right?" Mark said, his chest now puffed out, enjoying his moment to shine.

Coleman joined the brigade of shaking heads.

"Vijay," Mark whispered.

"Vijay?"

"Vijay. He insisted that nobody on our team ever has to sign an NCA. It was his one stipulation, and the only one he ever really fought for."

"Vijay?" Coleman said again.

"In exchange for his technical expertise," Steve said.

"Our technical expertise," Mark corrected him.

"Right," Steve continued, looking over the whole group. "In exchange for all *their* technical expertise, Vijay insisted that nobody ever had to sign an NCA. Not even you or me, Rob. He knew that our projects could never get off the ground without the technology behind them. He used it as leverage, for a few reasons. There were salary and benefit negotiations, of course, but mainly he used it in the event he wanted to leave..."

"Or was forced to leave," Mark added, jabbing a thumb into his own chest.

"And he extended that to his whole team," Coleman said to himself.

"It's brilliant, isn't it?" Steve said. "He knew they couldn't say no. It's not like they could go out and find another Vijay."

"Vijay," Coleman said.

"Yeah," Steve added. "And your idea, Rob, is dead in the water without Vijay being such a pain the you-know-what."

"Pain in the ass," Mark translated for the group.

Coleman had walked behind the loveseat and had his back to the basement door. His arms were crossed and he surveyed the team, who all seemed brighter now than when they had arrived.

"Vijay," he said aloud again.

"Yep," Steve said. "You really need to thank him the next time you see him."

"Thank me for what?"

The accent was unmistakably British, the tone clipped and direct. The engineers turned to face the door and, all at once, a shout went up.

"Vijay!"

He stood in the doorway, his arms crossed similar to Coleman's, and he smirked at the group, enjoying the attention but not wishing to show that he enjoyed the attention. His socks were still pulled high, his shorts were higher, and he had a race number still pinned to his chest.

Mark, whose idea of fashion was a WOOKIE shirt and tattered jeans, felt compelled to speak for the ensemble.

"Dude, what are you wearing?"

CHAPTER 43

The engineers had all departed at Vijay's request, leaving just Steve and Coleman alone with him. They each sat on one of the paisley recliners, while Vijay stood behind the loveseat, gazing down at them with a look of disdain.

"Steven, this place is disgusting. Why do you not finish this basement? And get rid of this furniture. It is not fit for an animal."

"See?" Coleman said.

"Oh, sorry, I'm not made of money like you guys. Well, sorry, I'm not made of money like you, Vijay. Rob is out of work, too."

"As am I," Vijay said.

"What?" Coleman and Steve said at the same time.

"That man is a lunatic. A hooligan. He does not know his tail from his trunk. I am better off for having departed his company."

Vijay nodded, a self-satisfied smile on his face.

"Wait," Coleman said. "You quit?"

"Indeed I did," Vijay said. "I have never been so insulted in all my life. I catch the first flight out of Bangalore. I travel across the ocean. I am forced to supplicate myself in some asinine demonstration of athleticism. I am asked to bow at the knee of men who have no interest in my solutions or ideas. I am scolded, no, admonished! Upbraided! Rebuked by a man so caught up in his delusions that he thinks he walked on the moon!"

"Vijay, what happened?"

"I quit! I tried to run with them for a few minutes, and they would not listen to me, so I quit running. And then Neal saw fit to yell at me, so I quit the company."

Coleman and Steve laughed aloud, drawing a perplexed look from Vijay, who returned their laughter with two upraised arms.

"What?"

"So, just to be clear, Armstrong flew you all the way from India so that you could run the half-marathon in my place?"

"Yes," Vijay said, now pointing at Coleman. "And what a silly and pointless waste of time. What great statement are you trying to make by running for 13 miles?"

"13.1," Coleman said.

"Ah, you must be referring to the .1 that I completed."

They laughed again, not so much at him this time as with him.

"And while you were running your tenth of a mile," Steve said, "you talked technology with them?"

"I attempted to do so! I was in the process of explaining the integration between an identity tracker and their firewall deployment, and how both were impacted by their wireless architecture, and the necessity for..."

"We've got it, Vijay," Steve said. "But what did they say?"

"They essentially told me to shut my mouth and run! But I will not be spoken to that way. Not by you, Rob, and certainly not by the men who actually need to hear and understand the implications of their security status. I did not even get the chance to tell them how I breached their database of accounts!"

"Whoa," Steve said.

"Yeah, that's a big no-no," Coleman added. "Those guys are there to compete and build relationships. According to Armstrong, they don't even care so much about the technology. They just want to see if they can spend the next three years..."

"And hopefully more," Steve added.

"Right. They want to see if they can spend the next several years with you before they award such a big contract."

"Well it is a model for lunacy. If this is how business is conducted in your country, then I am happy to remain in my own."

"I like the outfit, by the way," Coleman said. "I'm sure that got their attention."

"Do not patronize me, Rob." Vijay looked down at his green tanktop and high socks, and he crossed his arms against his body, suddenly self-conscious.

"Sorry and no offense, Vijay, I just can't believe Armstrong would send you."

"Drastic measures," Steve said.

"Personally, I would have gone with Jennifer," Coleman continued. "She looks like a runner and I have no doubt that she would have kept her mouth shut."

"Perhaps you can pass that information along to Neal," Vijay said, with an edge in his voice. "I believe she is one of the few still employed."

They were quiet for a few moments, each lost in thought, and Vijay had turned his back to them and stared out a basement window at the wooded area just beyond Steve's backyard. The trees were beginning to show green leaves, and squirrels and birds presently used the branches as their playground. It was a soothing view that eased the tension Vijay had built up over the past few days.

"What do you think Armstrong will do next?" The question came from Steve.

Vijay exhaled deeply and relaxed his shoulders, turning back toward them.

"I do not know," he said, "and to be frank, I shan't desire to care."

From upstairs they heard an evenly pitched buzzing sound, like the starting of a lawnmower, and they listened for about 10 seconds until the noise disappeared all at once. Steve jumped up, realizing what it was.

"It's the garage door," he said, running toward the basement steps. "She's back!"

They watched Steve bound up the staircase, three steps at a time. Before he faded from view, he stopped and poked his face into the little corner where the stairs met the main floor.

"If you hear her start to come down, you guys make yourselves scarce. Especially you, Rob!"

Vijay gave him a look to say, "what was that all about?" But Coleman waved him off. He stood and moved back behind the reclining chair, where he leaned forward on his forearms. He had softened, his countenance was easy, less intense, and his eyes showed something like sadness. Vijay looked back at him, skeptical. It was a look he had never seen from Coleman before.

"Hey, Vijay," he said softly, almost humbly, "I owe you an apology. I probably owe you about 10 apologies."

Vijay narrowed his eyes, his first instinct telling him that he was being conned.

"Look, I've been hanging on pretty tight for a long time, and I've never really bothered to understand everything you bring to the table. I get technology a little bit, not as well as Steve does, and I guess I always just assumed that the stuff would work. That there wasn't really much to it. Sell it, install it, and everything runs like clockwork. I knew you were the man and had this sterling reputation throughout the industry, but I never made a point to understand why."

Coleman looked to Vijay to see if any of it was registering yet, but he received no reaction, and so continued.

"Well, the events of the past week have been quite clarifying and I've come to realize that I wasn't the driver behind any of it. That the deal doesn't ever get done without the technology behind it. And not just the technology. Your technology. I haven't given you the respect you deserve, Vijay, and I should have never antagonized you like I did. I feel bad about it, I ask for your forgiveness and, as a show of good faith, I've got an idea that I think will shine a spotlight on your contributions."

Still nothing. Coleman kept on.

"You told me once that you had turned down a bunch of offers to join start-ups, but I could tell that it weighed on you. I could tell that you had an entrepreneurial spirit and that you always wondered 'what if?' Well, Vijay, what if we joined forces? What if we brought the best of both of our skill sets together, and we did this on our own? What if you could hand-select your team? What if you had nobody breathing down your neck? What if you could reap the profits of your own inventions? What if there was no Armstrong to stand in your way?"

Vijay took two steps forward and placed his hands on the back of the loveseat. He looked across the table made of empty paint buckets with a scholarly, focused, inquisitive look. Coleman had his attention.

"What do you propose?" Vijay said.

Coleman told him. He recounted the entire conversation with the engineering team, explained the plan, detailed the strategy, and sprinkled in plenty of flattering asides related to Vijay's expertise and the necessity for his technical genius. Vijay said nothing. He barely even blinked as he took it all in. When Coleman was through, Vijay stepped back from the loveseat and paced back and forth for a bit, his arms crossed and his eyes focused on the ground. Coleman allowed him to think. At last, Vijay stopped and looked up.

"There is the question of the money."

"Yes."

"It will take a handsome sum to get started. Hardware is not inexpensive, Rob, and paychecks do not write themselves."

"Vijay," Coleman said, "don't worry about the money. I've got that covered."

Vijay nodded. "You should know that I refuse to sign a non-compete agreement, Rob. The same goes for every member of my team."

"Granted."

"And, Rob, should we proceed, we proceed as equal partners. Equal in all matters."

"Agreed, but on one condition."

"Yes?"

"Steve is our equal partner as well."

Vijay crossed his arms and narrowed his eyes again.

"We'll need an operational expert, Vijay. Somebody squared away who can keep us on track. Somebody who gets along with everybody on the team. Somebody who can always remain calm and see the bigger picture. Somebody who won't panic at the first sign of trouble."

Vijay didn't think long before replying.

"Agreed," he said.

Just at that moment, after Coleman had extolled his many virtues, Steve came barreling down the basement steps. He was looking back behind him and taking five steps at a time.

"Go, go, go!" he said. "She's coming!"

"What is the meaning of..."

Coleman didn't let him finish. He grabbed Vijay by the arm, and they were out the door.

CHAPTER 44

Coleman was doing something very unusual, far outside of his normal routine at these games, and the other parents watched with a mixture of interest, puzzlement, and more than a little hint of judgment. The rumor mill was already turning – Connor had apparently spilled to some teammates that his Mom had locked his Dad out of the house – and juicy, gossipy nuggets were on the tips of many lips. Coleman's irregular behavior only intensified their cravings.

The game was in progress, a bunch of 6-year-olds buzzing around the field, mostly chasing the ball, and celebrating pretty much any positive development. One curly-haired kid with glasses threw both arms in the air after redirecting a breakaway when he accidentally stumbled in front of the ball's path. A few of the parents on the sidelines cheered along with the kid, but Coleman had barely noticed.

He was on the opposite sideline, alone in one corner, and he was squatting close to the grass. Instead of watching the game, he surveyed the ground, checking its contours and noticing problem spots, specific areas where the kids had worn the natural grass down to bald patches of dirt. While the game was underway, he had very slowly paced off all four sides, walking heel-to-toe just beside the chalk lines. In all his years as a soccer player, from prodigy to All-American to failed professional, he had never really looked at a field in this way before.

Honestly, there wasn't much to it. Four sides, a couple of goals, some flat earth with adequate drainage, and a bunch of healthy sod should do the trick. Still, Coleman thought he could improve upon the rudimentary job done by the county parks and recreation department. But before he devoted his energies to landscape maintenance, he first needed to improve upon the reaction he was receiving from his wife.

Angie had started out among the pack, and then had subtly separated herself from the other parents when it became apparent that Coleman was politicking for town weirdo. Several times she had tried to wave him down, offering up her palms to question his activities, then pointing at the ground beside her in an effort to reel him back to the other side of the field and the perception of normalcy. Coleman had ignored her every entreaty. So, Angie, during a timeout, had raised the ante in the gossip game and crossed the field of play directly toward his location.

Coleman jumped up when he saw her approach. Her balled fists were tucked into her warm-up jacket, and her head was down, though he could tell that she still had her eyes trained on him. She had her hair pulled back in a ponytail that bounced with each step, and her tight gray yoga pants led down to fashionable little running shoes with electric orange laces. She didn't wear makeup, but a light layer of gloss wet her lips, and it was this that he couldn't stop ogling. She looked terrific.

"Hey," he said, hopefully, as she reached his corner.

"What are you doing? You look like an insane person over here, walking back and forth like that. The other parents are about two seconds from calling child services."

"Who cares what they think?" he said, waving them off. Angie looked back across the field and watched them watching her.

"I do," she said. "And so does Connor. He's going to get uninvited from every birthday party on the team."

"Relax," he said. "I'm just looking at the field."

"Why?"

"Don't worry about it. Just something I'm working on."

They turned toward the field as the whistle blew and instinctively took a step back from the chalk lines intersecting in the corner. The goalkeeper for the opposing team manned his cage on a direct line from where they stood, and eyed them with suspicion. Angie smiled at him, but Coleman returned the probing stare. The goalie made an elaborate show of footwork and stretched overenthusiastically in an effort to non-verbally explain to the intruders that this was his space and the goal would not be breached. They ignored him.

"You look really good," Coleman offered, breaking the brief silence. Play continued at the other end of the field, so the goalie was currently preening for his own benefit.

"That's a fine effort, but I think you know better," she said, training her eyes on the game.

Coleman mulled it for a moment, but pushed forward.

"Are we going to talk about it? Can we talk about it? Please?"

"Let me consider it," Angie said, pausing for just a beat. "No."

"Angie, come on..."

"I don't want to know. If I don't know, then I'll have to use my imagination and maybe my imagination won't be as bad as the reality."

"It's not that bad. I mean it."

"I don't want to know."

She kicked at the field with the toe of her shoe and averted her eyes. Play was returning in their direction, and the soccer ball had made it to about midfield. Angie clapped her encouragement, drawing a little sideways glance from the goalkeeper.

"Listen," Coleman said, practically whispering. "Whatever happened in reality, or your imagination, was nothing. It meant nothing. And it won't ever happen again."

She bit at her lower lip as she watched the action unfold. "How am I supposed to believe you?"

"I don't know. Maybe I can prove it to you. I'll try to prove it to you."

"That would take a lot of proof. A lot of proof."

"Well, if it helps, I haven't had a drink since then. And I don't really plan to."

"Good for you."

"And I'm here. I didn't always make it to these."

"I'm sure your son is thrilled."

Their son had gotten behind the defense and made a run at goal. He was three steps beyond the nearest defender and charging hard when the ball sailed through an open gap. He had to redirect his line to catch up with the ball, and the goalie was caught in no-man's-land, forced to choose between waiting for the shot and running out to attack the ball. He chose the aggressive tack, and sprinted forward to greet Connor in mid-stride.

Angie and Coleman braced themselves. It was a head-on collision in the making, and their expressions were those of terrified parents, not anxious spectators. Fortunately, the whistle went up, loud and shrill, cutting through the air, and the opponents both pulled up and peeled off from the ball's line. The teenage referee, mop-topped and overeager, indicated that Connor was offside. Badly offside. The ref reached down to grab the ball, placed it on a spot, and then blew the whistle again. The goalie booted the ball high and far, and it landed back at midfield.

The keeper threw them a little smirk on his way back to the goal. Angie glared at him until they broke eye contact.

"Whew," Coleman said for both of them. "You know, I can teach him how to avoid those situations. In the backyard. At home."

"Are you asking for visitation rights?"

"I'm asking to go back to the way it was."

"That's a big ask."

"I know."

"And the answer is still no," she said. "Besides, it's kind of hard to go back to the way things were when neither of us has a job."

"What if I could change that?"

Coleman didn't get too far in the weeds with the technological or operational challenges, like he had with Steve, Vijay, and the engineers, but he gave her his elevator pitch and laid out the basic structure of the plan. He noted the timelines, he was very candid about their odds of success, and he stressed the importance of her contributions. He didn't try to sell her. He just tried to explain the facts and the implications.

She considered things, but it was a loaded conversation, and she said the first thought that popped into her head.

"That sounds like it will take a lot of money."

Coleman agreed with a nod. "That's why I need your blessing. I also thought that maybe it's something we could do...together."

"Together?"

He nodded again.

They silently watched the game, each lost in their private thoughts. A scrum had broken out, where a dozen boys were bunched up in a crowd, with each trying to kick the ball free. The referee bounced along the fringes of the group, just waiting to blow his whistle.

Angie turned to look at Coleman, and she looked for a long while, as if trying to read his face, to check him for honesty.

The whistle blew, and Coleman clapped.

"I'll think about it," Angie said.

CHAPTER 45

The early service had at last dispersed, the older set taking their time to file out to the parking lot, where they would slowly climb into their large sedans, slowly drive away from the parking lot, and slowly fill up every pancake house within shouting distance. The Reverend was gracious and polite, though he delicately tried to hurry them along. He had spotted his much younger parishioner during the sermon, and he watched him from the corner of his eye as he said farewell to the slowest of the slow, who were now exiting through the red front doors.

Coleman sat alone in a pew about midway down the left side of the aisle. He fiddled with a church bulletin, rolling it into a tight tube, and squinted against the dusty haze that leaked through the stained glass windows. He had tried to blend in, but despite the blue sweater vest and creased khaki pants, he had stood out from the morning crowd, mainly due to his hair being any color other than white or silver. They had more or less attacked him during the neighborly greeting portion of the service, able to sniff out younger blood as if they were vampires. Coleman had done his level best to smile along when the old ladies reached into their purses and produced pictures of their grandkids, and he was beyond grateful when the hymns started up again and everyone went back to their seats.

When the red doors closed and the last of the stragglers were gone, the Reverend came over and joined him. He was beaming as he sat down and draped an arm over the back of the dark wood pew. They were alone in the sanctuary, apart from a few church volunteers scurrying back and forth to prepare the altar for the late service, and Coleman was a little startled at the volume of the Reverend's voice. He was accustomed to whispering in church.

"Where's the rest of the clan?"

"Just me this morning."

The Reverend looked him over, and his smile faded into a sympathetic pursing of the lips. Sneaking something past him was a difficult proposition.

"Anything you'd like to talk about, Robert?"

"Not right now," Coleman said. "I came to give you this."

He lifted the sweater vest and slid his hand beneath it into the breast pocket of his shirt. When his hand reappeared, it held a folded piece of paper, colored a pale blue, which he handed over. The Reverend accepted it and unfolded the paper.

His eyes grew wide.

He looked up at Coleman, who just nodded and returned his astonishment with a little smile.

"Are you certain?" the Reverend said, looking at the paper again.

"Yeah," Coleman said, turning his attention forward. He marveled at the heavy wooden cross that seemed to levitate in mid-air above the altar. The Reverend noticed and followed Coleman's eyes with his own.

"What is it, son?"

Coleman didn't answer immediately, and just stared at the cross, thinking, wondering. The Reverend sensed a moment of confession and didn't think of interrupting.

"How does it stay up there?"

"What do you mean?"

"The cross," Coleman said. "How does it stay up there?"

"Ah, that. It's suspended by very strong metal cords that you can barely see. You have to look closely."

Coleman looked closely, and he could just make them out in the light's reflection.

"Aren't you afraid it will fall on your head?"

The Reverend smiled. "In a word, yes. We have the tension checked and the cords tightened each year to prevent such a catastrophe."

"Interesting," Coleman said.

"I like to think of it as a reminder that life can change at a moment's notice. You could lose a job, you could have a death in the family, you could get cancer, your house could burn down...or you could get impaled by a falling cross inside of a church. You just never know."

Coleman nodded and kept his gaze on the gleaming wood.

"So it does no good to worry," the Reverend said. "All we can do is live our best lives, stay close to the ones we love, and keep our faith in Him. It's pretty simple, really."

"It doesn't seem that simple."

"I know," the Reverend said, "and that's why I still have a job. Are you sure you're okay?"

Coleman thought before responding. The organ pipes gleamed behind the floating cross, and there was a sense of calm and peace that filled the quiet sanctuary.

"I'm not sure," he said. "But I'm working on it."

Angie was on flower detail for the late service, and she slipped through the red doors with a pot under each arm. It was too early for Easter, but not too early for lilies, and she had picked up an assortment of white and pink arrangements from a nearby florist. She set the pots on the floor inside and slipped out to retrieve the others. She had dropped Connor off at Sunday School when they arrived, and she was thankful for the few blissful moments she could be alone with just her thoughts and the flowers.

She took a deep whiff from the second armful she had hauled inside. They smelled sweet and crisp, like the beginnings of spring that they heralded. She set them down beside the other pots and stood up to straighten and stretch her back. To fend off the morning chill, she wore a light black sweater over a long black skirt, not out of mourning, but because black was an easy color to match on short notice, and it always seemed like she was running late on Sunday mornings.

As she looked around the sanctuary, and made mental notes on where to place the arrangements, she spotted the Reverend and nearly kicked over a flowerpot.

He was walking across the altar, pointing up at the cross suspended from the ceiling, and he had one of his large hands on her husband's back.

What in the world?

She watched as they crossed to a door on the opposite side of the sanctuary, at the back of the church, and disappeared. When the door reopened, the Reverend was alone.

Angie went about her business, confused and wondering, and she didn't avoid the Reverend, but she didn't approach him either. He appeared to be in a hurry, and he gave her a beaming smile as he passed by on the way to his inner offices.

She saw him next during the late service. He was in his purple robe, standing behind the pulpit, and he was smoothing out his notes as he prepared to launch into the sermon.

Angie was seated toward the back, off to the side, in a pew by herself. It was mostly younger families at that hour, and she didn't want to field any questions about her status or the whereabouts of her husband and child.

She took the church bulletin from her lap and opened it to see the chosen topic for the day's sermon. Immediately, her shoulders slumped and she crossed her arms as she leaned back against the pew.

Sermon: *Forgiveness & the Art of Letting Go.*

CHAPTER 46

Later that afternoon, after she had changed into jeans and a long-sleeve t-shirt, Angie was interrupted from her computer work by the sound of a muscular engine in the driveway.

She was working on her resume, the first time she had given it a thought since Connor was born. She had found a good template online, and her prior experience in marketing flowed nicely onto the page, but she was having some difficulty trying to convert her responsibilities as a mother into workplace accomplishments. This was wildly frustrating, and she typed out the entries, if only to see their absurdity on the screen:

- o Kept small human being alive for 6+ years and counting.
- o Prepared and/or arranged all meals for approximately 2,000 consecutive days.
- o Cleaned and managed disposal of all human excrement until small human being obtained ability to do so himself.
- o Sacrificed own body (which used to be pretty nice, thank you very much) and most of sanity in pursuit of happy life for small human being.

It was hopeless. She felt defeated from the start, and the rumbling outside was almost a welcome distraction from the futile task before her. Angie got up from the computer and walked barefoot down the hall to the front door.

She peered outside through the window. A silver pickup truck was parked outside, with a bed full of dark mulch. It had backed in and three men were unloading the mulch with shovels into a giant pile on the driveway surface.

"What in the world?" she said aloud.

When the last of the pile had been swept out of the flatbed, the three men hopped down and climbed back into the truck's cabin. She couldn't tell for certain, but one sort of looked like Steve. One of the others wore a t-shirt with a picture of Yoda. And the third, the man behind the wheel, slowly driving the truck out of the driveway and down the street, was unmistakably her husband.

☺

When they returned, Angie was slicing up an apple for Connor, and she was startled when the wheelbarrows rolled into the backyard. She walked over to the kitchen window, the small one over the sink, and pulled back the sheer curtains covering it. Steve and Mark each had a heaping load of mulch piled into a wheelbarrow, and they had proceeded to attack the flowerbeds on either side of the lawn.

She didn't see her husband, but she could hear the sounds of metal on metal coming from the driveway, so she turned from the sink and walked briskly down the hall. She opened the front door and stepped down onto the path leading to the driveway.

Coleman was standing in the back of the silver four-door truck, and he was shoveling more mulch into a third wheelbarrow. He waved when he saw her, and Angie walked toward him.

"What is this?"

"Mulch!" he said, wiping sweat from his forehead with the sleeve of his t-shirt. He propped the shovel's wooden handle against his chest while he wiped his palms on his athletic shorts, then returned to transferring small dark piles of mulch into a bigger pile in the wheelbarrow below.

"I can see that," Angie said, wincing a little at the pungent, earthy odor, "but why?"

"You said you needed some," Coleman said, breathing heavier with each thrust into the pile. He topped off the load and hopped down from the open liftgate onto the driveway. He landed on both feet, and Angie noticed that there was no complaint upon impact and no protest from either foot.

"Well, that's very nice, but I figured you would pay someone to do it."

"I am! Steve and Mark out there are my employees for the day."

"Didn't they get fired, too?"

"Yep, so they were available. Of course, I have to help them at their houses in exchange, but I figured it was a fair trade."

Angie walked along the side of the pickup toward the front. It shined from a fresh wax, and the black tires looked wet and glossy, the polished rims gleaming in the sunlight.

"What's with the truck?" she said.

"You like it?"

"I don't know."

"It's my new ride," Coleman beamed. "Well, 'nused.' I bought it used."

"What happened to the BMW?"

"Sold it. You know, this truck was about a third of the price, and it can do so much more."

"I can see that."

Coleman lifted the handles on his wheelbarrow and took the path toward the front door. He gave her a nod as he brushed past. He was sweaty, dirty from the mulch, and tired from the work, but he looked happy.

"You're just full of surprises," she said, turning to watch as he dumped his pile into a flower bed to the left of the front stoop.

He looked back and grinned.

"Oh, I'm just getting started."

They arrived early the next morning, early enough to wake her, and she jumped out of bed and quickly threw on a bathrobe. The noise was coming from the backyard.

It sounded like a tropical storm. Sheets of water pounded the second-floor windows. Relentless waves crashed against the siding. A sudsy mixture dripped down from the gutters. Underneath it all, the steady rumble of an engine powered the onslaught.

"What in the world?" Angie said, rushing downstairs to the French doors that opened onto the back patio.

Through the windows, she could see them standing on the grass, shoulder to shoulder, staring up toward the roof. The guy named Mark, whose gray shirt dripped water beneath the visage of Darth Vader, held what looked like a long gun in his arms, and he took target practice at the house. Coleman and Steve flanked him on either side, and all three men were giggling.

"Rob?" she shouted above the din, as she opened the doors and ran outside.

He saw her first, and he raised a palm in her direction. She stopped on the patio and looked up to where the gun was shooting. A strong flow of water gushed from Mark's gun and swept across wide stretches of the house, coating the windows and cleansing any dirt from the siding. Coleman reached down and turned off the small red engine, which sat propped up on two wheels.

"Hey!" he said, when the rumbling had ceased.

Angie didn't say anything. She just raised her arms and, with wide eyes, waited for a response.

"We're power washing it!" Coleman said. "The painters come tomorrow."

☺

Later that day, as dusk crept into night, Coleman returned in the silver pickup. This was the surprise he looked forward to most, not so much for the looks on their faces, as for something else he had in mind. He parked in the driveway, turned off the radio, and peeked into the back of the crew cabin.

He had to admit, it was pretty darn cute.

Coleman had specifically chosen this time to deliver the package. After all these years of living across the street, he knew the lady's schedule. For a few minutes, he waited impatiently, tapping his fingertips against the console, and watched through the rearview mirror.

There she was!

The lady had obviously just returned home from work, as evidenced by the tan pantsuit and heels clacking against her sidewalk. The rat dog was with her, not even on a leash, and it was already yipping at something by the oak tree in her yard. She stood there with her arms crossed, not a care in the world, and let the little dog yap.

Coleman's package immediately perked up in the backseat.

"Good girl," he whispered. "Good girl."

It was a fuzzy little bundle of blonde and golden joy and it bounced in the back, sniffing and sensing the dog across the street. A tiny retriever pup, with the soft, shallow breath of new life and paws too big for its little legs, paced back and forth on the seat, yearning to get outside.

Coleman was positively giddy. He could have eaten the dog up, it was so cute, but they would get to that later. First, the pup had a mission.

He connected a red leash to the matching collar, and he gently picked the dog up and lifted her to his lap in the front seat. He pet her behind the ears and nuzzled her wet little nose, cooing and baby-talking the entire time.

Stealthily he opened the truck door and looked across the street. As expected, the lady was snooping, eyeing the truck and looking to see who had just climbed out. Coleman ducked back inside and smiled at the puppy.

"You ready?"

She lifted up on her hind legs and pawed at the air, panting and pleading with him. She was ready.

Coleman lifted her onto the ground, but restrained her with the leash. He glanced both ways to make sure no cars were coming, then looked across the street and loudly cleared his throat.

He got their attention. The neighbor locked eyes with him, and the rat dog yelped. Then, all at once, Coleman dropped the leash and shouted.

"Whoops!"

The puppy was gone in a flash, darting across the street into the neighbor's front yard, a barrel of golden energy with a red leash trailing behind.

She ran straight for the rat dog. Even as a puppy, she was in a superior weight class, and the annoying little mutt across the street let out a terrified warbling sound.

It wasted no time. Turning on its stubby little legs, the rat dog ran as fast it could for the lady's front door.

The neighbor wasn't far behind.

They got through the storm door just as the puppy arrived on the front step, barking and bouncing, pressing its nose against the glass, trying to get to the other dog.

"Sorry about that!" Coleman said, not at all sorry, as he jogged across the street and into her lawn. "I'll get her."

He stole one more look at the rat dog, a look of supreme confidence – a look of victory – before the neighbor slammed the interior door in their faces.

Coleman reached down and picked up the puppy into his arms, cradling and caressing her as he crossed the street back to their house.

"What a good little girl," he said, over and over again.

CHAPTER 47

Armstrong paced in the small terminal as he awaited their arrival. It was a completely unexpected detour – he knew they would be on the East Coast, but not as far south as Raleigh – and their notification to meet that afternoon had been a command, not a request.

The small hub for private aviation was set apart from the two larger commercial terminals at Raleigh-Durham International. Shaped like an arrow that pointed toward the sky, the terminal's elevated two levels were all glass, and light poured through the windows and filled the airy waiting area. The architects had added a nice flourish to the building, an oeuvre dedicated to the aviators who traveled through the area, but Armstrong had a sinking feeling as he looked up and studied the piece. It was an artistic rendering of an airplane wing, slightly angled upward, that jutted out above the front door about midway up the glass facade. It stretched out over the entrance, its smooth underbelly providing a canopy for those deplaning and walking toward the terminal.

Armstrong thought it looked more like a plank, and he was afraid they would make him walk it.

He paced for a few more minutes, checking email on his phone to pass the time, until an attendant crossed the circular lobby to tell him they would be landing momentarily. Armstrong took several deep breaths to steel himself and watched through the first-floor windows as the jet touched down.

It was a Learjet 60XR from Bombardier, top of the line, and its white outer coating gleamed in the reflected sunlight. Its turned-up wingtips were accented red, a color scheme that continued along the sides of the cabin in sleek stripes. The jet barely registered a sound as it landed, far quieter than its larger sister craft on the commercial side. Only a few seconds after touchdown, the Lear was already turning into the general aviation groundspace, its long, conical nose pointing directly toward him.

Armstrong had more than a passing interest in such things, and he briefly forgot the unstated purpose of their visit as he admired the aircraft. His daydream ended abruptly, however, as the plane came to a complete stop and the cabin door opened in two sections, the top lifting in an arc above three steps that unfurled to the ground.

There was a brief pause, and then a man briskly hopped down the steps. He wore creased black pants, a white short-sleeve dress shirt with gold-striped epaulets, a black tie, and a black hat with matching golden wings.

The pilot.

Armstrong took one final breath and greeted the man with a big smile. The smile went unreturned as the pilot opened the door and stepped inside.

"Mister Armstrong?"

"That's me."

"They're ready for you. Follow me, please."

Armstrong thought they would have come inside the terminal, with its conference rooms and clean bathrooms and wireless Internet access. But he did as he was told and followed just behind the pilot. The sun was warm and beat against his bald pate. He stole a glance at the small cabin windows, but they were darkened and he could see nothing. The pilot stood off to the side as they reached the jet and motioned him inside.

Armstrong climbed the steps and ducked down as he entered. The cabin was dark and it took a few seconds for his eyes to adjust. When they did, he looked right into the stern faces of the CEO and the COO.

After all that build-up and the overwhelming air of wealth and success that radiated from a private jet, the cabin was a bit of a disappointment. They always were. Armstrong wasn't surprised – apart from the gadgets and technology, the spartan accoutrements were even worse in the spacecraft he had toured. It was definitely better than the commercial liners but, still, he had hoped for a little more *oomph* from the executive aircraft.

Six individual seats stretched out before him, with a couch and a small bar area situated in the back. The trimmings were a dark wood and the interior walls were clean and cream-colored. Other than the handheld devices mounted beside each seat, there wasn't much more in the way of entertainment. The seats had high backs and movable arms, and they matched the color of the walls.

In the first two rows, the seats faced one other, and this is where they sat, staring him down. The CEO pointed with his index finger for Armstrong to sit across from him. A small table that collapsed into the wall separated them. The COO, who sat in the other row, moved to the edge of his chair and leaned forward to create a little triangle between the three men.

"Thanks for having me out," Armstrong said nervously. "Nice plane."

"It will be a short visit," the CEO said.

"We're on our way to New York, then Washington," the COO added.

"But after the events of this week, we thought we'd better check up on you."

Armstrong looked from the CEO to the COO, then back again. His nervousness changed to confusion.

"I'm sorry, I don't follow," he said.

"We received 37 phone calls from a Kumar Vijay."

"Vijay Kumar?" Armstrong said.

"Vijay Kumar," the CEO corrected himself. "We received 37 calls, with 37 different messages attached to them, Neal, each one more detailed than the last."

"He refused to stop calling unless someone spoke to him," the COO said. "Of course, we were far too busy, so we had our assistant field his calls and jot down his messages."

"Neal, we need to know if you're in control of things here."

The CEO had leaned forward and looked Armstrong directly in the eye. Armstrong instinctively leaned back in his seat.

"Well, yes. Of course! Everything is perfectly under control. We just had a difference of opinion. A personality clash, really, and we had to release him. It sounds like he was lashing out."

"A personality clash?" the COO said.

"Yes, big time," Armstrong said. "They didn't like him at all. The Bank, I mean. Five minutes with Vijay, and they were running away from him. Literally, running away."

"And you deemed it necessary to fire him?"

"Yes!" Armstrong said, a bit too forcefully. "I mean, yes." He lowered his voice and leaned forward, placing his palms atop the table that separated him from the CEO.

"Look, gentlemen, this deal is too important. We can't have any impediments like this. I was doing what was right for the company."

The executives paused. This was one of their corporate mantras, and Armstrong had just thrown it back at them. Their tone softened and became more businesslike.

"He can be replaced?" the CEO said.

"Absolutely. The design is already done. We own that. We'll bring in a new technical lead once we have the contracts in hand."

"In one of his many messages, he claimed that nobody can do what he does. That he is the only engineer in the industry who understands the security technologies he is building."

"Vijay Kumar has delusions of grandeur," Armstrong said.

"And then, in another message, he threatened to use it against us," the COO said. "He mentioned that he never signed a non-compete."

"Is this going to be a problem, Neal?" The CEO had leaned almost all the way across the table.

"No! Definitely not. It's a common practice with engineers. Look, the guy can barely hold a normal conversation with other human beings. It's not like he's going to up and start his own company from scratch. He doesn't have the skill set."

"And if he joins up with a competitor?" the COO said.

"Won't happen. I've already laid that groundwork with a few well-placed calls of my own. In the interests of plausible deniability, I won't tell you what I said, but rest assured that he is persona non grata. Nobody in the industry will touch him."

"Good," the CEO said, leaning back and looking over at his COO. "Good."

The COO nodded, but asked for verification. "You're sure of all this, Neal?"

"Absolutely. Without question."

"We don't have to tell you what's at stake, do we?" the CEO said.

"No, sir, you do not." Armstrong clenched his jaw and tried to stifle a nervous gulp.

"Good," the CEO said. "Because, Neal?"

"Yes, sir?"

"You do whatever it takes to close this deal."

"Whatever it takes," the COO said.

Armstrong paused before speaking and looked them in the eye, starting with the COO and concluding with the big boss. He was confident now, having weathered the storm, and he allowed a hint of bluster into his reply.

"It's in the bag," he said.

"Good," the CEO said, returning the bluster. "Because if it's not, guess who else will be persona non grata?"

CHAPTER 48

During the final three missions of the Apollo Space Program in 1971 and 1972, the astronauts had hauled with them a Lunar Roving Vehicle, more commonly known as the "moon buggy." The battery-powered rovers were capable of transporting one or two NASA spacemen over distances of five or fewer miles in the moon's low-gravity atmosphere. With four tires and an elongated body, the rovers bounced along the moon's surface, kicking up lunar dust as they went. One of the many great, but unsung, achievements of NASA's early years, the three LRVs used on the Apollo 15, 16, and 17 missions remain on the moon today.

Armstrong would have rather been there with them.

He would have rather been anywhere other than his current location, which was bouncing along a muddy, wooded trail in a far more raucous fashion than the moon buggy had ever known.

He bounced on two tires, not four, and unlike the rovers, he had no batteries to power him – only his legs, his ambition, and utter fear. Armstrong wondered if the astronauts had been afraid when they first fired up their moon buggies, if they worried about flipping over, losing control of their steering, crashing into a canyon, or floating away into space.

He feared all of the above.

The entirety of the engineering team had staged a walk-out the day before. Armstrong had earlier had his eye on Jennifer, the tall, lithe woman on Vijay's team – she looked like an athlete and he had planned to threaten her with her job in order to join this latest foray into athletic adventure. When he summoned her, however, his entreaties had gone unreturned, and when he went to the bullpen area where the engineers worked, he found the open space of gadgetry, toys, and office debris completely clean and completely empty. The only remaining trace of their existence was a brief message written on a whiteboard in big black block letters, that simply stated:

WE OUT.

And, thus, Armstrong found himself that morning on a mountain bike, careening down a wooded hill, barely maintaining control of his rattling handlebars.

His teeth chattered as he bounced along the uneven terrain of knotty tree roots, hidden rocks, and hardened mud. His surgically-replaced hip screamed at the shock and trauma felt by each rotation of the tires. His eyes watered and he held each breath tight in his chest, afraid he would lose his balance if he let it go.

They had been mildly surprised when Armstrong showed up solo, with a specialty mountain bike racked to the back of his Benz. The bike was obviously brand new, and the outfit he sported clearly selected by a salesman at the bike shop. Long stretchy shorts, charcoal gray, with matching socks pulled high up to his knees. A red long-sleeve, sweat-wicking shirt, and a funky acid green helmet that matched the color of his bike. His shoes were white, each with three velcro straps, and they looked more equipped to handle Mount Everest than an everyday bike trail. He had fumbled at first, unracking his bike and getting it set for the day's event, and he was a little surprised when they made no effort whatsoever to help him.

He was more surprised, though, by their line of questioning. In the previous events with Coleman and Vijay, they had never once expressed an interest in talking business. Today, that's all they wanted to discuss.

Armstrong was forced to field questions about Vijay, about the architecture, about security specifications, about service-level agreements, about data-sharing portals, and insurance against loss of proprietary information. He was quite pleased with his own handling of the conversation – he could deflect and redirect with the best of them – but he could sense that their collective mood had changed. The pleasantries were missing, the camaraderie gone. They treated him like just another vendor, and they spared no feelings when they started down the trail.

It was located across from their headquarters, a mountain bike course that wound through the tall trees, up and down hills, through rushing streams and, in some places, over rocky jumps. For the Bankers, this was part of a weekly routine, and they knew every nook, every cranny, every hollow, every gap.

Armstrong knew none of it, and he lagged far behind.

He lost sight of them almost immediately, and he felt himself involuntarily yelling for them to hold up and show him the path. They either didn't hear or flat-out ignored him.

He carried on, trying to pedal hard enough to maintain some sort of shouting distance between them, yet taking it slow enough to stay on the narrow trail. He kept his eyes forward, on the lookout for sharp turns and hidden obstacles.

His lack of cardio training did him no favors, as he struggled up a hill, pushing hard against the pedals, his thighs burning with every thrust. As he crested the top, he could see the trail falling off before him. It carved the hill straight down to a small valley that cut across a moving stream. Exhausted from the climb, he let himself fall forward, picking up speed as he rolled down the hill.

The path was narrow, and he ducked beneath branches poking out over the trail, his helmet scraping against the wood. He could feel mud kicking up from the tires, splattering against his exposed skin. Each revolution hurtled him faster down the hill, the bike's shock absorbers bouncing like pogos over the rocky ground.

He was moving fast – too fast – when he reached the dip in the landscape, caught between control and reckless abandon as he approached the stream.

He could see water gurgling over rocks in the bed, and he guessed that the depth was sufficient to allow passage without launching airborne above the flow. He braced himself, crouching down against the handlebars, pressing his feet into their pedals and setting his jaw against the coming blows.

He guessed wrong.

The stream was deeper than expected.

His front tire dipped into the water and immediately submerged. The back tire was still rolling forward, but the front had stopped, and the motion served as an undesired brake.

With the physics of space and time pushing him forward, Armstrong flipped over the handlebars.

His feet landed first, one plunged deep into the water, and the other smashed hard against the top of a jutting rock.

The cracking sound was loud and unambiguous.

Even the Bankers, far ahead and moving fast, could hear the shriek that followed next, piercing the morning air and resounding through the wooded trail.

CHAPTER 49

He parked the truck in the driveway and looked across the street as he climbed out. No sign of the neighbor or her little dog. Just as he suspected, they had been exploring the joys of their own backyard ever since the arrival of the new Alpha on the block. He grinned a deep and satisfied grin, and then double-timed it up the walk to the front door.

He had returned to his normal business casual attire, creased khakis and a blue button-down with sleeves rolled up, and there was an ease and comfort about him as he waited on the porch. She noticed it through the window before she even opened the door.

"It's a little early, no?"

She wore her morning uniform – the college sweatshirt, yoga pants and running shoes she threw on before getting Connor off to school – and she self-consciously hid beneath her crossed arms after pulling the door wide.

"Good morning, Mrs. Coleman."

She hesitated and questioned him with her eyes. "Good morning," she said deliberately. "What's going on? Is everything okay?"

"Everything is wonderful. I came to give you this."

Coleman reached into his back pocket and produced a white business envelope. It was thin and sealed and professionally addressed with block letters. He had foregone the stamp in favor of delivery by hand.

"What now?" she said, sounding exasperated. "Look, I got the flowers. All the flowers. I appreciate the gesture. But you can stop now. I get the point."

Coleman pulled the envelope back. "Is it working?" he said hopefully.

"I'm not sure yet."

"Yet?" he said, more hope bubbling to the surface. He pursed his lips to fight back a smile.

She narrowed her eyes.

"Good enough," Coleman said, reading the signs. "But that's not why I'm here. This is something else entirely."

"Something else?"

"This is a business trip."

She stepped back and eyed him coolly.

"I haven't said yes to that," she reminded him.

"I know. But it's not that either."

"Then what is it?"

They could hear the little yapper across the street, even from its own backyard. The shrill and horrible sound carried up and over the roof and beyond the home's sides, reaching their front door in distant yelps. The sound was faint, but it was more than enough, particularly for a canine of such fine stock as the exquisite golden retriever puppy that came barreling down the hallway. Coleman caught the pup before she could hit the front lawn, and he picked her up and held her close to his chest. She whined and whimpered and laid her big paws on him, desperate to get after her nemesis across the street.

"Hey, what did you name her?"

"Neal Armstrong," Angie said, not skipping a beat.

"Very funny."

She actually smiled at her own joke and, for just the flicker of a second, they almost shared a moment.

"No," she said, reverting to form. "We talked about it, but we weren't coming up with anything good, so we went with something we already liked."

"And?"

"Say hello to Molly."

"Hello, Molly girl. Sweet Molly girl." Coleman talked like a baby and cooed in the pup's ear. "Wait, isn't that..."

Angie nodded. "Second place when we were discussing names for girls."

"So first place is still available?"

She nodded.

"Does that mean..."

She cut him off. "It means that I'm not sure yet."

"Good enough," Coleman said.

He set Molly down inside the hallway and patted her rump to send her on her way back to the kitchen. As he stepped back, he extended the envelope.

"So what is it?" she said, accepting it.

"I told you, it's business. Just read it. I think you'll like what it has to say."

Coleman turned and practically skipped down the path to his truck. The sun was bright, the birds were chirping, and the air was getting warmer and warmer as spring descended upon them. Unable to contain his enthusiasm, he turned back.

"This is not charity, and this is not me trying to win you back. We need you, Angie. Please think about it."

CHAPTER 50

A few days later, the basement at Steve's house had taken on a completely different appearance. It still looked like a war zone, but some structure was beginning to take shape. Coleman had sprung for all the materials as both a "thank you" for helping out at his house, and also as an "I'm sorry" for getting the poor guy fired. Steve was enjoying the attention. He felt like a tycoon, barking orders and watching his vision gradually become a reality from the fruits of their manual labor.

Sheets of drywall leaned against the wood studs that covered the basement's concrete walls. Sawhorses supported the sheets that would go up next, and the empty paint buckets, which had originally served as their conference table, were now filled with drywall nails. The team members scurried about the basement, helping one another prop a sheet up against the studs, or holding it in place while another teammate handled the nail gun.

The great thing about engineers, Coleman thought, was that they could usually engineer just about anything. A few 2x4's and a little drywall were no great shakes for this team and, by leveraging Mark's construction experience from putting himself through college, the team was able to slap walls up on Steve's basement rather quickly.

Even Vijay was there, though he was taking more of an advisory role, seated far back in a corner in one of the reclining chairs with his laptop balanced on his legs. Every few minutes, he would summon Coleman or Steve, show them something on the screen, and they would inevitably nod their assent.

Despite the absence of a non-compete agreement, they still had to start from scratch and produce new documentation in line with The Bank's Request for Proposal. Vijay was piecing together the architectural plans, diagrams, and specifications, and Steve would later fill in the numbers. It was up to Coleman to deliver the deal.

They had never seen Vijay so eager and upbeat before, and Coleman and Steve privately agreed that their equal partnership had made all the difference. Even though they had no clients, and they currently worked out of Steve's unfinished basement, and The Bank was still a big, big longshot, Vijay felt adequately respected, heard, and compensated for the first time in his career.

The engineers, too, had never been so motivated. The promise of profit-sharing, once there were profits, had given them a seat at the table, a voice for the first time, and their enthusiasm was on display, as they joked and laughed and worked together at something as unrelated to their expertise as a roughed-in basement.

Coleman also sprung for the pizza that arrived just past high noon. Steve's wife had been directing any visitors down the side yard to the basement door, and Coleman paid the delivery guy in cash and sent him on his way. They ate without talking much, hungry from the work, and listened to the strains of the classic rock songs piping through the radio.

Finishing his slice, Coleman wiped his hands off on his jeans, and was the first to grab a hammer and get back to work. Setting a good example, he thought to himself. He had been reading some of those management books that Steve had pushed on him and, instead of mocking Steve like he normally would, he had obliged and taken some of the lessons to heart. The others noticed, and they finished too, quietly cleaning up and getting back to their stations with little chatter.

Despite leaving the windows and the basement door wide open, there was a knock against the framing. The group looked up from their work. When they saw who it was, Steve turned off the radio.

Coleman set down his tools and took a step toward the door. He had shared his plan for both the marketing and the financing of their company with the entire team, and they immediately understood the significance of their visitor and the power she held.

Nobody breathed.

She looked around at each of them, studying the faces of the motley crew, privately questioning her decision one last time, before she turned to Coleman and smiled.

"I'm in," Angie said. "For all of it."

The team had taken to celebrating even the smallest of victories, and this counted as their biggest accomplishment to date.

A loud cheer went up, joined even by Vijay, that crept up the stairway, rose through the ceiling, and awakened Steve's wife just as she had settled in for an afternoon nap.

CHAPTER 51

"Welcoooooome to The Asylum!"

The shaggy-haired DJ waved from his booth and performed a full spin on his heels as the latest vehicle arrived. House music, laced with British acid pop, rang out over the loudspeakers. At least that's what the DJ had said, behind his mud-splattered ski goggles. Coleman had no idea – to him, it all sounded like too much bass and too little melody – and he watched as the throbbing beats sent the young man into calisthenic fits, a herky-jerky fusion of popping, locking, and general spazzing out.

Coleman had backed his truck into an open space, and he sat outside on the open tailgate and let his legs dangle just above the squishy ground. He had purposely timed his arrival to miss the start. His foot felt much better, but it was still a little tender, and he was in no shape to compete with Asylum jockeys of their caliber.

"Goooooooodbye from The Asylum!"

The DJ waved a farewell to a departing car. Coleman watched it go, and then climbed down from his truck, gently placing his brown loafers onto the moist ground. He would have to clean them later, but it would be a small price to pay for a potentially huge return on investment.

He stood and took a few deep breaths, mentally preparing his speech. He had worked on it all week, and ran it past everyone. There was no shortage of feedback, especially from the engineers, and he thought he had done a decent job of keeping the good parts and throwing away the rest. He tucked his dress shirt in tight and smoothed out the crease in his pants.

They were walking toward him.

He had watched their race from afar and, as expected, the President had won again, followed shortly by the Swede and then the Italian. They wore those ridiculous shoes with each toe defined, like the feet of a gorilla, and Coleman stifled a nervous snort as he watched them approach. He reached

227

into the back of his truck, and lifted out three clean beach towels, which he handed out with a smile when they were within arm's length.

"Mister Coleman?" the President said, cautiously accepting a towel. "To what do we owe the privilege?"

"Here you go, guys," Coleman said, passing towels to the other two.

"The race is over," the Italian said, wiping backward on his head so that his hair was slick and pressed down.

"We won," the Swede said.

"You always do," Coleman said.

"Almost always," the President corrected him.

"Right. Almost always."

Normally, recognition like that would have caused Coleman to swell with a healthy amount of pride, but the presentation now rattling through his mind offered an overdose of humility. He clasped his hands in front of him and looked at his feet for just a moment, before raising his eyes to meet their inquisitive stares.

"I owe you an apology," he said. "A big apology."

"An apology for what?" the President said.

"I was fired."

"Fired?" the Italian said.

"Fired," Coleman repeated, "with no severance, no recommendation, and definitely no farewell party."

"Why were you fired?" the Swede said.

"Because of you guys."

"Because of us?"

"Because of The Bank. I was fired because I blew the deal."

There was a brief stoppage in the background music, and the President looked behind him as the DJ called up another techno song on his laptop and began running in place to the beat.

"We don't follow," the President said, turning back. "There was no deal to blow. We are still in the evaluation phase. Nothing has been committed."

"And that's why I'm here," Coleman said, taking a step back until he felt the truck's open tailgate. He slid himself up onto the grooved surface and leaned forward, so that his elbows rested on his knees.

"Look," he said, addressing the President, "the first time we met, you said something that stuck with me, and I haven't been able to shake it since."

"What did I say?"

"You said that we needed more honesty in this world."

The President perked up and placed his hands on his hips. His breathing had slowed from the race, but the rise in his chest was still evident with every word he spoke.

"Honesty in all things. Yes, I remember."

"Well, in addition to an apology, I owe you some honesty," Coleman said. "I didn't miss the half-marathon because of another account, or because I went to India, or because of any fabricated delay."

"Then why did you miss it?" the Italian asked.

Coleman looked him deep in the eye.

"I missed it – and I got fired – because I had the gout."

It was as if the DJ had even heard the admission. Abruptly, the techno music stopped and a very awkward silence lingered over the proceedings. The Swede and the Italian looked at one another and started laughing.

"The gout?" the Italian said. "You got the gout?"

"Yeah," Coleman said, "in both feet."

"Wait, isn't that something that happens to fat and lazy people?" the Swede said, confused.

"The Disease of Kings, right?"

"No, it's more of a condition than a disease. And it can happen to anyone. It can be hereditary. There are a whole host of..." Coleman stopped himself from trying to explain it. "Never mind. The point is, I got the gout..."

"In both feet," the Italian said incredulously.

"Yes, unfortunately in both feet. And I could barely walk. That's why I didn't show for the half-marathon, and that's why Armstrong fired me."

"The gout," the Swede said for confirmation, as if unable to process the information.

"Yes," Coleman said.

They laughed again, a sputtering little laugh, and shook their heads, but the President had remained quiet. The music came back on, some classical piece of Mozart rudely layered with a thumping bass beat beneath a chorus of elegant strings and woodwinds. The President turned up his nose at the selection but returned to the conversation, his countenance serious and probing.

"Mister Armstrong thought your only purpose was to compete with us in the athletic arena."

"Yes."

"And once you suffered from your..."

"Condition."

"Condition," the President repeated, "you no longer served a purpose."

"Correct."

"And you were summarily dismissed."

"Fired, yes."

"Interesting," the President said. "And quite clarifying."

Coleman hopped down from the liftgate. The three men keyed in on his feet as he landed, curious to see if there were any remaining effects, but it was a soft and uneventful touchdown into the muddy earth. He reached into the flatbed and pulled a black bag toward him. Unzipping it, he produced a laptop. He opened it, waited just a second for the screen to flicker on, and he stood back.

It was a formal entry into The Bank's Request for Proposal.

They huddled around the laptop, focused on the screen, but listening intently to the pitch. Coleman started from the beginning, and left no detail to the imagination. From the gout to the gestation of their small company, he laid it all out there for them.

He explained how he and his wife had pulled every dollar of equity from their home in order to front the money for salaries and benefits and all the little and large expenses that popped up during the birth of a business.

With one notable exception, he told them about his team, about the engineers and their brilliance, about his operational expert, about his marketing guru. He explained how the technology in their little company was better, how their structure was leaner, how decisions were made faster, how the team was more nimble and able to react to changing conditions more rapidly.

He explained how The Bank would be their first client and, therefore, would get all their attention.

He gave them the numbers, a steep discount from what Armstrong and the other competitors were proposing.

Finally, closing the laptop shut, he looked the President in the eye and he asked him for the business.

The three men simultaneously crossed their arms and stood there shoulder to shoulder, thoughtfully considering Coleman's proposal, sentries of The Asylum.

"Highly interesting. Dare I say intriguing? But there is one component you failed to mention. One individual, to be exact."

The President leaned forward and spoke forcefully. "What of Mister Kumar?"

Coleman's response was short, direct, and filled with the pride he had swallowed earlier.

"Vijay Kumar is with us."

At this, they each took a step back and Coleman could hear them exhale.

As the three men looked at one another, a car started nearby and, as it drove away, the DJ yelled into his microphone.

"Gooooooodbye from The Asylum!"

CHAPTER 52

It was a unique way of awarding a contract but, as everyone in the room had experienced throughout the bid process, The Bank executives were anything but ordinary.

"It is important to face your competition," the President explained in his opening remarks, after each team had arrived and settled into the plush auditorium chairs. "To look them in the eye, win or lose, so that each may take the measure of the victor or the vanquished."

He, alone with his two executive advisors, stood on a small elevated stage, looking out over the group of aspirants. The auditorium was darkened, illuminated only by dim track lighting along the edges of the floor and three bright stage lights shining on each of the men. It was the first time any of the exclusive group had seen them in a formal business setting, and they cut a fine pose, almost regal in their tailored suits. The President stood a step forward from the other two, and his height, athletic posture, and the open movement of his arms commanded the room.

"We subjected you to an unorthodox discovery process, probably unlike any sale you have made in your careers."

This drew a smattering of nervous laughter from a few of the group seated closer to the front.

"For that, we thank you for your patience and your participation. I suppose it is true that most of us will do just about anything for money, right?"

He turned to his executives, who nodded theatrically, eliciting more laughter from the audience.

They were all there – a small group from IntelliSec, seated off to the side, and a larger group from SecureIntell seated in the middle toward the front. Armstrong was there, too, seated alone in the front row on the aisle, with a pair of crutches propped against the seat beside him. His chin rested on his interlocked fingers, and he looked sullen and remained quiet, not joining in the forced expressions of mirth from the others.

"It was a rigorous test of your determination, your will, and your desire to succeed," the President continued. "You all performed admirably."

Armstrong averted his eyes and looked down at his left foot, covered by a thick plaster cast from the top of the ankle down to the toes, which were exposed and wiggled free in the cold conditioned air. He had drawn little constellations and stenciled colorful pictures of the planets on his cast.

"But in the end, we could only choose one entity to manage, maintain, and protect our Internet security interests."

Members from the other teams moved forward in their seats and glanced around at one other, sensing the moment of truth at hand.

Armstrong stared at his foot.

"We selected the team that combined the spirit of our competition with the sound technological expertise, architecture, and support required to secure our fiduciary, regulatory, and financial interests."

As if they were one body, everyone in the auditorium inched forward to the edges of their seats.

"We also selected a team that best honored our wishes for honesty during the process. A team that, even when things went a little sideways, or flaws were encountered, they informed us, kept us apprised of the situation and, ultimately, won our trust."

At the mention of honesty, most everyone in the room now joined Armstrong in staring at their feet.

"In winning our trust, they also won our business. In the interests of privacy, we won't disclose numbers, but we would like to congratulate and award our contract to..."

A collective holding of the breath.

"Asylum Digital Security. Congratulations, gentlemen!"

Only the President, the Italian, and the Swede clapped. The rest of the auditorium was stone silent, apart from the confused murmurs of "*Asylum?*" and "*Who are they?*" that bubbled up from the losing groups.

From the back of the auditorium, three other men clapped in almost perfect symmetry with the executives from The Bank.

Armstrong heard them and turned in his chair.

Rob Coleman.

Steve Wellman.

Vijay Kumar.

With grins wider than the expanse of the Milky Way Galaxy, they waved back at him.

The executives had the audacity to throw a small reception for all parties involved in the bidding process, but only the gentlemen from Asylum attended, for obvious reasons. The others had scurried from the auditorium, racing through the lobby, and out to their cars.

On their way to the stage to join The Bankers, the Asylum team made a point to walk down Armstrong's side of the aisle, and they gave a wide berth as he limped past them on his crutches.

"Oh, hey, Mister Armstrong!" Steve said. "Have a really great day!"

Armstrong glared at him and continued on.

"Neal, what's wrong?" Vijay said, in his British lilt. "Do you have the gout?"

"Get out of my way," Armstrong grumbled, clanking up the aisle.

"Neal, wait up," Coleman said, his voice gentle and nearly apologetic.

Armstrong stopped.

"Listen, we don't want to be sore winners about the whole thing."

"When did you know?" Armstrong snapped.

"We signed the contracts yesterday. But we had nothing to do with the whole dog and pony show. That was all them."

"Well, it's rude and you don't deserve this. We'll take action, you know."

"Oh, I know you will. We've got lawyers now, too, Neal. And we've also got their lawyers." Coleman nodded toward the stage, where Steve and Vijay were vigorously shaking hands with the executives. "You do what you have to do, but I'm pretty sure you'll just be wasting your money."

Armstrong's face was red, and he looked ready to spit fire back at Coleman, but he took a long breath through his beak nose and turned up the aisle. Coleman watched him limp along and then called to him.

"Hey Neal? We feel bad about the whole thing. We really do. Without you, Asylum never comes together. So we got you a gift. A little token of our appreciation. We hope you enjoy it."

Armstrong ignored him and made his way through the building and out to the parking lot. The bike rack was long gone from his car, and he threw his crutches into the trunk, then steadied himself until he could flop into the driver's seat and pull away.

All the way back to the office, Coleman's words rattled around in his head.

A gift. A little token of our appreciation.

It made no sense, until Armstrong pulled into the parking lot. As he drove toward his normal spot, he slammed on the brakes, the seatbelt catching him as he lunged forward.

His spot was occupied by a colorful inflated castle. A generator beside it pumped air into the bright red, yellow, and blue cushions, and the structure swayed back and forth in the blowing breeze.

Armstrong closed his eyes and dropped his chin to his chest.

It was a moon bounce.

Back at The Bank headquarters, conversation had turned to business, and Coleman noticed the dull, glazed look overtaking the three executives as Vijay explained some important, yet mind-numbingly tedious, technological detail. Coleman smoothly changed course and redirected matters to a lighter topic.

"Sorry, guys, he's a much better engineer than he is a runner."

This drew a laugh from all but Vijay, who had a notion to argue, but stopped when Steve wrapped an arm around his shoulder and squeezed tight.

The President, appreciative of the course correction, smiled and clapped his hands together.

"That reminds me, Mister Coleman, you owe us a rematch, do you not?"

"The Asylum," the Swede said.

"This time you won't be so lucky," the Italian added.

Coleman laughed and nodded affirmatively.

"Okay, you'll get your rematch," he said, "but first you have to play on my turf."

"Your turf?" the President said.

"You'll see," Coleman said. "And, gentlemen, I would advise you to wear cleats."

CHAPTER 53

It took many weeks, and it wasn't without its hiccups, but the athletic complex shaped up quite nicely. The Reverend had underestimated the breadth of his extra land. By removing a small section of trees and leveling off some mild hills, they were able to squeeze in two youth soccer fields, a regulation softball diamond, a pavilion area with picnic tables and outdoor grills, additional parking, and an expansive playground for the kids, anchored by a huge wooden boat that was supposed to resemble Noah's Ark, but ended up looking more like the Jolly Roger.

Once the deal closed with The Bank, Coleman had kicked in another hundred grand out of his own commission, doubling the initial amount he had donated. The Reverend was giddy with the unexpected bounty of riches, and had wanted to name the fields in Coleman's honor.

Coleman wouldn't allow it.

Insisting that it was a place for the kids and their families, he thought that it should go unnamed and let them be known simply as the fields by the church. That pleased the Reverend very much, and so they became known.

It also pleased the Reverend very much that those same fields had recently spurred an uptick in church attendance.

Coleman was rightly proud of the complex, and he had been spending a lot of time there lately, both during construction when he helped oversee the project, and afterward, once the fields were complete. While things were amicable with Angie, and they were still legally married, he had been living alone in a nearby apartment, a month-to-month corporate rental. They were getting along quite well at work, too, but she hadn't been able to turn the corner yet and allow him back in the house.

In order to spend as much time with his son as possible, Coleman had arranged for Connor's soccer team to practice at the church fields. He had taken on a more active role with the boys, too, serving now as the lead assistant.

He also got to see Molly quite a bit – Angie usually dropped the dog off with Connor – and she was growing fast, awkwardly learning how to manage her big paws and longer limbs. He had even trained her how to retrieve a stray soccer ball by rolling it with her nose.

Another thing Coleman did, with a whole lot of nudging from the Reverend, was to start up a recreational adult league. It consisted of a few ex-players, but mainly middle-aged guys who wanted a more exciting exercise routine than just jogging. The quality of play ranged from pretty bad to bloody awful, but it didn't really matter. The guys were fun to be around, and it gave Coleman something to do after work.

That afternoon's game took place in conjunction with the youth soccer practice on the next field. Most of the guys on the team were fathers of the boys anyway, so it was an effort to squeeze two commitments into one slot of time. The only difference was that Coleman had invited the guys from The Bank. As requested, they showed up in soccer cleats and all the latest gear.

"Hey, you basically funded this complex," he had told the President, "I figured you should get a look at it."

Beginning to feel his oats as a business owner, Coleman cannily placed the President on his own team, with the Reverend as their goalkeeper, and stuck the Italian and the Swede on a team with Steve and Vijay.

All game long, Coleman controlled the pace of play and steadily fed the ball to the President near the goal. The Bank executives were not nearly as adept at soccer as they were at extreme sports, but it was pretty tough to miss when the President had the ball in open space and only Vijay Kumar standing between him and the goal. By the end of the game, the Italian and the Swede had a deeper appreciation for Coleman's soccer prowess, and the President had a hat trick.

They agreed that the next event would move back to their turf. They had recently discovered a passion for rollerblading, and they were all excited and going and on and on about it, but Coleman was distracted and only heard bits and pieces.

Off in one corner of the youth field, Angie stood alone. He caught her eye, and she waved to him and mouthed a hello. It was the same way she would have greeted him before.

Coleman waved back and ignored the executives.

He couldn't stop looking at his wife.

CHAPTER 54

Steve's wife had finally kicked them out of the basement right around the time the first payments from The Bank had cleared. They had been spending roughly 10 to 12 hours per day down there, huddled around temporary folding tables and Steve's drum kit, and the ongoing gifts of manicure, massage, and mid-day mimosa no longer had any impact. Mrs. Wellman had a beautiful newly-finished basement, and she wanted to enjoy it.

Fortunately for the team, business was looking good. To swoop in at the last minute and swipe The Bank deal out from under some of the major industry players had brought them plenty of attention, and contracts from some smaller regional banks were beginning to trickle in.

In her role as Marketing Director, Angie Coleman had gotten them some well-placed press in the industry publications and was instrumental in their brand creation and the development of their website and company logo – a dark and impenetrable fortress that sat atop a pair of healthy, happy feet.

Vijay Kumar helped out with the marketing, too. It had always been a desire of his but, like all things with Vijay, he liked to be pursued, and after much encouragement, pleading, and begging, he had at last moved to America. As a partner in the company, they had been sending him to any industry conference that would have him and, as the center of attention, he was doing a fine job of providing keynote speeches and whitepapers that, above all else, promoted his own expertise. Vijay had also started a cricket team, but the others had yet to join him in this pursuit, apart from one unenthusiastic exception.

Steve and his spreadsheets were seamlessly managing the flow of funds, and his financial and statistical models had the infant company prepared for any scenario. The business plan that he liked best, however, was the one that had them ready for rapid growth. He had thrived in his new role as a partner and, with the increase in confidence, he had become surprisingly bold. In exchange for a healthy profit-sharing plan, Steve had convinced everyone on the team to sign a non-compete agreement. They were together for the long haul – even Vijay, who only signed after much bellyaching and a written agreement to join his cricket team. Steve's only complaint was the use of his basement as office space, but that was about to change.

Armstrong had followed through with his threat and sued them, but the litigation was very short-lived after two of the engineers – Jennifer and Mark – countersued, claiming they were subjected to a hostile work environment with a hint of sexual harassment. When rumors of the countersuit made the industry trades, Armstrong's company quietly dropped their own legal action, not needing any additional bad publicity. They also quietly dropped Neal Armstrong, who was said to be interviewing for an upper management position with a discount airline.

Rob Coleman had learned more about corporate real estate than he ever cared to know. In a normal company, this job would have fallen to their operational expert, but Steve and his basement had done more than enough, so Coleman reluctantly volunteered. After weeks of meeting with realtors and scouting area office complexes, he had chosen a two-story, mixed-use facility, with restaurants, coffee shops, and boutique stores interspersed among the business tenants. It checked all the boxes: it was in the heart of the Research Triangle Park, it was near enough to The Bank, and it was only about a 15-minute drive to the airport.

It also had a pond with a fountain, traced by a path for walking, jogging, and biking.

Coleman had parked his pickup beside the curb outside of their new offices. As he unloaded boxes, he paused for a moment to admire the signage announcing the new home of Asylum Digital Security.

It was a warm day, pushing toward the summer months, and he had worked up a good sweat as he hauled their humble beginnings up the sidewalk toward the front doors. The painters would arrive tomorrow, and the furniture movers would be there as soon as the paint was dry.

Despite the heat, the sweat, and the strain on his back, Coleman smiled as he worked.

While making his way back down the path for one final load of boxes, Angie pulled up in her minivan and lowered the window.

"You need any help?" she said.

"No, I'm good. Last load right here." He wiped his forehead against his sleeve and approached the open window.

"Okay," she said. "Well, listen, I'm on my way to get Connor from school and then we're headed to the grocery store."

"Sounds good," he said. "Hey, go ahead and work from home tomorrow. They'll be painting in here and we won't be able to get in yet."

Angie nodded and thought for a moment.

"Do you want to work from home tomorrow, too? Our home, I mean?"

"Really?"

"Yeah," she said softly. "Why don't you join us for dinner tonight, too."

"Okay."

"And save some of the empty boxes for your things."

"Oh," Coleman said, his spirits beginning to sink. "You need me to move some stuff out?"

"No," Angie said, looking up at him. "I want you to move some stuff in."

It took a moment to register but, when it did, he was beaming. He said goodbye to her and went over to his truck to grab the last two boxes, which he stacked and carried up the path in both arms. He walked a little funny, presumably from the weight of the boxes.

Angie noticed. She hadn't pulled away yet. Concerned, she called after him.

"Hey, are you limping again?"

Coleman stopped and turned back, holding the boxes to one side so he could see her. He shook his head, held her eye, and then he smiled.

"Strutting," was all he said.

THE END

OAKLINE BOOKS

www.oaklinebooks.com

ABOUT THE AUTHOR

Ryan Stallings is the author of the *American Heroes Series* for children. His novels, *Bully!* and *Flight!,* have received critical acclaim for their humorous and educational depictions of Theodore Roosevelt and the Wright Brothers as they romp through present-day America. *Limping Along* is his first novel for adults.

He lives in North Carolina with his wife and three kids, and he currently walks without a limp.